AGENT OF THE TERRAN EMPIRE

Fenross said thickly, 'A barbarian horde streaked in yesterday, shot up all the defence posts, landed, and in three hours had put Fort Lone to the torch.'

'That's not our department, sir, unless we're wanted to track down just who did it,' Flandry ventured. 'So why pick on me?'

'The barbarians have made away with her Highness, the Lady Megan of Luna, princess of the blood and the Emperor's favourite granddaughter! We need you.'

'I should say you do, dear chief.' Modesty was not a failing of Flandry's. 'All right, I'll flit directly over. Cheers.' He cut the circuit and went back on to the balcony.

The girl watched him with eyes like blued silver. 'What is it, Nick?' she asked quietly.

Flandry's mouth twisted. 'I'm not sure yet, but I think I've just been condemned to death.'

Agent of the Terran Empire

Poul Anderson

CORONET BOOKS
Hodder and Stoughton

First published 1965 by Chilton Books,
Philadelphia, Penn.

Coronet Edition 1977

Printed in Great Britain for
Hodder & Stoughton Paperbacks, a
division of Hodder & Stoughton Ltd.,
Mill Road, Dunton Green, Sevenoaks, Kent,
(Editorial Office: 47 Bedford Square, London, WC1 3DP)
by Cox & Wyman Ltd,
London, Reading and Fakenham

ISBN 0 340 21245 4

TIGER
BY
THE
TAIL

Captain Flandry opened his eyes and saw a metal ceiling. Simultaneously, he grew aware of the thrum and quiver which meant he was aboard a spaceship running on ultradrive.

He sat up with a violence that sent the dregs of alcohol swirling through his head. He'd gone to sleep in a room somewhere in the stews of Catawrayannis, with no prospect or intention of leaving the city for an indefinite time — let alone the planet! Now —

The chilling realisation came that he was not aboard a human ship. Humanoid, yes, from the size and design of things, but no vessel ever built within the borders of the Empire, and no foreign make that he knew of.

Even from looking at this one small cabin, he could tell. There were bunks, into one of which he had fitted pretty well, but the sheets and blankets were of plastic weave. They seemed — he looked more closely — the sheets seemed to be of some vegetable fibre, the blankets of long bluish-grey hair. There were a couple of chairs and a table in the middle of the room, wooden, and they must have seen better days for they were elaborately handcarved in an intricate interwoven design new to Flandry — and planetary art-forms were a hobby of his. The way and manner in which the metal plating had been laid was another indication, and —

He sat down again, buried his whirling head in his hands, and tried to think. There was a thumping in his head and a vile taste in his mouth which liquor didn't ordinarily leave — at least not the stuff he'd been drinking — and now that he remembered, he'd gotten sleepy much earlier than one would have expected when the girl was so good-looking —

Drugged — oh, no! *Tell me I'm not as stupid as a stereofilm hero! Anything but that!*

But who'd have thought it, who'd have looked for it? Certainly the people and beings on whom he'd been trying to get a lead would never try such a stunt. Besides, none of them had been around, he was sure of it. He'd simply been out building part of the elaborate structure of demimonde acquaintances and information which would eventually, by exceedingly indirect routes, lead him to those he was seeking. He'd simply been out having a good time — *quite* a good time, in fact — and —

And now someone from outside the Empire had him. And now what?

He got up, a little unsteadily, and looked around for his clothes. No sign of them. And he'd paid three hundred credits for that outfit, too. He stamped savagely over to the door. It didn't have a photocell attachment; he jerked it open and found himself looking down the muzzle of a blaster.

It was of different design from any he knew, but it was quite unmistakable. Captain Flandry sighed, relaxed his taut muscles, and looked more closely at the guard who held it.

He was humanoid to a high degree, perhaps somewhat stockier than Terrestrial average — and come to think of it, the artificial gravity was a little higher than one gee — and with very white skin, long tawny hair and beard, and oblique violet eyes. His ears were pointed and two small horns grew above his heavy eyebrow ridges, but otherwise he was manlike enough. With civilised clothes and a hooded cloak he could easily pass himself off for human.

Not in the getup he wore, of course, which consisted of a kilt and tunic, shining beryllium-copper cuirass and helmet, buskins over bare legs, and a murderous-looking dirk. As well as a couple of scalps hanging at his belt.

He gestured the prisoner back, and blew a long hollow blast on a horn slung at his side. The wild echoes chased each other down the long corridor, hooting and howling with a primitive clamour that tingled faintly along Captain Flandry's spine.

He thought slowly, while he waited: No intercom, apparently not even speaking tubes laid the whole length of the ship. And household articles of wood and animal and vegetable fibres, and that archaic costume there — They were barbarians, all right. But no tribe that he knew about.

That wasn't too surprising, since the Terrestrial Empire and the half-dozen other civilised states in the known Galaxy ruled over several thousands of intelligent races and had some contact with nobody knew how many thousands more. Many of the others were, of course, still planet-bound, but quite a few tribes along the Imperial borders had mastered a lot of human technology without changing their fundamental outlook on things. Which is what comes of hiring barbarian mercenaries.

The peripheral tribes were still raiders, menaces to the border planets and merely nuisances to the Empire as a whole. Periodically they were bought off, or played off against each other — or the Empire might even send a punitive expedition out. But if one day a strong barbarian race under a strong leader should form a reliable coalition — then *vae victis*!

A party of Flandry's captors, apparently officers, guardsmen, and a few slaves, came down the corridor. Their leader was tall and powerfully built, with a cold arrogance in his pale-blue eyes that did not hide a calculating intelligence. There was a golden coronet on his head, and the robes that swirled around his big body were rainbow-gorgeous. Flandry recognised some items as having been manufactured within the Empire. Looted, probably.

They came to a halt before him and the leader looked him up and down with a deliberately insulting gaze. To be thus surveyed in the nude could have been badly disconcerting, but Flandry was immune to embarrassment and his answering stare was bland.

The leader spoke at last, in strongly accented but fluent Anglic: 'You may as well accept the fact that you are a prisoner, Captain Flandry.'

They'd have gone through his pockets, of course. He asked levelly, 'Just to satisfy my own curiosity, was that girl in your pay?'

'Of course. I assure you that the Scothani are not the brainless barbarians of popular Terrestrial superstition, though —' a bleak smile — 'it is useful to be thought so.'

'The Scothani? I don't believe I've had the pleasure —'

'You have probably not heard of us, though we have had some contact with the Empire. We have found it convenient to remain in obscurity, as far as Terra is concerned, until the time is ripe. But — what do you think caused the Alarri to invade you, fifteen years ago?'

Flandry thought back. He had been a boy then, but he had, of course, avidly followed the news accounts of the terrible fleets that swept in over the marches and attacked Vega itself. Only the hardest fighting at the Battle of Mirzan had broken the Alarri. Yet it turned out that they'd been fleeing still another tribe, a wild and mighty race who had invaded their own system with fire and ruin. It was a common enough occurrence in the turbulent barbarian stars; this one incident had come to the Empire's notice only because the refugees had tried to conquer it in turn. A political upheaval within the Terrestrial domain had prevented closer investigation before the matter had been all but forgotten.

'So you were driving the Alarri before you?' asked Flandry with as close an approximation to the right note of polite interest as he could manage in his present condition.

'Aye. And others. The Scothani have quite a little empire now, out there in the wilderness of the Galaxy. But, since we were never originally contacted by Terrestrials, we have, as I say, remained little known to them.'

So — the Scothani had learned their technology from some other race, possibly other barbarians. It was a familiar pattern, Flandry could trace it out in his mind. Spaceships landed on the primitive world, the initial awe of the natives gave way to the realisation that the skymen weren't so very different after all — they could be killed like anyone else; traders, students, labourers, mercenary warriors visited the more advanced worlds, brought back knowledge of their science and technology; factories were built, machines produced, and some local king used the new power to impose his rule on all his planet; and then, to unite his restless subjects, he had to turn their faces outward, promise plunder and glory if they followed him out to the stars —

Only the Scothani had carried it farther than most. And lying as far from the Imperial border as they did, they could build up a terrible power without the complacent, politics-ridden Empire being more than dimly aware of the fact — until the day when —

Vae victis!

II

'Let us have a clear understanding,' said the barbarian chief. 'You are a prisoner on a warship already light years from Llynathawr, well into the Imperial marches and bound for Scotha itself. You have no chance of rescue, and mercy depends entirely on your own conduct. Adjust it accordingly.'

'May I ask why you picked me up?' Flandry's tone was mild.

'You are of noble blood, and a highranking officer in the

Imperial intelligence service. You may be worth something as a hostage. But primarily we want information.'

'But I —'

'I know.' The reply was disgusted. 'You're very typical of your miserable kind. I've studied the Empire and its decadence long enough to know that. You're just another worthless younger son, given a high-paying sinecure so you can wear a fancy uniform and play soldier. You don't amount to anything.'

Flandry let an angry flush go up his cheek. 'Look here —'

'It's perfectly obvious,' said the barbarian. 'You come to Llynathawr to track down certain dangerous conspirators. So you register yourself in the biggest hotel in Catawrayannis as Captain Dominic Flandry of the Imperial Intelligence Service, you strut around in your expensive uniform dropping dark hints about your leads and your activities — and these consist of drinking and gambling and wenching the whole night and sleeping the whole day!' A cold humour gleamed in the blue eyes. 'Unless it is your intention that the Empire's enemies shall laugh themselves to death at the spectacle.'

'If that's so,' began Flandry thinly, 'then why —'

'You will know something. You can't help picking up a lot of miscellaneous information in your circles, no matter how hard you try not to. Certainly you know specific things about the organisation and activities of your own corps which we would find useful information. We'll squeeze all you know out of you! Then there will be other services you can perform, people within the Empire you can contact, documents you can translate for us, perhaps various liaisons you can make — eventually, you may even earn your freedom.' The barbarian lifted one big fist. 'And in case you wish to hold anything back, remember that the torturers of Scotha know their trade.'

'You needn't make melodramatic threats,' said Flandry sullenly.

The fist shot out, and Flandry fell to the floor with darkness whirling and roaring through his head. He crawled to hands and knees, blood dripping from his face, and vaguely he heard the voice: 'From here on, little man, you are to address me as befits a slave speaking to a crown prince of Scotha.'

The Terrestrial staggered to his feet. For a moment his fists clenched. The prince smiled grimly and knocked him down again. Looking up, Flandry saw brawny hands resting on blaster butts. Not a chance, not a chance.

Besides, the prince was hardly a sadist. Such brutality was the normal order among the barbarians — and come to think of it, slaves within the Empire could be treated similarly.

And there was the problem of staying alive.

'Yes, sir,' he mumbled.

The prince turned on his heel and walked away.

They gave him back his clothes, though someone had stripped the gold braid and the medals away. Flandry looked at the soiled, ripped garments and sighed. Tailor-made — !

He surveyed himself in the mirror as he washed and shaved. The face that looked back was wide across the cheekbones, straight-nosed and square-jawed, with carefully waved reddish-brown hair and a moustache trimmed with equal attention. Probably too handsome, he reflected, wiping the blood from under his nose, but he'd been young when he had the plasti-cosmetician work on him. Maybe when he got out of this mess he should have the face made over to a slightly more rugged pattern to fit his years. He was in his thirties now, after all — getting to be a big boy, Dominic.

The fundamental bone structure of head and face was his own, however, and so were the eyes: large and bright, with a hint of obliquity, the iris of that curious grey which can seem any colour, blue or green or black or gold. And the trim, medium-tall body was genuine too. He hated exercises, but went through a dutiful daily ritual since he needed sinews and co-ordination for his work. And, too, a man in condition was something to look at among the usually flabby nobles of Terra; he'd found his figure no end of help in making his home leaves pleasant.

Well, can't stand here admiring yourself all day, old fellow. He slipped blouse, pants, and jacket over his silkite undergarments, pulled on the sheening boots, tilted his officer's cap at an angle of well gauged rakishness, and walked out to meet his new owners.

The Scothani weren't such bad fellows, he soon learned. They were big brawling lusty barbarians, out for adventure and loot and fame as warriors; they had courage and loyalty and a wild streak of sentiment that he liked. But they could also fly into deadly rages, they were casually cruel to anyone that stood in their way, and Flandry acquired a not too high respect for their brains. It would have helped if they'd washed oftener, too.

14

This warship was one of a dozen which Cerdic, the crown prince, had taken out on a plundering cruise. They'd sacked a good many towns, even some on nominally Imperial planets, and on the way back had sent down a man in a lifeboat to contact Cerdic's agents on Llynathawr, which was notoriously the listening post of this sector of the Empire. Learning that there was something going on which a special agent from Terra had been investigating, Cerdic had ordered him picked up. And that was that.

Now they were homeward bound, their holds stuffed with loot and their heads stuffed with plans for further inroads. It might not have meant much, but — well — Cerdic and his father Penda didn't seem to be just ordinary barbarian chiefs, nor Scothania an ordinary barbarian nation.

Could it be that somewhere out there among the many stars someone had finally organised a might that could break the Empire? Could the Long Night really be at hand?

Flandry shoved the thought aside. He had too much to do right now. Even his own job at Llynathawr, important as it was, could and would be handled by someone else — though not, he thought a little sadly, with the Flandry touch — and his own immediate worry was here and now. He had to find out the extent of power and ambition of the Scothani; he had to learn their plans and get the information to Terra, and somehow spike them even a little. After that there might be time to save his own hide.

Cerdic had him brought to the captain's cabin. The place was a typical barbarian chief's den, with the heads of wild beasts on the walls and the hides on the floors, old shields and swords hung up in places of honour, a magnificent golden vase stolen from some planet of artists shining in a corner. But there were incongruous modern touches, a microprint reader and many bookrolls from the Empire, astrographic tables and computer, a vodograph. The prince sat in a massive carven chair, a silkite robe flung carelessly over his broad shoulders. He nodded with a certain affability.

'Your first task will be to learn Scothanian,' he said without preliminary. 'As yet almost none of our people, even nobles, speak Anglic, and there are many who will want to talk to you.'

'Yes, sir,' said Flandry. It was what he would most have desired.

'You had better also start organising all you know so you can present it coherently,' said the prince. 'And I, who have lived in the Empire, will be able to check enough of your statements to tell whether you are likely speaking the truth.' He smiled mirthlessly. 'If there is reason to suspect you are lying, you will be put to the torture. And one of our Sensitives will then get at the truth.'

So they had Sensitives, too. Telepaths who could tell whether a being was lying when pain had sufficiently disorganised his mind were as bad as the Empire's hypnoprobes.

'I'll tell the truth, sir,' he said.

'I suppose so. If you co-operate, you'll find us not an ungrateful people. There will be more wealth than was ever dreamed of when we go into the Empire. There will also be considerable power for such humans as are our liaison with their race.'

'Sir,' began Flandry, in a tone of weak self-righteousness, 'I couldn't think of —'

'Oh, yes, you could,' said Cerdric glumly. 'I know you humans. I travelled incognito throughout your whole Empire, I was on Terra itself. I posed as one of you, or when convenient as just another of the subject races. I *know* the Empire — its utter decadence, its self-seeking politicians and pleasure-loving mobs, corruption and intrigue everywhere you go, collapse of morals and duty-sense, decline of art into craft and science into stagnancy — you were a great race once, you humans, you were among the first to aspire to the stars and we owe you something for that, I suppose. But you're not the race you once were.'

The viewpoint was biased, but enough truth lay in it to make Flandry wince. Cerdric went on, his voice rising: 'There is a new power growing out beyond your borders, young peoples with the strength and courage and hopefulness of youth, and they'll sweep the rotten fragments of the Empire before them and build something new and better.'

Only, thought Flandry, *only first comes the Long Night, darkness and death and the end of civilisation, the howling peoples in the ruins of our temples and a myriad petty tyrants holding their dreary courts in the shards of the Empire. To say nothing of the decline of good music and good cuisine, taste in clothes and taste in women and conversation as a fine art.*

'We've one thing you've lost,' said Cerdric, 'and I think ultimately that will be the deciding factor. Honesty. Flandry, the Scothani are a race of honest warriors.'

'No doubt, sir,' said Flandry.

'Oh, we have our evil characters, but they are few and the custom of private challenges soon eliminates them,' said Cerdic. 'And even their evil is an open and clean thing, greed or lawlessness or something like that; it isn't the bribery and conspiracy and betrayal of your rotten politicians. And most of us live by our code. It wouldn't occur to a true Scothani to do a dishonorable thing, to break an oath or desert a comrade or lie on his word of honour. Our women aren't running loose making eyes at every man they come across; they're kept properly at home till time for marriage and then they know their place as mothers and houseguiders. Our boys are raised to respect the gods and the king, to fight, and to speak truth. Death is a little thing, Flandry, it comes to everyone in his time and he cannot stay it, but honour lives forever.

'We don't corrupt ourselves. We keep honour at home and root out disgrace with death and torture. We live our code. And that is really why we will win.'

Battleships help, thought Flandry. And then, looking into the cold bright eyes: '*He's fanatic. But a hell of a smart one. And that kind makes the most dangerous enemy.*

Aloud he asked, humbly: 'Isn't any stratagem a lie, sir? Your own disguised travels within the Empire — '

'Naturally, certain manoeuvres are necessary,' said the prince stiffly. 'Nor does it matter what one does with regard to alien races. Especially when they have as little honour as Terrestrials.'

The good old race-superiority complex, too. Oh, well.

'I tell you this,' said Cerdic earnestly, 'in the hope that you may think it over and see our cause is just and be with us. We will need many foreigners, especially humans, for liaison and intelligence and other services. You may still accomplish something in a hitherto wasted life.'

'I'll think about it, sir,' said Flandry.

'Then go.'

Flandry got.

The ship was a good three weeks en route to Scotha. It took Flandry about two of them to acquire an excellent working knowledge of the language, but he preferred to simulate

17

difficulty and complained that he got lost when talk was too rapid. It was surprising how much odd information you picked up when you were thought not to understand what was being said. Not anything of great military significance, of course, but general background, stray bits of personal history, attitudes and beliefs — it all went into the neat filing system which was Flandry's memory, to be correlated with whatever else he knew or learned into an astonishingly complete picture.

The Scothani themselves were quite friendly, eager to hear about the fabulous Imperial civilisation and to brag of their own wonderful past and future exploits. Since there was obviously nothing he could do, Flandry was under the loosest guard and had virtually the freedom of the ship. He slept and messed with the warriors, swapped bawdy songs and dirty jokes, joined their rough-and-tumble wrestling matches to win surprised respect for his skill, and even became the close friend and confidant of some of the younger males.

The race was addicted to gambling. Flandry learned their games, taught them some of the Empire's, and before the trip's end had won back his stolen finery plus several other outfits and a pleasantly jingling purse. It was — well — he almost hated to take his winnings from these overgrown babies. It just never occurred to them that dice and cards could be made to do tricks.

The picture grew. The barbarian tribes of Scotha were firmly united under the leadership of the Frithian kings, had been for several generations. Theoretically it was an absolute monarchy, though actually all classes except the slaves were free. They had conquered at least a hundred systems outright, contenting themselves with exacting tribute and levies from most of these, and dominated all others within reach. Under Penda's leadership, a dozen similar, smaller barbarian states had already formed a coalition with the avowed purpose of invading the Empire, capturing Terra, destroying the Imperial military forces, and making themselves masters. Few of them thought beyond the plunder to be had, though apparently some of them, like Cerdic, dreamed of maintaining and extending the Imperial domain under their own rule.

They had a formidable fleet — Flandry couldn't find out its exact size — and its organisation and technology seemed far superior to that of most barbarian forces. They had a great industry, mostly slave-manned with the Scothan overlords supervising. They had shrewd leaders, who would wait till one of the Empire's recurring political crises had reduced its fighting strength, and who were extremely well informed about their enemy. It looked — bad!

Especially since they couldn't wait too long. Despite the unequalled prosperity created by industry, tribute, and piracy, all Scotha was straining at the leash, nobles and warriors in the whole coalition foaming to be at the Empire's throat; a whole Galactic sector had been seized by the same savage dream. When they came roaring in — well, you never could tell. The Empire's fighting strength was undoubtedly greater, but could it be mobilised in time? Wouldn't Penda get gleeful help from two or three rival imperia? Couldn't a gang of utterly fearless fanatics plough through the mass of self-seeking officers and indifferent mercenaries that made up most of the Imperial power today?

Might not the Long Night really be at hand?

III

Scotha was not unlike Terra — a little larger, a little farther from its sun, the seas made turbulent by three small close moons. Flandry had a chance to observe it telescopically — the ship didn't have magniscreens — and as they swept in, he saw the mighty disc roll grandly against the Galactic star-blaze and studied the continents with more care than he showed.

The planet was still relatively thinly populated, with great forests and plains standing empty, archaic cities and villages huddled about the steep-walled castles of the nobles. Most of its industry was on other worlds, though the huge military bases were all on Scotha and its moons. There couldn't be more than a billion Scothani all told, estimated Flandry, probably less, and many of them would live elsewhere as overlords of the interstellar domain. Which didn't make them less formidable. The witless hordes of humankind were more hindrance than help to the Empire.

Cerdic's fleet broke up, the captains bound for their estates. He took his own vessel to the capital, Iuthagaar, and brought it down in the great yards. After the usual pomp and ceremony of homecoming, he sent for Flandry.

'What is your attitude towards us now?' he asked.

'You are a very likeable people, sir,' said the Terrestrial, 'and it is as you say — you are a strong and honest race.'

'Then you have decided to help us actively?' The voice was cold.

'I really have little choice, sir,' shrugged Flandry. 'I'll be a prisoner in any case, unless I get to the point of being trusted. The only way to achieve that is to give you my willing assistance.'

'And what of your own nation?'

'A man must stay alive, sir. These are turbulent times.'

Contempt curled Cerdic's lip. 'Somehow I thought better of you,' he said. 'But you're a human. You could only be expected to betray your oaths for your own gain.'

Surprise shook Flandry's voice. 'Wasn't this what you wanted, sir?'

'Oh, yes. I suppose so. Now come along. But not too close — you make me feel a little sick.'

They went up to the great grey castle which lifted its windy spires over the city, and presently Flandry found himself granted an audience with the King of Scothania.

It was a huge and dimlit hall, hung with the banners and shields of old wars and chill despite the fires that blazed along its length. Penda sat on one end, wrapped in furs against the cold, his big body dwarfed by the dragon-carved throne. He had his eldest son's stern manner and bleak eyes, without the prince's bitter intensity — a strong man, thought Flandry, hard and ruthless and able — but perhaps not too bright.

Cerdic had mounted to a seat on his father's right. The queen stood on his left, shivering a little in the damp draft, and down either wall reached a row of guardsmen. The fire shimmered on their breastplates and helmets and halberds; they seemed figures of legend, but Flandry noticed that each warrior carried a blaster too.

There were others in evidence, several of the younger sons of Penda, grizzled generals and councillors, nobles come for a visit. A few of the latter were of non-Scothan race and did not seem to be meeting exceptional politeness. Then there were the hangers-on, bards and dancers and the rest, and slaves scurrying about. Except for its size — and its menace — it was a typical barbarian court.

Flandry bowed the knee as required, but thereafter stood erect and met the king's eye. His position was anomalous,

20

officially Cerdic's captured slave, actually — well, what was he? Or what could he become in time?

Penda asked a few of the more obvious questions, then said slowly: 'You will confer with General Nartheof here, head of our intelligence section, and tell him what you know. You may also make suggestions if you like, but remember that false intentions will soon be discovered and punished.'

'I will be honest, your majesty.'

'Is any Terrestrial honest?' snapped Cerdic.

'I am,' said Flandry cheerfully. 'As long as I'm paid, I serve faithfully. Since I'm no longer in the Empire's pay, I must perforce look about for a new master.'

'I doubt you can be much use,' said Penda.

'I think I can, your majesty,' answered Flandry boldly. 'Even in little things. For instance, this admirably decorated hall is so cold one must wear furs within it, and still the hands are numb. I could easily show a few technicians how to install a radiant heating unit that would make it like summer in here.'

Penda lifted his bushy brows. Cerdic fairly snarled: 'A Terrestrial trick, that. Shall we become as soft and luxurious as the Imperials, we who hunt vorgari on ski?'

Flandry's eyes, flitting around the room, caught dissatisfied expressions on many faces. Inside, he grinned. The prince's austere ideals weren't very popular with these noble savages. If they only had the nerve to —

It was the queen who spoke. Her soft voice was timid: 'Sire, is there any harm in being warm? I — I am always cold these days.'

Flandry gave her an appreciative look. He'd already picked up the background of Queen Gunli. She was young, Penda's third wife, and she came from more southerly Scothan lands than Iuthagaar; her folk were somewhat more civilised than the dominant Frithians. She was certainly a knockout, with that dark rippling hair and those huge violet eyes in her pert face. And that figure too — there was a suppressed liveliness in her; he wondered if she had ever cursed the fate that gave her noble blood and thus a political marriage.

For just an instant their eyes crossed.

'Be still,' said Cerdic.

Gunli's hand fell lightly on Penda's. The king flushed. 'Speak not to your queen thus, Cerdic,' he said. 'In truth this

21

Imperial trick is but a better form of fire, which no one calls unmanly. We will let the Terrestrial make one.'

Flandry bowed his most ironical bow. Cocking an eye up at the queen, he caught a twinkle. She knew.

Nartheof made a great show of blustering honesty, but there was a shrewd brain behind the hard little eyes that glittered in his hairy face. He leaned back and folded his hands behind his head and gave Flandry a quizzical stare.

'If it is as you say — ' he began.

'It is,' said the Terrestrial.

'Quite probably. Your statements so far check with what we already know, and we can soon verify much of the rest. If, then, you speak truth, the Imperial organisation is fantastically good.' He smiled. 'As it should be — it conquered the stars, in the old days. But it's no better than the beings who man it, and everyone knows how venial and cowardly the Imperials are today.'

Flandry said nothing, but he remembered the gallantry of the Sirian units at Garrapoli and the dogged courage of the Valatian Legion and — well, why go on? The haughty Scothani just didn't seem able to realise that a state as absolutely decadent as they imagined the Empire to be wouldn't have endured long enough to be their own enemy.

'We'll have to reorganise everything,' said Nartheof. 'I don't care whether what you say is true or not, it makes good sense. Our whole setup is outmoded. It's ridiculous, for instance, to give commands according to nobility and blind courage instead of proven intelligence.'

'And you assume that the best enlisted man will make the best officer,' said Flandry. 'It doesn't necessarily follow. A strong and hardy warrior may expect more of his men than they can give. You can't all be supermen.'

'Another good point. And we should eliminate swordplay as a requirement; swords are useless today. And we have to train mathematicians to compute trajectories and everything else.' Nartheof grimaced. 'I hate to think what would have happened if we'd invaded three years ago, as many hotheads wanted to do. We would have inflicted great damage, but that's all.'

'You should wait at least another ten or twenty years and really get prepared.'

'Can't. The great nobles wouldn't stand for it. Who wants to

22

be duke of a planet when he could be viceroy of a sector? But we have a year or two yet.' Nartheof scowled. 'I can get my own service whipped into shape, with your help and advice. I have most of the bright lads. But as for some of the other forces — gods, the dunderheads they have in command! I've argued myself hoarse with Nornagast, to no use. The fool just isn't able to see that a space fleet the size of ours must have a special co-ordinating division equipped with semantic calculators and — The worst of it is, he's a cousin to the king, he ranks me. Not much I can do.'

'An accident could happen to Nornagast,' murmured Flandry.

'Eh?' Nartheof gasped. 'What do you mean?'

'Nothing,' said Flandry lightly. 'But just for argument's sake, suppose — well, suppose some good swordsman should pick a quarrel with Nornagast. I don't doubt he has many enemies. If he should unfortunately be killed in the duel, you might be able to get to his majesty immediately after, before anyone else, and persuade him to appoint a more reasonable successor. Of course, you'd have to know in advance that there'd be a duel.'

'Of all the treacherous, underhanded — !'

'I haven't done anything but speculate,' said Flandry mildly. 'However, I might remind you of your own remarks. It's hardly fair that a fool should have command and honour and riches instead of better men who simply happen to be of lower degree. Nor, as you yourself said, is it good for Scothania as a whole.'

'I won't hear of any such Terrestrial vileness.'

'Of course not. I was just — well, speculating. I can't help it. All Terrestrials have dirty minds. But we did conquer the stars once.'

'A man might go far, if only — no!' Nartheof shook himself. 'A warrior doesn't bury his hands in muck.'

'No. But he might use a pitchfork. Tools don't mind dirt. The man who wields them doesn't even have to know the details . . . But let's get back to business.' Flandry relaxed even more lazily. 'Here's a nice little bit of information which only highly placed Imperials know. The Empire has a lot of arsenals and munitions dumps which are guarded by nothing but secrecy. The Emperor doesn't dare trust certain units to guard such sources of power, and he can't spare enough reliable legions to watch them all. So obscure, uninhabited planets are used.' Nartheof's eyes were utterly intent now. 'I know of only one, but it's a good prospect. An uninhabited, barren system not many parsecs inside the border, the second planet honeycombed with underground works that are crammed with spaceships, atomic bombs, fuel — power enough to wreck a world. A small, swift fleet could get there, take most of the stores, and destroy the rest before the nearest garrison could ever arrive in defence.'

'Is that *true*?'

'You can easily find out. If I'm lying, it'll cost you that small unit, that's all — and I assure you I've no desire to be tortured to death.'

'Holy gods!' Nartheof quivered. 'I've got to tell Cerdic now, right away. —'

'You could. Or you might simply go there yourself without telling anyone. If Cerdic knows, he'll be the one to lead the raid. If you went, you'd get the honour — and the power —'

'Cerdic would not like it.'

'Too late then. He could hardly challenge you for so bold and successful a stroke.'

'And he is getting too proud of himself. He could stand a little taking down.' Nartheof chuckled, a deep vibration in his shaggy breast. 'Aye, by Valtam's beard, I'll do it! Give me the figure now —'

Presently the general looked up from the papers and gave Flandry a puzzled stare. 'If this is the case, and I believe it is,' he said slowly, 'it'll be a first-rate catastrophe for the Empire. Why are you with us, human?'

'Maybe I've decided I like your cause a little better,' shrugged Flandry. 'Maybe I simply want to make the best of my own situation. We Terrestrials are adaptable beasts. But I have enemies here, Nartheof, and I expect to make a few more. I'll need a powerful friend.'

'You have one,' promised the barbarian. 'You're much too useful to me to be killed. And — and — damn it, human, somehow I can't help liking you.'

IV

The dice rattled down on to the table and came to a halt. Prince Torric swore good-naturedly and shoved the pile of coins towards Flandry. 'I just can't win,' he laughed. 'You have the gods with you, human.'

For a slave, I'm not doing so badly, thought Flandry. *In fact, I'm getting rich.* 'Fortune favours the weak, highness,' he smiled. 'The strong don't need luck.'

'To Theudagaar with titles,' said the young warrior. He was drunk; wine flushed his open face and spread in puddles on the table before him. 'We're too good friends by now, Dominic. Ever since you got my affairs in order — '

'I have a head for figures, and of course Terrestrial education helps — Torric. But you need money.'

'There'll be enough for all when we hold the Empire. I'll have a whole system to rule, you know.'

Flandry pretended surprise. 'Only a system? After all, a son of King Penda — '

'Cerdic's doing,' Torric scowled blackly. 'The dirty avagar persuaded Father that only one — himself, of course — should succeed to the throne. He said no kingdom ever lasted when the sons divided power equally.'

'It seems very unfair. And how does he know he's the best?'

'He's the oldest. That's what counts. And he's conceited enough to be sure of it.' Torric gulped another beakerful.

'The Empire has a better arrangement. Succession is by ability alone, among many in a whole group of families.'

'Well — the old ways — what can I do?'

'That's hardly warrior's talk, Torric. Admitting defeat so soon — I thought better of you!'

'But what to *do* — ?'

'There are ways. Cerdic's power, like that of all chiefs, rests on his many supporters and his own household troops. He isn't well liked. It wouldn't be hard to get many of his friends to give allegiance elsewhere.'

'But — treachery — would you make a brotherslayer of me?'

'Who said anything about killing? Just — dislodging, let us say. He could always have a system or two to rule, just as he meant to give you.'

'But — look, I don't know anything about your sneaking Terrestrial ways. I suppose you mean to dish — disaffect his allies, promise them more than he gives ... What's that word — bribery? — I don't know a thing about it, Dominic. I couldn't do it.'

'You wouldn't have to do it,' murmured Flandry. 'I could help. What's a man for, if not to help his friends?'

Earl Morgaar, who held the conquered Zanthudian planets in fief, was a noble of power and influence beyond his station. He was also notoriously greedy.

He said to Captain Flandry: 'Terrestrial, your suggestions about farming out tax-gathering have more than doubled my income. But now the natives are rising in revolt against me, murdering my troops wherever they get a chance and burning their farms rather than pay the levies. What do they do about that in the Empire?'

'Surely, sir, you could crush the rebels with little effort,' said Flandry.

'Oh, aye, but dead men don't pay tribute either. Isn't there a better way? My whole domain is falling into chaos.'

'Several ways, sir.' Flandry sketched a few of them — puppet native committees, propaganda shifting the blame on to some scapegoat, and the rest of it. He did not add that these methods work only when skilfully administered.

'It is well,' rumbled the earl at last. His hard gaze searched Flandry's impassively smiling face. 'You've made yourself useful to many a Scothanian leader since coming here, haven't you? There's that matter of Nartheof — he's a great man now because he captured that Imperial arsenal. And there are others. But it seems much of this gain is at the expense of other Scothani, rather than of the Empire. I still wonder about Nornagast's death.'

'History shows that the prospect of great gain always stirs up internal strife, sir,' said Flandry. 'It behooves the strong warrior to seize a dominant share of power for himself and so reunite his people against their common enemy. Thus did the early Terrestrial emperors end the civil wars and become the rulers of the then accessible universe.'

'Ummm — yes. Gain — power — wealth — aye, some *good* warrior — '

'Since we are alone, sir,' said Flandry, 'perhaps I may remark that Scotha itself has seen many changes of dynasty.'

'Yes — of course, I took an oath to the king. But suppose, just suppose the best interests of Scothania were served by a newer and stronger family — '

They were into details of the matter within an hour. Flandry suggested that Prince Kortan would be a valuable ally — but beware of Torric, who had ambitions of his own —

There was a great feast given at the winter solstice. The town and the palace blazed with light and shouted with music and drunken laughter. Warriors and nobles swirled their finest robes about them and boasted of the ruin they would wreak in the Empire. It was to be noted that the number of alcoholic quarrels leading to bloodshed was unusually high this year, especially among the upper classes.

There were enough dark corners, though. Flandry stood in one, a niche leading to a great open window, and looked over the glittering town lights to the huge white hills that lay silent beyond, under the hurtling moons. Above were the stars, bright with the frosty twinkle of winter; they seemed so near that one could reach a hand up and pluck them from the sky. A cold breeze wandered in from outside. Flandry wrapped his cloak more tightly about him.

A light footfall sounded on the floor. He looked about and saw Gunli the queen. Her tall young form was vague in the shadow, but a shaft of moonlight lit her ace with an unearthly radiance. She might have been a lovely girl of Terra, save for the little horns and — well —

These people aren't really human. They look human, but no people of Terra were ever so — simple-minded! Then with an inward grin: *But you don't expect a talent for intrigue in women, Terrestrial or Scothan. So the females of this particular species are quite human enough for anyone's taste.*

The cynical mirth faded into an indefinable sadness. He — damn it, he liked Gunli. They had laughed together often in the last few months, and she was honest and warm-hearted and — well, no matter, no matter.

'Why are you here all alone, Dominic?' she asked. Her voice was very quiet, and her eyes seemed huge in the cold pale moonlight.

'It would hardly be prudent for me to join the party,' he answered wryly. 'I'd cause too many fights. Half of them out there hate my insides.'

'And the other half can't do without you,' she smiled. 'Well I'm as glad not to be there myself. These Frithians are savages. At home — ' She looked out the window and sudden tears glittered in her eyes.

'Don't weep, Gunli,' said Flandry softly. 'Not tonight. This is the night the sun turns, remember. There is always new hope in a new year.'

'I can't forget the old years,' she said with a bitterness that shocked him.

Understanding came. He asked quietly: 'There was someone else, wasn't there?'

'Aye. A young knight. But he was of low degree, so they married me off to Penda, who is old and chill. And Jomana was killed in one of Cerdic's raids —' She turned her head to look at him, and a pathetic attempt at a smile quivered on her lips. 'It isn't Jomana, Dominic. He was very dear to me, but even the deepest wounds heal with time. But I think of all the other young men, and their sweethearts —'

'It's what the men want themselves.'

'But not what the women want. Not to wait and wait and wait till the ships come back, never knowing whether there will only be his shield aboard. Not to rock her baby in her arms and know that in a few years he will be a stiffened corpse on the shores of some unknown planet. Not — well —' She straightened her slim shoulders. 'Little I can do about it.'

'You are a very brave and lovely woman, Gunli,' said Flandry. 'Your kind has changed history ere this.' And he sang softly a verse he had made in the Scothan bardic form:

> 'So I see you standing,
> sorrowful in darkness.
> But the moonlight's broken
> by your eyes tear-shining —
> moonlight in the maiden's
> magic net of tresses.
> Gods gave many gifts, but,
> Gunli, yours was greatest.'

Suddenly she was in his arms . . .

Sviffash of Sithafar was angry. He paced up and down the secret chamber, his tail lashing about his bowed legs, his fanged jaws snapping on the accented Scothanian words that poured out.

'Like a craieex they treat me!' he hissed. 'I, king of a planet and an intelligent species, must bow before the dirty barbarian Penda. Our ships have the worst positions in the fighting line and the last chance at loot. The swaggering Scothani on Sithafar treat my people as if they were conquered peasants, not warrior allies. It is not to be endured!'

Flandry remained respectfully silent. He had carefully nursed the reptile king's smouldering resentment along ever since the being had come to Iuthagaar for conference, but he wanted Sviffash to think it was all his own idea.

'By the Dark God, if I had a chance I think I'd go over to the Terran side!' exploded Sviffash. 'You say they treat their subjects decently?'

'Aye, we've learned it doesn't pay to be prejudiced about race, your majesty. In fact, many nonhumans hold Terrestrial citizenship. And of course a vassal of the Empire remains free within his own domain, except in certain matters of trade and military force where we must have uniformity. And he has the immeasurable power and wealth of the Empire behind and with him.'

'My own nobles would follow gladly enough,' said Sviffash. 'They'd sooner loot Scothanian than Terrestrial planets, if they didn't fear Penda's revenge.'

'Many other of Scotha's allies feel likewise, your majesty. And still more would join an uprising just for the sake of the readily available plunder, if only they were sure the revolt would succeed. It is a matter of getting them all together and agreeing —'

'And you have contacts everywhere, Terrestrial. You're like a spinner weaving its web. Of course, if you're caught I shall certainly insist I never had anything to do with you.'

'Naturally, your majesty.'

'But if it works — hah!' The lidless black eyes glittered and a forked tongue flickered out between the horny lips. 'Hah, the sack of Scotha!'

'No, your majesty. It is necessary that Scotha be spared. There will be enough wealth to be had on her province planets.'

'Why?' The question was cold, emotionless.

'Because you see, your majesty, we will have Scothan allies who will co-operate only on that condition. Some of the power-seeking nobles . . . and then there is a southern nationalist movement which wishes separation from the Frithian north . . . and I may say that it has the secret leadership of the queen herself . . .'

29

Flandry's eyes were as chill as his voice: 'It will do you no good to kill me, Duke Asdagaar. I have left all the evidence with a reliable person who, if I do not return alive, or if I am killed later, will take it directly to the king and the people.'

The Scothan's hands clenched white about the arms of his chair. Impotent rage shivered in his voice: 'You devil! You crawling worm!'

'Name-calling is rather silly coming from one of your history,' said Flandry. 'A parricide, a betrayer of comrades, a breaker of oaths, a mocker of the gods — I have all the evidence, Duke Asdagaar. Some of it is on paper, some is nothing but the names of scattered witnesses and accomplices each of whom knows a little of your career. And a man without honour, on Scotha, is better dead. In fact, he soon will be.'

'But how did you learn?' Hopelessness was coming into the duke's tone; he was beginning to tremble a little.

'I have my ways. For instance, I learned quite a bit by cultivating the acquaintance of your slaves and servants. You highborn forget that the lower classes have eyes and ears, and that they talk among themselves.'

'Well —' The words were almost strangled. 'What do you want?'

'Help for certain others. You have powerful forces at your disposal —'

Spring winds blew softly through the garden and stirred the trees to rustling. There was a deep smell of green life about them; a bird was singing somewhere in the twilight, and the ancient promise of summer stirred in the blood.

Flandry tried to relax in the fragrant evening, but he was too tense. His nerves were drawn into quivering wires and he had grown thin and hollow-eyed. So too had Gunli, but it seemed only to heighten her loveliness; it had more than a hint of the utterly alien and remote now.

'Well, the spaceship is off,' said the man. His voice was weary. 'Aethagir shouldn't have any trouble getting to Ifri, and he's a clever lad. He'll find a way to deliver my letter to Admiral Walton.' He scowled, and a nervous tic began over his left eye. 'But the timing is so desperately close. If our forces strike too soon, or too late, it can be ruinous.'

'I don't worry about that, Dominic,' said Gunli. 'You know how to arrange these things.'

'I've never handled an empire before, my beautiful. The next several days will be touch and go. And that's why I want you to leave Scotha now. Take a ship and some trusty guards and go to Alagan or Gimli or some other out-of-the-way planet.' He smiled with one corner of his mouth. 'It would be a bitter victory if you died in it, Gunli.'

Her voice was haunted. 'I should die. I've betrayed my lord — I am dishonoured —'

'You've saved your people — your own southerners, and ultimately all Scotha.'

'But the broken oaths —' She began to weep, quietly and hopelessly.

'An oath is only a means to an end. Don't let the means override the end.'

'An oath is an oath. But Dominic — it was a choice of standing by Penda or by — you —'

He comforted her as well as he could. And he reflected grimly that he had never before felt himself so thoroughly a skunk.

V

The battle in space was, to the naked eye, hardly visible — brief flashes of radiation among the swarming stars, occasionally the dark form of a ship slipping by and occulting a wisp of the Milky Way. But Admiral Walton smiled with cold satisfaction at the totality of reports given him by the semantic integrator.

'We're mopping them up,' he said. 'Our task force has twice their strength, and they're disorganised and demoralised anyway.'

'Whom are we fighting?' wondered Chang, the executive officer.

'Don't know for sure. They've split into so many factions you can never tell who it is. But from Flandry's report, I'd say it was — what was that outlandish name now? — Duke Markagrav's fleet. He holds this sector, and is a royalist. But it might be Kelry, who's also anti-Terrestrial — but at war with Markagrav and in revolt against the king.'

'Suns and comets and little green asteroids!' breathed Chang. 'This Scothanian hegemony seems just to have disintegrated. Chaos! Everybody at war with everybody else, and hell take the hindmost! How'd he do it?'

'I don't know.' Walton grinned. 'But Flandry's the Empire's ace secret service officer. He works miracles before breakfast. Why, before these barbarians snatched him he was handling the Llynathawr trouble all by himself. And you know how he was doing it? He went there with everything but a big brass band, did a perfect imitation of a political appointee using the case as an excuse to do some high-powered roistering, and worked his way up towards the conspirators through the underworld characters he met in the course of it. They never dreamed he was any kind of danger — as we found out after a whole squad of men had worked for six months to crack the case of his disappearance.'

'Then the Scothanians have been holding the equivalent of a whole army, and didn't know it!'

'That's right,' nodded Walton. 'The biggest mistake they ever made was to kidnap Captain Flandry. They should have played safe and kept some nice harmless cobras for pets!'

Iuthagaar was burning. Mobs rioted in the streets and howled with fear and rage and the madness of catastrophe. The remnants of Penda's army had abandoned the town and were fleeing northward before the advancing southern rebels. They would be harried by Torric's guerrillas, who in turn were the fragments of a force smashed by Earl Morgaar after Penda was slain by Kortan's assassins. Morgaar himself was dead and his rebels broken by Nartheof. The earl's own band had been riddled by corruption and greed and had fallen apart before the royalists' counterblow.

But Nartheof was dead too, at the hands of Nornagast's vengeful relatives. His own seizure of supreme power and attempt at reorganisation had created little but confusion, which grew worse when he was gone. Now the royalists were a beaten force somewhere out in space, savagely attacked by their erstwhile allies, driven off the revolting conquered planets, and swept away before the remorselessly advancing Terrestrial fleet.

The Scothanian empire had fallen into a hundred shards, snapping at one another and trying desperately to retrieve their own with no thought for the whole. Lost in an incomprehensibly complex network of intrigue and betrayal, the great leaders fell, or pulled out of the mess and made hasty peace with Terra. War and anarchy flamed between the stars — but limited war, a petty struggle really. The resources and organisation for real war and its attendant destruction just weren't there any more.

A few guards still held the almost deserted palace, waiting for the Terrestrials to come and end the strife. There was nothing they could do but wait.

Captain Flandry stood at a window and looked over the city. He felt no great elation. Nor was he safe yet. Cerdic was loose somewhere on the planet, and Cerdic had undoubtedly guessed who was responsible.

Gunli came to the human. She was very pale. She hadn't expected Penda's death and it had hurt her. But there was nothing to do now but go through with the business.

'Who would have thought it?' she whispered. 'Who would have dreamed we would ever come to this? That mighty Scotha would lie at the conqueror's feet?'

'I would,' said Flandry tonelessly. 'Such jerry-built empires as yours never last. Barbarians just don't have the talent and the knowledge to run them. Being only out for plunder, they don't really build.

'Of course, Scotha was especially susceptible to this kind of sabotage. Your much-vaunted honesty was your own undoing. By carefully avoiding any hint of dishonourable actions, you became completely ignorant of the techniques and the preventive measures. Your honour was never more than a latent ability for dishonour. All I had to do, essentially, was to point out to your key men the rewards of betrayal. If they'd been really honest, I'd have died at the first suggestion. Instead, they grabbed at the chance. So it was easy to set them against one another until no one knew whom he could trust.' He smiled humourlessly. 'Not many Scothani objected to bribery or murder or treachery when it was shown to be to their advantage. I assure you, most Terrestrials would have thought further, been able to see beyond their own noses and realised the ultimate disaster it would bring.'

'Still — honour is honour, and I have lost mine and so have all my people.' Gunli looked at him with a strange light in her eyes. 'Dominic, disgrace can only be wiped out in blood.'

He felt a sudden tightening of his nerves and muscles, an awareness of something deadly rising before him. 'What do you mean?'

She had lifted the blaster from his holster and skipped out of reach before he could move. 'No — stay there!' Her voice was shrill. 'Dominic, you are a cunning man. But are you a brave one?'

He stood still before the menace of the weapon. 'I think — ' He groped for words. No, she wasn't crazy. But she wasn't really human, and she had the barbarian's fanatical code in her as well. Easy, easy, or death would spit at him. 'I think I took a few chances, Gunli.'

'Aye. But you never fought. You haven't stood up man to man and battled as a warrior should.' Pain racked her thin lovely face. She was breathing hard now. 'It's for you as well as him, Dominic. He has to have his chance to avenge his father — himself — fallen Scotha — and you have to have a chance too. If you can win, then you are the stronger and have the right.'

Might makes right. It was, after all, the one unbreakable law of Scotha. The old trial by combat, here on a foreign planet many light-years from green Terra —

Cerdic came in. He had a sword in either hand, and there was a savage glee in his bloodshot eyes.

'I let him in, Dominic,' said Gunli. She was crying now. 'I had to. Penda was my lord — but kill him, kill him!'

With a convulsive movement, she threw the blaster out of the window. Cerdic gave her an enquiring look. Her voice was almost inaudible: 'I might not be able to stand it. I might shoot you, Cerdic.'

'Thanks!' He ripped the word out, savagely. 'I'll deal with you later, traitress. Meanwhile — ' A terrible laughter bubbled in his throat — 'I'll carve your — friend — into many small pieces. Because who, among the so-civilised Terrestrials, can handle a sword?'

Gunli seemed to collapse. 'O gods, O almighty gods — I didn't think of that — '

Suddenly she flung herself on Cerdic, tooth and nail and horns, snatching at his dagger. 'Get him, Dominic!' she screamed. '*Get him!*'

The prince swept one brawny arm out. There was a dull smack and Gunli fell heavily to the floor.

'Now,' grinned Cerdic, 'choose your weapon!'

Flandry came forward and took one of the slender broadswords. Oddly, he was thinking mostly about the queen, huddled there on the floor. Poor kid, poor kid, she'd been under a greater strain than flesh and nerves were meant to bear. But give her a chance and she'd be all right.

Cerdic's eyes were almost dreamy now. He smiled as he crossed blades. 'This will make up for a lot,' he said. 'Before you die, Terrestrial, you will no longer be a man — '

Steel rang in the great hall. Flandry parried the murderous slash and raked the prince's cheek. Cerdic roared and plunged, his blade weaving a net of death before him. Flandry skipped back, sword ringing on sword, shoulders to the wall.

They stood for an instant, straining blade against blade, sweat rivering off them, and bit by bit the Scothan's greater strength bent Flandry's arm aside. Suddenly the Terrestrial let go, striking out almost in the same moment, and the prince's steel hissed by his face.

He ran back and Cerdic rushed him again. The Scothan was wide open for the simplest stop thrust, but Flandry didn't want to kill him. They closed once more, blades clashing, and the human waited for his chance.

It came, an awkward move, and then one supremely skilful twist. Cerdic's sword went spinning out of his hand and across the room and the prince stood disarmed with Flandry's point at his throat.

For a moment he gaped in utter stupefaction. Flandry laughed harshly and said: 'My dear friend, you forget that deliberate archaism is one characteristic of a decadent society. There's hardly a noble in the Empire who hasn't studied *scientific* fencing.'

Defeat was heavy in the prince's defiant voice: 'Kill me, then. Be done with it.'

'There's been too much killing, and you can be too useful.' Flandry threw his own weapon aside and cocked his fists. 'But there's one thing I've wanted to do for a long, long time.'

Despite the Scothan's powerful but clumsy defence, Flandry proceeded to beat the living hell out of him.

'We've saved Scotha, all Scotha,' said Flandry. 'Think, girl. What would have happened if you'd gone on into the Empire? Even if you'd won — and that was always doubtful, for Terra is mightier than you thought — you'd only have fallen into civil war. You just didn't have the capacity to run an empire — as witness the fact that your own allies and conquests turned on you the first chance they got. You'd have fought each other over the spoils, greater powers would have moved in, Scotha would have been ripe for sacking. Eventually you'd have gone down into Galactic oblivion. The present conflict was really quite small; it took far fewer lives than even a successful invasion of the Empire would have done. And now Terra will bring the peace you longed for, Gunli.'

'Aye,' she whispered. 'We deserve to be conquered.'

'But you aren't,' he said. 'The southerners hold Scotha now, and Terra will recognise them as the legal government — with you the queen, Gunli. You'll be another vassal state of the Empire, yes, but with all your freedoms except the liberty to rob and kill other races. And trade with the rest of the Empire will bring you a greater and more enduring prosperity than war ever would.

'I suppose that the Empire is decadent. But there's no reason why it can't some day have a renaissance. When the vigorous new peoples such as yours are guided by the ancient wisdom of Terra, the Galaxy may see its greatest glory.'

She smiled at him. It was still a wan smile, but something of her old spirit was returning to her. 'I don't think the Empire is so far gone, Dominic,' she said. 'Not when it has men like you.' She took his hands. 'And what will you be doing now?'

He met her eyes, and there was a sudden loneliness within him. She was very beautiful.

But it could never work out. Best to leave now, before a bright memory grew tarnished with the day-to-day clashing of personalities utterly foreign to each other. She would forget him in time, find someone else, and he — well — 'I have my work,' he said.

They looked up to the bright sky. Far above them, the first of the descending Imperial ships glittered in the sunlight like a falling star.

WARRIORS
FROM
NOWHERE

'Crime,' said Captain Dominic Flandry of the Terran Empire's Naval Intelligence Corps, 'is entirely a matter of degree. If you shoot your neighbour in order to steal his property, you are a murderer and a thief, and will be psycho-revised and enslaved. If, however, you gather a band of lusty fellows, knock off a couple of million people, and take their planet, you are a great conqueror, a world hero, and your name goes down in the history books. Sooner or later, this inconsistency seeps into the national consciousness and causes a desire for universal peace. That is known as decadence, especially among historical philosophers who never had to do any of the actual fighting. The Empire is currently in the early stages of decadence, which is the most agreeable time to inhabit: peace and pleasure, and the society not yet rotted so far that chaos sets in. One might say the Empire is a banana just starting to show brown spots.'

He was not jailed for his remarks because he made them in private, sitting on the balcony of his lodge on Varrak's southern continent and enjoying his usual noontime breakfast. His flamboyantly pyjamaed legs were cocked up on the rail. Sighting over his coffee cup and between his feet, he saw the mountainside drop steeply down to a green sun-flooded wilderness. The light played over a lean, straight-boned face and a long hard body which made him look anything but a petty noble of a sated imperium. But his business — maintaining the status quo of a realm threatened by internal decay and outside aggression — was a strenuous one.

His current mistress, Ella, offered him a cigarette and he inhaled it into lighting. She was a stunning blonde whom he had bought a few weeks previously in the planet's one city, Fort Lone. He gathered that she was of the old pioneer stock, semi-aristocrats who had fallen on evil times and been sold for debt. With such people he sympathised, but there was nothing he could do about the system; and she could have worse owners than himself.

He took another sip of coffee, wiped his moustache, and drew a breath to resume his musings. An apologetic cough brought his head around, and he saw his valet, the only other being in the lodge. This was a slim humanoid from Shalmu, with a hairless green skin, prehensile tail, and impeccable manners. Flandry had christened him Chives and taught him several things which made him valuable in more matters than laying out a dress suit. 'Pardon me, sir, Admiral Fenross is calling from the city.'

Flandry cursed and got up. 'Fenross! What's he doing on this planet? Tell him to — no, never mind, it's anatomically impossible.' He sauntered into the study, frowning. There was no love lost between him and his superior, but Fenross wouldn't call a man on furlough unless it was urgent.

The screen held a gaunt, sharp, red-haired face which dripped sweat past dark-shadowed eyes. 'There you are! Put in your scrambler, combination 770.' When Flandry had adjusted the dials, the admiral said harshly: 'Furlough cancelled. Get busy at once.' With a sudden break in his voice: 'Though God knows what you can do. But it means all our heads.'

Flandry sucked in his cheeks with a long drag of smoke. 'What is it — sir?'

'The sack of Fort Lone was more than a raid — '

'What sack?'

'You don't KNOW?'

'Haven't tuned the telescreen for a week, sir. I wanted to rest.'

Fenross snarled something and said thickly, 'Well, then, a barbarian horde streaked in yesterday, shot up all the defence posts, landed, and in three hours had put the place to the torch and looted all the available wealth. Also took about a thousand citizens, mostly women. They made a clean getaway before the nearest naval base was even alerted. No telling where they came from or where they went.'

Flandry cursed again, vividly. He knew the situation. The Taurian sector of the Empire was meant as a buffer; beyond it lay the wild stars, an unexplored jungle swarming with barbarian hordes who had gotten spaceships and atomic blasters too soon and used them only to plunder. There was always war on these marches, raids and punitive expeditions. But still — an attack on Varrak! He found it hard to believe.

'That's not our department, sir, unless we're wanted to track down just who did it,' he ventured. 'The Navy does the fighting, I'm told. So why pick on me?'

40

'You and every other man in the sector. Listen, Flandry, the barbarians have made away with her Highness, the Lady Megan of Luna, princess of the blood and the Emperor's favourite grand-daughter!'

'Hmmm — so.' Not a muscle stirred in Flandry's countenance, but he felt his belly grow tense and cold. 'I . . . see. What clues have you got?'

'Not many. One officer did manage to hide in the ruins and take a solidographic film — just a few minutes' worth. It may give us a lead; perhaps the xenological division can identify the raiders from it. But still — ' Fenross paused, it obviously hurt him to say so, but he got it out: 'We need you.'

'I should say you do, dear chief.' Modesty was not a failing of Flandry's. 'All right, I'll flit directly over. Cheers.' He cut the circuit and went back on to the balcony. Chives was clearing away the breakfast dishes and Ella sat smoking. 'So long, children. I'm on my way.'

The girl watched him with eyes like blued silver. 'What is it, Nick?' she asked quietly.

Flandry's mouth twisted. 'I'm not sure yet, but I think I've just been condemned to death.'

It was like a scene from hell.

Against a tumbled, blazing background of ruin, the barbarians were raging in an armoured swarm: huge burly men in helmet and cuirass, some carrying archaic swords. The picture was focused on a dais where a dozen young women were huddled, stripped alike of clothing and hope, the wildness of terror fading before despair. Some of them were being carried off towards a disc-shaped spaceship, others were still in the middle of the horde. They were being sold. Great gems, silver and gold, the loot of the city, were being tossed at the gnomish unhuman figure which squatted on the dais and handed down each purchase to a grinning conqueror.

The film ended. Flandry looked past the shattered walls of the building where he sat, to the smoking desolation which had been Fort Lone. Imperial marines were on guard, a relief station had been set up, a heavy battlewagon hung in the sky — all of which was too late to do much good.

'Well,' snapped Fenross, 'what d'you make of it?'

Flandry turned the enlarger knob, until one of the solid-seeming images stood gigantic before him. 'Definitely human,' he said. 'Except for that dwarf creature, I'd say they were all of Terrestrial race.'

'Of course! I know that much, you idiot. They must be from some early colony out here which got lost and reverted to barbarism. There have been such cases before. But which one? Is it even on record?'

'The spaceship is an odd design. I think there are some beings in the Merseian hegemony who still build that type, but it's not what I would expect barbarians imitating our boats to have.'

Fenross gulped and his knuckles whitened on the table edge. 'If the Merseians are behind this — '

Flandry gestured at the dwarf. 'Tall, dark, and handsome there may offer a clue to their origin. I don't know. I'll have to consult the files. But I must say this raid has a strange pattern. Varrak is light-years inside the border. There are plenty of tempting spots closer than this to the Wilderness. Then, the raiders knew exactly where to shoot and bomb to knock out all the defences. And, of course, they got the princess. Looks very much as if they had inside help, doesn't it?'

'I thought of that too. Every survivor of the garrison is being hypnoprobed, but so far none of them have known anything.'

'I doubt that any will. Our enemy is too smooth an operator to leave such clues. If he had collaborators in the fort, they left with the raiders and we'll list them as "missing, presumed disintegrated in action". But what's the story on her Highness?'

Fenross groaned. 'She was taking a tour of the outer marches. Those meatheads back on Terra should have known better than that! Or maybe the Imperial whim overruled them. The Lady Megan has the Emperor around her little finger. Anyhow, she went incognito, with a secret-service detachment to guard her, of course. But the raiders just smashed down the walls of the place where she was staying, shot all her guards, and made off with her and her servants.'

'Again,' said Flandry, 'it looks like inside information. Why else should they hit Varrak, except to get the princess? The looting was just a sideline. And apparently they knew precisely where she was housed.' He took out a cigarette and inhaled nervously. 'What d'you think their motive is? Ransom?'

'I hope to God it's just money. But I'm afraid — These barbarian kings aren't stupid. I'm afraid her ransom will be political and military concessions which we can ill afford. Especially if the raiders, as you suggest, are really Merseian agents. The Emperor will give it to them, regardless.' Fenross laid his head on his clenched fists. 'This could mean the beginning of the end for Terra.'

'I suppose his Majesty has not yet been informed?'

'Of course not! I know him. His first act on learning the news will be to have everybody who could possibly be responsible executed. That includes you and me, in case you don't know. I think we can suppress the information for a couple of weeks, maybe a month, but certainly no longer. If we don't get her back before then — ' Fenross drew a finger across his throat.

Flandry scowled. He was uncommonly fond of living. 'What are you doing?' he asked.

'Alerting all our agents. We'll comb the Wilderness. We'll fill the whole damned Merseian Empire with spies. But — I'm afraid we haven't time to do anything. Space is too big — ' Fenross turned angry eyes on his subordinate. 'Well, don't just sit there! Get going!'

'No sense duplicating effort, darling sir.' Flandry calculated his insolence deftly. 'I've got a notion of my own, if you'll give me a free hand to play with it. I'll want access to all the files, including the most confidential.'

'Go ahead,' mumbled Fenross. 'Enjoy yourself while you can.'

Flandry got up. 'It might stimulate my mind if a small reward were offered,' he said mildly.

The lodge was as good a place as any to begin his work. Tele-stats from the central files could be sent directly to him there, on scrambled circuit. A monitor in his receiver, responding to the Secret order, printed the material in code on tapes which would disintegrate within an hour. Flandry sat in dressing gown and slippers, wading through metre after metre of information; much of it had cost lives, some of it was worth an empire. It was the job of Intelligence to know everything about everyone in the attainable galaxy. Chives kept him supplied with coffee and cigarettes.

Ella stole up behind him near dawn and laid a hand on his head. 'Aren't you ever coming to bed, Nick?' she asked.

'Not yet,' he grunted. 'I'm on the track of a hunch. And if my notion is right, we have to move fast; there'll be less than the two weeks beloved Fenross, may he rot in hell, is counting on.

43

Our enemy will see that his august Majesty gets the news before then.'

She nodded, the light sliding down her long gold hair, and sat down at his feet. Slowly the sun rose.

'Stars and planets and little pink asteroids,' muttered Flandry at last. 'I may have the answer. Electronic cross-filing is a wonderful invention.'

She regarded him wordlessly. He rubbed his chin, feeling its unshaven bristles scratchy on his palm. 'But what I'm going to do with the answer, I don't know. Talk about sticking your head in a lion's mouth — '

He paced the floor restlessly. 'Chives is a handy fellow with a gun or a set of burglar's tools,' he said, 'but I need someone else.'

'Can I help, Nick?' asked Ella. 'I'd be glad to. You have been good to me.'

He regarded her a moment. Tall and lithe and fair, with something in her of the strength which had won this world from jungle — 'Ella,' he enquired suddenly, 'can you shoot?'

'I used to hunt ferazzes in the mountains,' she said.

'And — look — what would you say if I set you free? Not only that, but hunted up all the rest of your family and bought them free and set them up with some land of their own. The reward would cover that, with a bit to spare for my next poker game.'

Sudden tears were in her eyes. 'I don't have any words,' she said.

'But would you risk death, torture, degradation — whatever punishment a crazy all-powerful mind could think of, if we failed? You aren't so badly off now. Will you set it all on a turn of the cards?'

'Of course,' she said quietly, and rose to her feet.

He laughed and slapped her in a not very brotherly fashion. 'All right! You can come out on the target range and prove what you said about shooting while Chives packs.'

In Flandry's private speedster it was a three-day flit to Vor. After rehearsing what must be done, he spent the time amusing himself and his companions. There might not be another chance.

Vor had been settled early in the days of Imperial expansion, and had become a rich world, the natural choice of capital for the duke who governed the Taurian Sector. It was like another Terra — less grandiose, more bustling and businesslike — and the Sector itself was almost an empire within the Empire, a powerful realm of many stars whose ruler sat high in the councils of the Imperium.

Flandry left Chives in the boat at the main spaceport, and gave the postmaster a sizeable bribe to forget that his vessel was more heavily armed than a civilian craft ought to be. He and Ella caught a flittercab downtown and got a penthouse in one of the better hotels. Flandry never stinted himself when he was on expense account, but this time the penthouse had a business reason. You could land a spaceboat on the roof if a quick getaway became necessary.

He called the ducal palace that evening and got through to the chief social secretary. 'Captain Sir Dominic Flandry of his Majesty's Intelligence Corps,' he said pompously to the effeminate face. 'I would like an audience with his Grace. There is some business to discuss.'

'I am afraid, sir, that — '

A telescreen buzzed by the secretary's elbow. 'Excuse me.' He spoke to it. When he faced back around, his expression was obsequious. 'Of course, sir. His Grace would be pleased to see you at fourteen hundred tomorrow.'

'Good,' said Flandry. 'I'll buy you a lollipop sometime, Junior.' He switched off and laughed at Ella's astonished face. 'That does it,' he told her. 'Someone was monitoring the secretary, and when he got my name, let the secretary know in no uncertain terms that my presence is urgently desired at the palace — or, at least, that an invitation would allay my suspicions for a while.'

There were no lights on, but by the radiance of Vor's one great moon he saw her bite her lip. 'That doesn't sound good,' she said.

'It sounds very much as if my notion is right. Look here.' Flandry had been over all the points a dozen times, but he liked to hear himself talk. 'The Intelligence Corps is highly efficient if you point it in the right direction. In this case, the kidnapping was so designed that Fenross is pointed in a hundred different directions, none of them correct. He's tackling the hopeless job of investigating a million barbarian stars and the hostile Merseian Empire. But I, having a nasty suspicious mind, thought that there might be elements within our own territory

45

which would not mind having the Emperor's favourite grand-daughter for a guest.

'That alien-type spaceship was meant as a clue towards Merseia, but I didn't like it. Merseia is too far away from here for Wilderness barbarians to copy from them; and if the raid was their doing, why should they give themselves away so blatantly? Likewise, ordinary barbarian looters would not have come to Varrak in the first place, and wouldn't have had such accurate information in the second place. Even Merseia was unlikely to know about the princess' tour. Oh, they were genuine enough outlanders, you could see that on them — but who hired them, and who provided the leadership?

'That little gnome thing gave me a hunch. He was obviously in some position of authority, or he wouldn't have been demanding loot in exchange for those girls — the raiders would simply have taken the women themselves. The files held no information on a race of that exact description, but I did find out that his Grace, Duke Alfred of Tauria, has a number of aliens in his household, some of them from unknown regions where only a few human ships have ventured.

'Well, it seems logical. Before long, some barbarian king is going to demand a goodly chunk of this sector as Megan's ransom. She may be returned then, with her memory wiped clean of the circumstances, or she may not. The important thing is that the king will get the territory. The Emperor will suppose we can fight a war to get it back. But the king will be a puppet of Alfred's, and it'll be Alfred's own army which bears the brunt of that campaign. The duke, pretending all the time to be on our side, will see to it that we're beaten back and lose the rest of Tauria to boot. Then he can set himself up as an independent ruler, or he can make a deal with some rival empire like Merseia. In either case, we lose one of our main bulwarks.

'At least,' finished Flandry, 'that's how I'd work the business.'

Ella shivered, and there was something haunted in her eyes. 'War,' she whispered. 'Killing, burning, looting, enslaving — no!'

'It's up to us to stop it,' said Flandry. 'I can't tell Fenross my suspicions yet; even if he believed me, which is doubtful, the Taurian division of the Corps is probably full of Alfred's agents. He'd find out and take steps to halt us. We'd probably

46

all find ourselves jailed for treason. Now by announcing myself here, I must have alarmed his Grace. He'll want to know if I'm really on his trail — '

A shadow blocked out the moon and moved across the floor. Flandry peered cautiously through the window. Below the great skyscraper, the night city flared and blazed with a million jewelled lights, all the way up to the huge fortress-like castle on the hill. But there was a flitter landing on his roof.

'Quick work,' muttered Flandry between his teeth. His blaster slid from its holster. 'I thought the duke would wait to see me, but apparently not.'

Ella cradled a repeater rifle in her arms. In the darkened room, a shaft of moonlight threw her face into white, unreal relief. 'They may be innocent,' she said.

'They wouldn't land here without asking if they were.' Flandry saw half a dozen dark forms get out and start towards the penthouse. Moonrays glittered on metal. 'Local assassins, I daresay, hired to nab us. Let 'em have it!'

His blaster roared, a thunderbolt leaped through the windowpane and wrapped one man in flame. The others yelled, scattering. Ella's rifle spoke, and someone reeled on the edge of the roof and toppled horribly over the wall. Bullets cracked against the house.

'If this were ordinary innocent robbery, the police would be down on us like hawks,' observed Flandry. 'But they've been warned off here for tonight.' His nostrils dilated. 'Sleepy gas! Get your mask!'

The fight snarled for minutes. Two men came behind the house, blew open the door with a grenade, and sprang into the living room. Ella cut them down as Flandry fired out the window. Then there was silence.

'That's all,' said Flandry. His voice came muffled through the mask. 'Clumsy job. Friend Alfred must be rattled. Well, we'll give him time to think up something really fiendish for us.' He stepped over to the service screen and punched its button. 'I trust the manager has also been told to mind his own business tonight . . . Hello, service? I'm afraid there's a bit of a mess in our place. Can you send someone up to clean it?'

The audience hall was huge, and earlier dukes had furnished it with a luxury of gold and tapestry which was somewhat overwhelming. The present master hadn't bothered to remove this, but his more austere personality showed in the comfortless furniture and the armed guards who formed an unmoving wall on either side. Flandry felt dwarfed, but he walked with his usual swagger up to the throne, where he delivered a sweeping bow. In colourful clothes and ceremonial sword, he outshone the man who sat there.

Duke Alfred was big, his muscles running towards middle-aged paunch but hardness still on the blocky grey-bearded face. Flandry had met him briefly, some years before, and marked him for a dangerous man. 'Be at ease,' he said. His voice and the expressionless countenance did not echo the hospitable words. 'Whom have you here?' He nodded at Ella, who crouched abjectly on the carpet.

'A small present for your Grace,' said Flandry. 'She may amuse you.' There was nothing suspicious about that; one customarily brought gifts when visiting a noble, and both of them had been X-rayed for weapons as they entered.

'Hm.' Interest and appreciation flickered in the duke's eyes. 'Look at me, wench.' Ella raised a timid face. She was quite an actress, as Flandry had already learned. 'Good. Take her to the harem.' A gigantic four-armed Gorzunian slave kowtowed and led her out.

'Well,' said Alfred, 'what did you wish to see me about?'

'A trifling matter, your Grace, but it may be that you can furnish information my service needs.' Flandry spun a plausible tale of investigating some Merseian agents who were being sent to stir up discord in the outer provinces. Tactfully, he mentioned the fight last night and his belief that the enemy knew who was trailing them and had tried to wipe him out. Perpaps the duke had some news of their activities? So far they had not manifested themselves in Tauria but it was as well to make sure.

No, there was nothing. If any such news did come, the duke would certainly make it known to the Corps. Meanwhile, he was a busy man. Good day, Captain.

Flandry backed out. When he got to the castle gates, his spine crawled. Alfred was not going to let him get away so easily. There was bound to be another attempt to capture him and hypnoprobe him to find out if he really suspected anything. And this time the duke wasn't going to trust hired thugs.

Flandry went downtown to the local Corps office and filed a routine report on his ostensible mission. Alfred's men would be bound to check up on that much. More surreptitiously, he fetched a standard disguise kit and weapons from the locker where he had left them.

He ate a lonely supper in a restaurant, thinking rather wistfully of Ella, and dawdled over his liqueur. Two men who had entered shortly after him and taken a nearby table idled too, but rather awkwardly.

Flandry studied them without seeming to do so. One was a small, clever-looking chap, the other was big and rangy and had a military bearing. He must be one of the household guards, out of uniform for the occasion. He would do.

Flandry got up and strolled into the street. His shadows followed, mingling with the crowd. He could have shaken them easily enough, but that wasn't his intention. Give them every break instead; they were hard-working men and deserved a helping hand.

He caught a flittercab. 'Know any dives?' he asked fatuously. 'You know, music, girls, anything goes, but not too expensive.'

'Sure, sir.' The cabbie grinned and flew towards the slums which fringed the town. They landed on the twenty-fifth flange of a tall building which blinked with garishly obscene lights. Another cab spiraled down behind them.

Flandry spent a while in the bar, amused at the embarrassment of his shadows, and then picked a girl, a slim thing with a red insolent mouth. She snuggled against him as they went down the corridor. A door opened for them and they went through.

'Sorry, sister.' Flandry pulled out his stunner and let her have a medium beam. She'd be out for hours. He laid her on the bed and stood waiting, the weapon in his hand.

It was not long before the door opened again. His followers were there. Had they bribed or threatened the madam? Flandry's stunner dropped the smaller man.

The big one was on him like a tiger — a skilled twist, and the gun clanged free against the wall. Flandry drove a knee upward. Pain lanced through him as it jarred against body armour. The guardsman got a hold which should have pinned him. Flandry writhed free with a trick he knew, whirled about and delivered a rabbit punch that had all his weight behind it. The guardsman fell.

For a moment Flandry, panting, hesitated. It was safest to murder those two, but — He settled for giving his victims a hypo to keep them cold. Then he stepped out the window on to the emergency landing and signalled for a cab on his wrist-phone. When it arrived the driver looked into a blaster muzzle.

'We've got three sleepers to get rid of,' said Flandry cheerfully. 'On your way, friend, unless you want to add a corpse to the museum. You tote them.'

They left town well behind and found a region of woods, where they landed. Flandry stunned and hypoed the driver, and laid all four out under a tree. As an afterthought he folded their hands on their breasts and put white flowers in their fingers.

Now to work! He stripped them and took out his kit. The ID machine got busy, recording every detail of the guardsman's appearance. When he was finished, he threw his loot in the cab and took off. The sleepers would take till tomorrow to wake up, and then, without clothes or money, would need another day or more to reach an area where they could get help and report what had happened. By that time the affair would be over, one way or another.

As the autopilot flew him back, Flandry studied the guardsman's papers. At the edge of town he abandoned the cab and took another to the spaceport. He was sure there would be ducal agents watching there. They saw him enter his boat, get clearance for interstellar space, and take off. Presumably his mission was finished, or else he was scared and hightailing it for safety. In either case the enemy would tend to write him off, which would help matters considerably.

What the agents did not see was Flandry and Chives hard at work disguising the Terran. Much can be done with plastic face masks, false fingertips and the rest. It wouldn't pass a close examination, but Flandry was hoping there wouldn't be one. When he got through, he was Lieutenant Roger Bargen of the ducal household guards. The boat landed near a village some fifty kilometres from town. Flandry caught the morning monorail back.

He did not report to his colonel when he entered the castle. That would have been asking for a hypnoprobe. But it was pretty clear that Bargen's job had been secret, none of his mess-mates would have known of it — so if they saw Bargen scurrying around the place, too busy for conversation, it would not occur to them that anything had gone wrong. Of course, the deception could only last a few hours, but Flandry was betting that he would only need that long.

In fact, he reflected grimly, *I'm betting my life.*

Ella the slave, who had been Ella McIntyre and a free woman of Varrak's hills, did not like the harem. There was something vile about its perfumed atmosphere, and she hoped the duke would not send for her that night. If he did — well, that was part of the price. But she was left alone. There was a dormitory for the lesser inmates, like a luxurious barracks, and a wide series of chambers for them to lounge in, and silent non-human slaves to bring them food. She prowled restlessly about as the day waned. The other women watched her but said little; such new arrivals must be fairly common.

But she had to make friends, fast. The harem was the most logical place for the duke to hide his prisoner, secrecy and seclusion were the natural order of things here. But it would be a gossipy little world. She picked an alert-looking girl with wide bright eyes, and wandered up to her and smiled shyly. 'Hello,' she said. 'My name is Ella.'

'Just come in, I suppose?'

'Yes. I'm a present. Ummm — ah — how is it here?'

'Oh, not such a bad life. Not much to do. Gets a little boring.' Ella shivered at the thought of a lifetime inside these walls, but nodded meekly. The other girl wanted to know what was going on outside, and Ella spent some hours telling her.

The conversation finally drifted the way she hoped. Yes — something strange. The whole western suite had been sealed off, with household troopers on guard at the door to the hallway. Somebody new must be housed there, and speculation ran wild on the who and why.

Ella held her tension masked with a shivering effort. 'Have you any idea who it might be?' she asked brightly.

'I don't know. Maybe some alien. His Grace has funny tastes. But you'll find that out, my dear.'

Ella bit her lips.

That night she could not sleep at all. It was utterly dark, a thick velvety black full of incense, it seemed to strangle her. She wanted to scream and run, run between the stars till she was back in the loved lost hills of Varrak. A lifetime without seeing the sun or feeling the hill-wind on her face! She turned wearily, wondering why she had ever agreed to help Flandry.

But if he lived and came to her, she could tell him what he

51

wanted to know. *If* he lived! And even if he did, they were in the middle of a fortress. He would be flayed alive, and she — *God, let me sleep. Just let me sleep and forget.*

The fluorotubes came on again with morning, a cold dawn. She bathed in the swimming pool and ate her breakfast without tasting. She wondered if she looked as tired and haggard as she felt.

A scaled hand touched her shoulder. She whirled about with a little shriek and looked into a beaked reptile face. It spoke hissingly: 'You are the new concubine?'

She tried to answer but her throat tightened up.

'Come.' The guard turned and strode away. Numbly, she went after him. The chatter in the harem died as she went by, and the eyes that followed were frightened. A girl was not summoned by an armed guard for pleasure.

They went down a long series of chambers. At the end there was a door. It opened at the guard's gesture, and he waved her in. As he followed, the door closed behind him.

The room was small and bare. It held a chair with straps and wires and a switchboard; she recognised the electronic torture machine which left no marks on the flesh. In another chair crouched a being who was not human. Its small hunched body was wrapped in gorgeous robes, and great lustreless eyes regarded her from the bulging hairless head.

'Sit down.' A thin hand waved her to the electronic chair, and she took it helplessly. 'I want to talk to you. You will do well to answer without lies.' The voice was high and squeaky, but there was nothing ridiculous about the goblin who spoke. 'for your information, I am Sarlish of Jagranath, which lies beyond the Empire; I am his Grace's chief intelligence officer, so you see this is no routine matter. You were brought here by a man of whom I have suspicions. Why?'

'As — a gift — sir,' she whispered.

'*Timeo Danaos et dona ferentes*,' said Sarlish surprisingly. 'I did not learn of it till this morning, or I would have investigated sonner. You are just a common slave?'

'Yes — sir — he bought me on Varrak before coming here — '

'Varrak, eh? I'd like to hypnoprobe you, but that would leave you in no fit state for his Grace tonight if you should be innocent. I think — ' Sarlish stroked his meagre chin contemplatively. 'Yes. A bit of pain will disorganise your mind enough so that if you are lying, the proper questions will bring

52

out inconsistencies. After that we can see about the probe. I am sorry.' He gestured to the guard.

Ella leaped up, yelling. The guard snatched for her and she ducked free, driving a kick at his belly. He grunted and stepped back. She threw herself at the door. As it opened, the reptile hands closed on her arm. Whirling, she brought the extended fingers of her free hand into his eyes. He screamed and backed away.

'Ah, so,' murmured Sarlish. He took out a stunner and aimed it judicially at the struggling pair.

'I wouldn't try that, Dollie,' said a voice in the doorway.

Sarlish spun about to face a blaster. 'Bargen!' he cried dropping his weapon. Then, slowly: 'No, Captain Flandry, isn't it?'

'In person, and right in the traditional nick of time.' The blinded guard lurched towards him. Flandry shot him with a narrow beam. Sarlish sprang from his chair at fantastic speed and scuttled between his legs, bringing him down. Ella leaped over the Terran and caught the gnome with a flying tackle. Sarlish hissed and clawed. She twisted at his neck in sheer self-defence, and suddenly the thin spine snapped and Sarlish kicked once and was still.

'Nice going!' Flandry scrambled to his feet. With a quick motion, he peeled off the face mask. 'Too hot in this damned thing. All right, did you find our princess?'

'This way.' A swift cold gladness was in the girl. She bent and picked up the dead guard's blaster. 'I'll show you. But can we — ?'

'Not by ourselves. But I've signalled Chives. Got at a radio just before coming here. Though how he's going to find exactly where we are, I don't know. I've had to assume you'd succeeded —' Flandry zigzagged to avoid a flock of screaming girls. 'Wow! No wonder the duke has non-human servants here!'

'Behind that wall — we'll have to go around, through the hall,' panted Ella.

'And be shot as we come? No, thanks!' Flandry began assembling scattered chairs and divans into a rough barricade before the wall. 'Cut our way through, will you?'

Plastic bubbled and smoked as Ella's flame attacked it. Flandry went on: 'I bluffed my way in here by saying I had to fetch someone. A girl told me where you'd been taken. Imagine the

53

only reason I got away with it is that no man would dare come in here unless he had orders from Alfred himself. But now there's the devil to pay, and I only hope Chives can locate us in time and not get himself blown out of the sky.' He looked along the barrel of his blaster, down the arched length to the room to the rest of the suite. 'Here they come!'

A troop of guards burst into sight. Flandry set his blaster to needle beam — that gave maximum range, but you had to be skilful to hit anything at such a distance. One of the men toppled. A curtain of fire raged before the others. The heat of it scorched his face. He picked off another man, and another. But the rest were circling around, getting within wide-beam range, and one shot could fry him. 'Get that wall cut!'

'Here goes!' Ella jumped back as the circle she had burned collapsed outward. A drop of molten plastic stung her skin. The barricade burst into flame as a beam caught it. She tumbled through the hole, heedless of its hot edges, and Flandry followed her.

The girl inside crouched against the wall, mouth open with terror. She was dark, with a pretty, vacuous face that showed the Imperial blood. 'Lady Megan?' snapped Flandry.

'Yes,' she whimpered. 'Who are you?'

'At your service, your highness — I hope.' Flandry sent a wide beam out through the hole in the wall. A man screamed his agony. The agent reflected bitterly how many brave folk — probably including Ella and himself — were dead because a spoiled brat had wanted a new kind of thrill.

The door swung inward. Ella blasted as it did, and there was a roar of disintegrating flesh and bone and armour. Flandry heaved a sofa up against the sagging door. Poor protection — they could only hold out for minutes.

He turned a sweating, smoke-blackened face to the princess. 'I take it you know the duke kidnapped you, your Highness?' he asked.

'Yes,' she winced. 'But he wasn't going to hurt me — '

'So you think! I happen to know he intended to kill you.' That wasn't exactly true, but it served its purpose. If they lived, Megan wouldn't get him in trouble for endangering her life. She even began babbling something about a reward, and Flandry hoped Ella would remember it later. If there was a later.

He had one advantage. The duke could not use heavy stuff to

54

blow them all up without killing his prisoner. But — He passed out three gas masks.

The outer wall glowed. A circle was being cut from it, big enough to let a dozen men through at a time. Flandry and Ella could blast the first wave, but the next would overpower them.

Smoke swirled heavy and bitter in the room. It was hot, stinking of sweat and blood. Flandry grinned crookedly. 'Well, darling,' he said, 'it was a nice try.' Ella's hand stroked his hair, briefly.

Something bellowed outside. The walls trembled, and he heard the rumble and crash of falling masonry. Outside, the noise of blasters and bullets grew to a storm.

'Chives!' whooped Flandry.

'What?' asked Megan faintly.

'Salade of Alfred au naturel with Chives,' burbled Flandry. 'You must meet Chives, your Highness. One of nature's noblemen. He — how the hell did he do it?'

A volcano growled outside, the walls glowed red, and then there was silence.

Flandry pulled the burning sofa away and risked a glance into the corridor. It was a ruin, scorched and tumbled by the full impact of a naval blaster canon. The attacking troopers had simply ceased to exist. A series of smashed walls showed open sky far beyond. Hovering in the wreckage was his own lean speedster.

'Chives,' said Flandry in awe, 'merely swooped up to the fortress at full drive, blew his way in with the guns and bombs, and opened up on the duke's men.'

The airlock swung wide, and a green head looked out. 'I would recommend haste, sir,' said Chives. 'The alarm is out, and they have fighting ships.'

He extended a ladder. Flandry and the girls tumbled up it, the airlock clanged shut behind them, and the boat took off with a yell. Behind it, a small cruiser lifted from the military field.

'How did you find us?' gasped Flandry. 'I didn't even know where the harem was myself when I called you.'

'I assumed there would be fighting, sir,' said Chives modestly. 'Blasters ionise the air. I used the radiation detectors to fix your direction as I approached.' He set the boat on autopilot and moved over to the tiny galley.

Flandry studied the viewscreens as the planet fell beneath them. 'That cruiser — ' he muttered. 'No — look at the radar —

we're distancing it. This can of ours has legs. We'll make it to Varrak all right.'

He glanced about the cabin. Ella was trying to soothe a hysterical Megan. She looked up to him for a moment and he saw glory in her eyes.

'Our only worry,' he said, 'is that dear Alfred might rise in open revolt now that he's exposed. If that happens, Merseia would probably move in and we'd have a general war on our hands.'

Chives looked up from the stove. 'His Grace was directing the assault on your stronghold, sir,' he said. 'When I fired on the soldiers, I fear I took the liberty of disintegrating the duke as well. Does her Highness take sugar or lemon in her tea?

HONOURABLE
ENEMIES

I

The door swung open behind him and a voice murmured gently: 'Good evening, Captain Flandry.'

He spun around, grabbing for his stun pistol in a wild reflex, and found himself looking down the muzzle of a blaster. Slowly, then, he let his hands fall and stood taut, his eyes searching beyond the weapon, and the slender six-fingered hand that held it, to the tall gaunt body and the sardonically smiling face behind.

The face was humanoid — lean, hawk-nosed, golden-skinned, with brilliant amber eyes under feathery blue brows, and a high crest of shing blue feathers rising from the narrow hairless skull. The being was dressed in a simple white tunic of his people, leaving his clawed avian feet bare, but insignia of rank hung bejewelled around his neck and a cloak like a gush of blood from his wide shoulders.

But they'd all been occupied elsewhere — Flandry had seen to that. What had slipped up — ?

With an effort, Flandry relaxed and let a wry smile cross his face. Never mind who was to blame; he was trapped in the Merseian chambers and had to think of a way to escape with a whole skin. His mind whirred with thought. Memory came — this was Aycharaych of Chereion, who had come to join the Merseian embassy only a few days before, presumably on some mission corresponding to Flandry's.

'Pardon the intrusion,' he said; 'it was purely professional. No offence meant.'

'And none taken,' said Aycharaych politely. He spoke faultless Anglic, only the faintest hint of his race's harsh accent in the syllables. But courtesy between spies was meaningless. It would be too easy to blast down the intruder and later express his immense regret that he had shot down the ace intelligence officer of the Terrestrial Empire under the mistaken impression that it was a burglar.

Somehow, though, Flandry didn't think that the Chereionite would be guilty of such crudeness. His mysterious people were too old, too coldly civilised, and Aycharaych himself had too great a reputation for subtlety. Flandry had heard of him before; he would be planning something worse.

'That is quite correct,' nodded Aycharaych. Flandry started — could the being guess his exact thoughts? 'But if you will pardon my saying so, you yourself have committed a bit of clumsiness in trying to search our quarters. There are better ways of getting information.'

Flandry gauged distances and angles. A vase on a table stood close to hand. If he could grab it up and throw it at Aycharaych's gun hand.—

The blaster waved negligently. 'I would advise against the attempt,' said the Chereionite.

He stood aside. 'Good evening, Captain Flandry,' he said.

The Terran moved towards the door. He couldn't let himself be thrown out this way, not when his whole mission depended on finding out what the Merseians were up to. If he could make a sudden lunge as he passed close —

He threw himself sideways with a twisting motion that brought him under the blaster muzzle. Hampered by a greater gravity than the folk of his small planet were used to, Aycharaych couldn't dodge quickly enough. But he swung the blaster with a vicious precision across Flandry's jaw. The Terran stumbled, clasping the Chereionite's narrow waist. Aycharaych slugged him at the base of the skull and he fell to the floor.

He lay there a moment, gasping, blood running from his face. Aycharaych's voice jeered at him from a roaring darkness: 'Really, Captain Flandry, I had thought better of you. Now please leave.'

Sickly, the Terran crawled to his feet and went out the door. Aycharaych stood in the entrance watching him go, a faint smile on his hard, gaunt visage.

Flandry went down endless corridors of polished stone to the suite given the Terrestrial mission. Most of them were at the feast, the ornate rooms stood almost empty. He threw himself into a chair and signalled his personal slave for a drink. A stiff one.

There was a light step and the suggestive whisper of a long silkite skirt behind him. He looked around and saw Aline Chang-Lei, the Lady Marr of Syrtis, his partner on the mission and one of Sol's top field agents for intelligence.

She was tall and slender, dark of hair and eye, with the high cheekbones and ivory skin of a mixed heritage such as most Terrans showed these days; her sea-blue gown did little more than emphasise the appropriate features. Flandry liked to look at her, though he was pretty well immune to beautiful women by now.

'What was the trouble?' she asked at once.

'What brings you here?' he responded. 'I thought you'd be at the party, helping distract everyone.'

'I just wanted to rest for a while,' she said. 'Official functions at Sol get awfully dull and stuffy, but they go to the other extreme at Betelgeuse. I wanted to hear silence for a while.' And then, with grave concern: 'But you ran into trouble.'

'How the hell it happened, I can't imagine,' said Flandry. 'Look — we prevailed on the Sartaz to throw a brawl with everybody invited. We made double sure that every Merseian on the planet would be there. They'd trust to their robolocks to keep their quarters safe — they have absolutely no way of knowing that I've found a way to nullify a robolock. So what happens? I no sooner get inside than Aycharaych of Chereion walks in with a blaster in his hot little hand. He anticipates everything I try and finally shows me the door. Finis.'

'Aycharaych — I've heard the name somewhere. But it doesn't sound Merseian.'

'It isn't. Chereion is an obscure but very old planet in the Merseian Empire. Its people have full citizenship with the dominant race, just as our empire grants Terrestrial citizenship to many non-humans. Aycharaych is one of Merseia's leading intelligence agents. Few people have heard of him, precisely because he is so good. I've never clashed with him before, though.'

'I know whom you mean now,' she nodded. 'If he's as you say, and he's here on Alfzar it isn't good news.'

Flandry shrugged. 'We'll just have to take him into account, then. As if this mission weren't tough enough!'

He got up and walked to the balcony window. The two moons of Alfzar were up, pouring coppery light on the broad reach of the palace gardens. The warm wind blew in with scent of strange flowers that had never bloomed under Sol and they caught the faint sound of the weird, tuneless music which the monarch of Betelgeuse favoured.

For a moment, as he looked at the ruddy moonlight and the thronging stars, Flandry felt a wave of discouragement. The

61

Galaxy was too big. Even the four million stars of the Terrestrial Empire were too many for one man ever to know in a lifetime. And there were the rival imperia out in the darkness of space, Gorrazan and Ythri and Merseia, like a hungry beast of prey —

Too much, too much. The individual counted for too little in the enormous chaos which was modern civilisation. He thought of Aline — it was her business to know who such beings as Aycharaych were, but one human skull couldn't hold a universe; knowledge and power were lacking.

Too many mutually alien races; too many forces clashing in space, and so desperately few who comprehended the situation and tried their feeble best to help — naked hands battering at an avalanche as it ground down on them.

Aline came over and took his arm. Her face turned up to his, vague in the moonlight, with a look he knew too well. He'd have to avoid her, when or if they got back to Terra; he didn't want to hurt her but neither could he be tied to any single human.

'You're discouraged with one failure?' she asked lightly. 'Dominic Flandry, the single-handed conqueror of Scothania, worried by one skinny bird-being?'

'I just don't see how he knew I was going to search his place,' muttered Flandry. 'I've never been caught that way before, not even when I was the worst cub in the Service. Some of our best men have gone down before Aycharaych. I'm convinced MacMurtrie's disappearance at Polaris was his work. Maybe it's our turn now.'

'Oh, come off it,' she laughed. 'You must have been drinking *sorgan* when they told you about him.'

'*Sorgan?*' His brows lifted.

'Ah, now I can tell you something you don't know.' She was trying desperately hard to be gay. 'Not that it's very important; I only happened to hear of it while talking with one of the Alfzarian narcotics detail. It's a drug produced on one of the planets here — Cingetor, I think — with the curious property of depressing certain brain centres such that the victim loses all critical sense. He has absolute faith in whatever he's told.'

'Hm. Could be useful in our line of work.'

'Not very. Hypnoprobes are better for interrogation, and there are more reliable ways of producing fanatics. The drug has an antidote which also confers permanent immunity. So it's not much use, really, and the Sartaz has suppressed its manufacture.'

'I should think our Intelligence would like to keep a little on hand, just in case,' he said thoughtfully. 'And of course certain nobles in all the empires, ours included, would find it handy for purposes of seduction.'

'What *are* you thinking of? she teased him.

'Nothing; I don't need it,' he said smugly.

The digression had shaken him out of his dark mood. 'Come on,' he said. 'Let's go join the party.'

She went along at his side. There was a speculative look about her.

II

Usually the giant stars have many planets, and Betelgeuse, with forty-seven, is no exception. Of these, six have intelligent native races, and the combined resources of the whole system are considerable, even in a civilisation used to thinking in terms of thousands of stars.

When the first Terrestrial explorers arrived, almost a thousand years previously, they found that the people of Alfzar had already mastered interplanetary travel and were in the process of conquering the other worlds — a process speeded up by their rapid adoption of the more advanced human technology. However, they had not attempted to establish an empire on the scale of Sol or Merseia, contenting themselves with maintaining hegemony over enough neighbour suns to protect their home. There had been clashes with the expanding powers around them, but generations of wily Sartazes had found it profitable to play their potential enemies off against each other; and the great states had, in turn, found it expedient to maintain Betelgeuse as a buffer against their rivals and against the peripheral barbarians.

But the gathering tension between Terra and Merseia had raised Betelgeuse to a position of critical importance. Lying squarely between the two great empires, she was in a position with her powerful fleet to command the most direct route between them and, if allied with either one, to strike at the heart of the other. If Merseia could get the alliance, it would very probably be the last preparation she considered necessary for war with Terra. If Terra could get it, Merseia would suddenly be in a deteriorated position and would almost have to make concessions.

So both empires had missions on Alfzar trying to persuade the Sartaz of the rightness of their respective causes and the immense profits to be had by joining. Pressure was being applied wherever possible; officials were lavishly bribed; spies were swarming through the system getting whatever information they could and — of course — being immediately disowned by their governments if they were caught.

It was normal diplomatic procedure, but its critical importance had made the Service send two of its best agents, Flandry and Aline, to Betelgeuse to do what they could in persuading the Sartaz, finding out his weaknesses, and throwing as many monkey wrenches as possible into the Merseian activities. Aline was especially useful in working on the many humans who had settled in the system long before and become citizens of the kingdom; quite a few of them held important positions in the government and the military. Flandry —

And now, it seemed, Merseia had called in *her* top spy, and the subtle, polite, and utterly deadly battle was on.

The Sartaz gave a hunting party for his distinguished guests. It pleased his sardonic temperament to bring enemies together under conditions where they had to be friendly to each other. Most of the Merseians must have been pleased, too; hunting was their favourite sport. The more citified Terrestrials were not at all happy about it, but they could hardly refuse.

Flandry was especially disgruntled at the prospect. He had never cared for physical exertion, though he kept in trim as a matter of necessity. And he had too much else to do.

Too many things were going disastrously wrong. The network of agents, both Imperial and bribed Betelgeusean — who ultimately were under his command — were finding the going suddenly rugged. One after another, they disappeared; they walked into Merseian or Betelgeusean traps; they found their best approaches blocked by unexpected watchfulness. Flandry couldn't locate the source of the difficulty, but since it had begun with Aycharaych's arrival, he could guess. The Chereionite was too damned smart to be true. Sunblaze, it just wasn't possible that anyone could have known about those Jurovian projects, or that Yamatsu's hiding place should have been

64

discovered, or — And now this damned hunting party! Flandry groaned.

His slave roused him in the dawn. Mist, tinged with blood by the red sun, drifted through the high windows of his suite. Someone was blowing a horn somewhere, a wild call in the vague mysterious light, and he heard the growl of engines warming up.

'Sometimes,' he muttered sourly, 'I feel like going to the emperor and telling him where to put our beloved empire.'

Breakfast made the universe slightly more tolerable. Flandry dressed with his usual finicky care in an ornate suit of skintight green and a golden cloak with hood and goggles, hung a needle gun and duelling sword at his waist, and let the slave trim his reddish-brown moustache to the micrometric precision he demanded. Then he went down long flights of marble stairs, past royal guards in helmet and corselet, to the courtyard.

The hunting party was gathering. The Sartaz himself was present, a typical Alfzarian humanoid — short, stocky, hairless, blue-skinned, with huge yellow eyes in the round, blunt-faced head. Other nobles of Alfzar and its fellow planets were present, more guardsmen, a riot of colour in the brightening dawn. There were the members of the regular Terrestrial embassy and the special mission, a harried and unhappy looking crew. And there were the Merseians.

Flandry gave them all formal greetings. After all, Terra and Merseia were nominally at peace, however many men were being shot and cities burning on the marches. His grey eyes looked sleepy and indifferent but they missed no detail of the enemy's appearance.

The Merseian nobles glanced at him with the thinly covered contempt they had for all humans. They were mammals, but with more traces of reptilian ancestry in them than Terrans showed. A huge-thewed two metres they stood, with a spiny ridge running from forehead to the end of the long, thick tail which they could use to such terrible effect in hand-to-hand battle. Their hairless skins were pale green, faintly scaled, but their massive faces were practically human. Arrogant black eyes under heavy brow ridges met Flandry's gaze with a challenge.

I can understand that they despise us, he thought. *Their civilisation is young and vigorous, its energies turned ruthlessly outward; Terra is old, satiated — decadent. Our whole policy is* directed towards maintaining the galactic status quo, not because we love peace but because we're comfortable the way things are. We stand in the way of Merseia's dream of an all-embracing galactic empire. We're the first ones they have to smash.

I wonder — historically, they may be on the right side. But Terra has seen too much bloodshed in her history, has too wise and weary a view of life. We've given up seeking perfection and glory; we've learned that they're chimerical — but that knowledge is a kind of death within us.

Still — I certainly don't want to see planets aflame and humans enslaved and an alien culture taking up the future. Terra is willing to compromise; but the only compromise Merseia will ever make is with overwhelming force. Which is why I'm here.

A stir came in the streaming red mist, and Aycharaych's tall form was beside him. The Chereionite smiled amiably. 'Good morning, Captain Flandry,' he said.

'Oh — good morning,' said Flandry, starting. The avian unnerved him. For the first time, he had met his professional superior, and he didn't like it.

But he couldn't help liking Aycharaych personally. As they stood waiting, they fell to talking of Polaris and its strange worlds, from which the conversation drifted to the comparative xenology of intelligent primitives throughout the galaxy. Aycharaych had a vast fund of knowledge and a wry humour matching Flandry's. When the horn blew for assembly, they exchanged the regretful glance of brave enemies. *It's too bad we have to be on opposite sides. If things had been different —*

But they weren't.

The hunters strapped themselves into their tiny one-man airjets. Each had a needle-beam projector in the nose, not too much armament when you hunted the Borthudian dragons. Flandry thought that the Sartaz would be more than pleased if the game disposed of some of his guests.

The squadron lifted into the sky and streaked northward for the mountains. Fields and forests lay in dissolving fog below them, and the enormous red disc of Betelgeuse was rising into a purplish sky. Despite himself, Flandry enjoyed the reckless speed and the roar of cloven air around him. It was godlike, this rushing over the world to fight the monsters at its edge.

In a couple of hours, they raised the Borthudian mountains,

gaunt windy peaks rearing into the upper sky, the snow on their flanks like blood in the ominous light. Signals began coming over the radio; scouts had spotted dragons here and there, and jet after jet broke away to pursue them. Presently Flandry found himself alone with one other vessel.

As they hummed over fanged crags and swooping canyons, he saw two shadows rise from the ground and his belly muscles tightened. Dragons!

The monsters were a good ten metres of scaled, snake-like length, with jaws and talons to rend steel. Huge leathery wings bore them aloft, riding the wind with lordly arrogance as they hunted the great beasts that terrorised villagers but were their prey.

Flandry kicked over his jet and swooped for one of them. It grew monstrously in his sights. He caught the red glare of its eyes as it banked to meet him. No running away here; the dragons had never learned to be afraid. It rose against him.

He squeezed his trigger and a thin sword of energy leaped out to burn past the creature's scales into its belly. The dragon held to its collision course. Flandry rolled out of its way. The mighty wings clashed metres from him.

He had not allowed for the tail. It swung savagely and the blow shivered the teeth in his skull. The airjet reeled and went into a spin. The dragon stooped down on it and the terrible claws ripped through the thin hull.

Wildly, Flandry slammed over his controls, tearing himself loose. He barrel-rolled, metal screaming as he swung about to meet the charge. His needle beam lashed into the open jaws and the dragon stumbled in midflight. Flandry pulled away and shot again, flaying one of the wings.

He could hear the dragon's scream. It rushed straight at him, swinging with fantastic speed and precision as he sought to dodge. The jaws snapped together and a section of hull skin was torn from the framework. Wind came in to sear the man with numbing cold.

Recklessly, he dived to meet the plunging monster, his beam before him like a lance. The dragon recoiled. With a savage grin, Flandry pursued, slashing and tearing.

The torn airjet handled clumsily. In midflight, it lurched and the dragon was out of his sights. Its wings buffeted him and he went spinning aside with the dragon after him.

The damned thing was forcing him towards the cragged

mountainside. Its peaks reached hungrily after him, and the wind seemed to be a demon harrying him closer to disaster. He swung desperately, aware with sudden grimness that it had become a struggle for life with the odds on the dragon's side.

If this was the end, to be shattered against a mountain and eaten by his own quarry — He fought for control.

The dragon was almost on him, rushing down like a thunderbolt. It could survive a collision, but the jet would be knocked to earth. Flandry fired again, struggling to pull free. The dragon swerved and came on in the very teeth of his beam.

Suddenly it reeled and fell aside. The other jet was on it from behind, raking it with deadly precision. Flandry thought briefly that the remaining dragon must be dead or escaped and now its hunter had come to his aid — all the gods bless him, whoever he was!

Even as he watched, the dragon fell to earth, writhing and snapping as it did. It crashed on to a ledge and lay still.

Flandry brought his jet to a landing nearby. He was shaking with reaction, but his chief emotion was a sudden overwhelming sadness. There went another brave creature down into darkness, wiped out by a senseless history that seemed only to have the objective of destroying. He raised a hand in salute as he grounded.

The other jet had already landed a few metres off. As Flandry opened his cockpit canopy, its pilot stepped out.

Aycharaych.

The man's reaction was almost instantaneous. Gratitude and honour had no part in the Service. Here was his greatest enemy, all unsuspecting, and it would be the simplest thing in the world to shoot him down. Aycharaych of Chereion, lost in a hunt for dangerous game, too bad — and remorse could come later, when there was time —

His needle pistol was halfway from the holster when Aycharaych's weapon was drawn. Through the booming wind, he heard the alien's quiet voice: 'No.'

He raised his own hands, and his smile was bitter. 'Go ahead,' he invited. 'You've got the drop on me.'

'Not at all,' said Aycharaych. 'Believe me, Captain Flandry, I will never kill you except in self-defence. But since I will always be forewarned of your plans, you may as well abandon them.'

The man nodded, too weary to feel the shock of the revelation which was here. 'Thanks,' he said. 'For saving my life, that is.'

'You're too useful to die,' replied Aycharaych candidly, 'But I'm glad of it.'

They took the dragon's head and flew slowly back towards the palace. Flandry's mind whirled with a gathering dismay.

There was only one way in which Aycharaych could have known of the murder plan, when it had sprung into instantaneous being. And that same fact explained how he knew of every activity and scheme the Terrestrials tried, and how he could frustrate every one of them while his own work went on unhampered.

Aycharaych could read minds!

III

Aline's face was white and tense in the red light that streamed into the room. 'No,' she whispered.

'Yes,' said Flandry grimly. 'It's the only answer.'

'But telepathy — everyone knows its limitations — '

Flandry nodded. 'The mental patterns of different races are so alien that a telepath who can sense them has to learn a different "language" for every species — in fact, for every individual among non-telepathic peoples, whose minds, lacking mutual contact, develop purely personal thought-types. Even then it's irregular and unreliable. I've never let myself be studied by any telepath not on our side, so I'd always considered myself safe.

'But Chereion is a very old planet. Its people have the reputation among the more superstitious Merseians of being sorcerers. Actually, of course, it's simply that they've discovered certain things about the nervous system which nobody else suspects yet. Somehow, Aycharaych must be able to detect some underlying resonance-pattern common to all intelligent beings.

'I'm sure he can only read surface thoughts, those in the immediate consciousness. Otherwise he'd have found out so much from all the Terrans with whom he must have had contact that Merseia would be ruling Sol by now. But that's bad enough!'

Aline said drearily, 'No wonder he spared your life; you've become the most valuable man on his side!'

'And not a thing I can do about it,' said Flandry. 'He sees me every day. I don't know what the range of his mind is — probably only a few metres; it's known that all mental pulses are weak and fade rapidly with distance. But in any case, every time he meets me he skims my mind, reads all my plans — I just can't help thinking about them all the time — and takes action to forestall them.'

'We'll have to get the Imperial scientists to work on a thought screen.'

'Of course. But that doesn't help us now.'

'Couldn't you just avoid him, stay in your rooms — '

'Sure. And become a complete ciper. I have to get around, see my agents and the rulers of Betelgeuse, learn facts and keep my network operating. And every single thing I learn is just so much work done for Aycharaych — with no effort on his part.' Flandry puffed a cigarette into lighting and blew nervous clouds of smoke. 'What to do, what to do?'

'Whatever we do,' said Aline, 'it has to be fast. The Sartaz is getting more and more cool towards our people. While we blunder and fail, Aycharaych is working — bribing, blackmailing, influencing one key official after another. We'll wake up some fine morning to find ourselves under arrest and Betelgeuse the loyal ally of Merseia.'

'Fine prospect,' said Flandry bitterly.

The waning red sunlight streamed through his windows, throwing pools of dried blood on the floor. The palace was quiet, the nobles resting after the hunt, the servants scurrying about preparing the night's feast. Flandry looked around at the weird decorations, at the unearthly light and the distorted landscape beyond the windows. Strange world under a strange sun, and himself the virtual prisoner of its alien and increasingly hostile people. He had a sudden wild feeling of being trapped.

'I suppose I should be spinning some elaborate counterplot,' he said hopelessly. 'And then, of course, I'll have to go down to the banquet and let Aycharaych read every detail of it — every little thing I know, laid open to his eyes because I just can't suppress my own thoughts — '

Aline's eyes widened, and her slim hand tightened over his. 'What is it?' he asked. 'What's your idea?'

'Oh — nothing, Dominic, nothing.' She smiled. 'I have some direct contact with Sol and — '

'You never told me that.'

'No reason for you to know it. I was just wondering if I should report this new trouble or not. Galaxy knows how those muddle-headed bureaucrats will react to the news. Probably yank us back and cashier us for incompetence.'

She leaned closer and her words came low and urgent. 'Go find Aycharaych, Dominic. Talk to him, keep him busy, don't let him come near me to interfere. He'll know what you're doing, naturally, but he won't be able to do much about it if you're as clever a talker as they say. Make some excuse for me tonight, too, so I don't have to attend the banquet — tell them I'm sick or something. Keep *him* away from me!'

'Sure,' he said with a little of his old spirit. 'But whatever you're hatching in that lovely head, be quick about it. He'll get at you mighty soon, you know.'

He got up and left. She watched him go, with a dawning smile on her lips.

Flandry was more than a little drunk when the party ended. Wine flowed freely at a Betelgeusean banquet, together with music, food, and dancing girls of every race present. He had enjoyed himself — in spite of everything — most of all, he admitted, he'd enjoyed talking to Aycharaych. The being was a genius of the first order in almost every field, and it had been pleasant to forget the dreadfully imminent catastrophe for a while.

He entered his chambers. Aline stood by a little table, and the muted light streamed off her unbound hair and the shimmering robe she wore. Impulsively, he kissed her.

'Good night, honey,' he said. 'It was nice of you to wait for me.'

She didn't leave for her own quarters. Instead, she held out one of the ornate goblets on the table. 'Have a nightcap, Dominic,' she invited.

'No, thanks. I've had entirely too many.'

'For me.' She smiled irresistibly. He clinked glasses with her and let the dark wine go down his throat.

It had a peculiar taste, and suddenly he felt dizzy, the room wavered and tilted under him. He sat down on his bed until it

had passed, but there was an — oddness — in his head tha
wouldn't go away.

'Potent stuff,' he muttered.

'We don't have the easiest job in the world,' said Aline softly
'We deserve a little relaxation.' She sat down beside him. 'Jus
tonight, that's all we have. Tomorrow is another day, and a
worse day.'

He would never have agreed before, his nature was too cool
and self-contained, but now it was all at once utterly reasonable. He nodded.

'And you love me, you know,' said Aline.

And he did.

Much later, she leaned close against him in the dark, her hair
brushing his cheek, and whispered urgently: 'Listen, Dominic,
I have to tell you this regardless of the consequences; you have
to be prepared for it.'

He stiffened with a return of the old tension. Her voice went
on, a muted whisper in the night: 'I've contacted Sol by courier robot and gotten in touch with Fenross. He has brains, and
he saw at once what must be done. It's a poor way, but the only
way.

'The fleet is already bound for Betelgeuse. The Merseians
think most of our strength is concentrated near Llynathawr, but
that's just a brilliant piece of deception — Fenross' work. Actually, the main body is quite near, and they've got a new energy
screen that'll let them slip past the Betelgeusean cordon without being detected. The night after tomorrow, a strong squadron will land in Gunazar Valley, in the Borthudians, and
establish a beachhead. A detachment will immediately move to
occupy the capital and capture the Sartaz and his court.'

Flandry lay rigid with shock. 'But this means war!' he
strangled. 'Merseia will strike at once, and we'll have to fight
Betelgeuse too.'

'I know. But the Imperium has decided we'll have a better
chance this way. Otherwise, it looks as if Betelgeuse will go to
the enemy by default.

'It's up to us to keep the Sartaz and his court from suspecting
the truth till too late. We have to keep them here at the palace.
The capture of the leaders of an absolute monarchy is always a
disastrous blow. Fenross and Walton think Betelgeuse will surrender before Merseia can get here.

'By hook or crook, Dominic, you've got to keep them unaware. That's your job; at the same time, keep on distracting Aycharaych, keep him off my neck.'

She yawned and kissed him. 'Better go to sleep now,' she said. 'We've got a tough couple of days ahead of us.'

He couldn't sleep. He got up when she was breathing quietly and walked over to the balcony. The knowledge was staggering. That the Empire, the bungling decadent Empire, could pull such a stroke and hope to get away with it!

Something stirred in the garden below. The moonlight was dim red on the figure that paced between two Merseian bodyguards. Aycharaych!

Flandry stiffened in dismay. The Chereionite looked up and he saw the wise smile on the telepath's face. *He knew.*

In the following two days, Flandry worked as he had rarely worked before. There wasn't much physical labour involved, but he had to maintain a web of complications such that the Sartaz would have no chance for a private audience with any Merseian and would not leave the capital on one his capricious journeys. There was also the matter of informing such Betelgeusean traitors as were on his side to be ready, and —

It was nerve-shattering. To make matters worse, something was wrong with him: clear thought was an effort; he had a new and disastrous tendency to take everything at face value. What had happened to him?

Aycharaych excused himself on the morning after Aline's revelation and disappeared. He was out arranging something hellish for the Terrans when they arrived, and Flandry could do nothing about it. But at least it left him and Aline free to carry on their own work.

He knew the Merseian fleet could not get near Betelgeuse before the Terrans landed. It is simply not possible to conceal the approximate whereabouts of a large fighting force from the enemy. How it had been managed for Terra, Flandry couldn't imagine. He supposed that it would not be too large a task force which was to occupy Alfzar — but that made its mission all the more precarious.

The tension gathered, hour by slow hour. Aline went her own way, conferring with General Bronson, the human Betelgeusean officer whom she had made her personal property. Perhaps he could disorganise the native fleet at the moment when Terra struck. The Merseian nobles plainly knew what

Aycharaych had found out; they looked at the humans with frank hatred, but they made no overt attempt to warn the Sartaz. Maybe they didn't think they could work through the wall of suborned and confused officials which Flandry had built around him — more likely, Aycharaych had suggested a better plan for them. There was none of the sense of defeat in them which slowly gathered in the human.

It was like being caught in spider webs, fighting clinging grey stuff that blinded and choked and couldn't be pulled away. Flandry grew haggard, he shook with nervousness, and the two days dragged on.

He looked up Gunazar Valley in the atlas. It was uninhabited and desolate, the home of winds and the lair of dragons, a good place for a secret landing — only how secret was a landing that Aycharaych knew all about and was obviously ready to meet?

'We haven't much chance, Aline,' he said to her. 'Not a prayer, really.'

'We'll just have to keep going.' She was more buoyant than he, seemed almost cheerful as time stumbled past. She stroked his hair tenderly. 'Poor Dominic, it isn't easy for you.'

The huge sun sank below the horizon — the second day, and tonight was the hour of decision. Flandry came out into the great conference hall to find it almost empty.

'Where are the Merseians, your Majesty?' he asked the Sartaz.

'They all went off on a special mission,' snapped the ruler. He was plainly ill pleased with the intriguing around him, of which he would be well aware.

A special mission — O almighty gods!

Aline and Bronson came in and gave the monarch formal greeting. 'With your permission, your Majesty,' said the general, 'I would like to show you something of great importance in about two hours.'

'Yes, yes,' mumbled the Sartaz and stalked out.

Flandry sat down and rested his head on one hand. Aline touched his shoulder gently. 'Tired, Dominic?' she asked.

'Yeah,' he said. 'I feel rotten. Just can't think these days.'

She signalled to a slave, who brought a beaker forward. 'This will help,' she said. He noticed sudden tears in her eyes. What was the matter?

74

He drank it down without thought. It caught at him, he gasped and grabbed the chair arms for support. 'What the devil —'

It spread through him with a sudden coolness that ran along his nerves towards his brain. It was like the hand that Aline had laid on his head, calming, soothing —

Clearing!

Suddenly he sprang to his feet. The whole preposterous thing stood forth in its raw grotesquerie — tissue of falsehoods, monstrosity of illogic!

The Fleet *couldn't* have moved a whole task force this close without the Merseian intelligence knowing of it. There *couldn't* be a new energy screen that he hadn't heard of. Fenross would never try so fantastic a scheme as the occupation of Betelgeuse before all hope was gone.

He didn't love Aline. She was brave and beautiful, but he didn't love her.

But he *had*. Three minutes ago, he had been desperately in love with her.

He looked at her through blurring eyes as the enormous truth grew on him. She nodded, gravely, not seeming to care that tears ran down her cheeks. Her lips whispered a word that he could barely catch.

'Goodbye, my dearest.'

IV

They had set up a giant televisor screen in the conference hall, with a row of seats for the great of Alfzar. Bronson had also taken the precaution of lining the walls with royal guardsmen whom he could trust — long rows of flashing steel and impassive blue faces, silent and moveless as the great pillars holding up the soaring roof.

The general paced nervously up and down before the screen, looking at his watch unnecessarily often. Sweat glistened on his forehead. Flandry sat relaxed; only one who knew him well could have read the tension that was like a coiled spring in him. Only Aline seemed remote from the scene, too wrapped in her own thoughts to care what went on.

'If this doesn't work, you know, we'll probably be hanged,' said Bronson.

'It ought to,' answered Flandry tonelessly. 'If it doesn't, I won't give much of a damn whether we hang or not.'

He was prevaricating there; Flandry was most fond of living, for all the wistful half-dreams that sometimes rose in him.

A trumpet shrilled, high brassy music between the walls and up to the ringing rafters. They rose and stood at attention as the Sartaz and his court swept in.

His yellow eyes were suspicious as they raked the three humans.

'You said that there was to be a showing of an important matter,' he declared flatly. 'I *hope* that is correct.'

'It is, your Majesty,' said Flandry easily. He was back in his element, the fencing with words, the casting of nets to entrap minds. 'It is a matter of such immense importance that it should have been revealed to you weeks ago. Unfortunately, circumstances did not permit that — as the court shall presently see — so your Majesty's loyal general was forced to act on his own discretion with what help we of Terra could give him. But if our work has gone well, the moment of revelation should also be that of salvation.'

'It had better be,' said the Sartaz ominously. 'I warn you — all of you — that I am sick of the spying and corruption the empires have brought with them. It is about time to cut the evil growth from Betelgeuse.'

'Terra has never wished Betelgeuse anything but good, your Majesty,' said Flandry 'and as it happens, we can offer proof of that. If — '

Another trumpet cut off his voice, and the warder's shout rang and boomed down the hall: 'Your Majesty, the Ambassador of the Empire of Merseia asks audience.'

The huge green form of Lord Korvash of Merseia filled the doorway with a flare of gold and jewelry. And beside him — Aycharaych!

Flandry was briefly rigid with shock. If that opponent came into the game now, the whole plan might crash to ruin. It was a daring, precarious structure which Aline had built; the faintest breath of argument could dissolve it — and then the lightnings would strike!

One was not permitted to bear firearms within the palace, but the duelling sword was a part of full dress. Flandry drew his with a hiss of metal and shouted aloud:

76

'Seize those beings! They mean to kill the Sartaz!'

Aycharaych's golden eyes widened as he saw what was in Flandry's mind. He opened his mouth to denounce the Terran — and leaped back in bare time to avoid the man's murderous thrust.

His own rapier sprang into his hand. In a whirr of steel, the two spies met.

Korvash the Merseian drew his own great blade in sheer reflex. 'Strike him down!' yelled Aline. Before the amazed Sartaz could act, she had pulled the stun pistol he carried from the holster and sent the Merseian toppling to the floor.

She bent over him, deftly removing a tiny needle gun from her bodice and palming it on the ambassador. 'Look, your Majesty,' she said breathlessly, 'he had a deadly weapon. We knew the Merseians planned no good, but we never thought they would dare —'

The Sartaz's gaze was shrewd on her. 'Maybe we'd better wait to hear his side of it,' he murmured.

Since Korvash would be in no position to explain his side for a good hour, Aline considered it a victory.

But Flandry — her eyes grew wide and she drew a hissing gasp as she saw him fighting Aycharaych. It was the swiftest, most vicious duel she had ever seen, leaping figures and blades that were a blur of speed, back and forth along the hall in a clamour of steel and blood.

'Stop them!' she cried, and raised the stunner.

The Sartaz laid a hand on hers and took the weapon away. 'No,' he said. 'Let them have it out. I haven't seen such a show in years.'

'Dominic —' she whispered.

Flandry had always thought himself a peerless fencer, but Aycharaych was his match. Though the Chereionite was hampered by gravity, he had a speed and precision which no human could ever meet, his thin blade whistled in and out, around and under the man's guard to rake face and hands and breast, and he was smiling — smiling.

His telepathy did him little or no good. Fencing is a matter of conditioned reflex — at such speeds, there isn't time for conscious thought. But perhaps it gave him an extra edge, just compensating for the handicap of weight.

Leaping, slashing, thrusting, parrying, clang and clash of

cold steel, no time to feel the biting edge of the growing weariness — dance of death while the court stood by and cheered.

Flandry's own blade was finding its mark; blood ran down Aycharaych's gaunt cheeks and his tunic was slashed to red ribbons. The Terran's plan was simple and the only one possible for him. Aycharaych would tire sooner, his reactions would slow — the thing to do was to stay alive that long!

He let the Chereionite drive him backward down the length of the hall, leap by leap, whirling around with sword shrieking in hand. Thrust, parry, riposte, recovery — *whirr, clang!* The rattle of steel filled the hall and the Sartaz watched with hungry eyes.

The end came as he was wondering if he would ever live to see Betelgeuse rise again. Aycharaych lunged and his blade pierced Flandry's left shoulder. Before he could disengage it, the man had knocked the weapon spinning from his hand and had his own point against the throat of the Chereionite.

The hall rang with the savage cheering of Betelgeuse's masters. 'Disarm them!' shouted the Sartaz.

Flandry drew a sobbing breath. 'Your Majesty,' he gasped, 'let me guard this fellow while General Bronson goes on with our show.'

The Sartaz nodded. It fitted his sense of things.

Flandry thought with a hard glee: *Aycharaych, if you open your mouth, so help me, I'll run you through.*

The Chereionite shrugged, but his smile was bitter.

'Dominic, Dominic!' cried Aline, between laughter and tears.

General Bronson turned to her. He was shaken by the near ruin. 'Can you talk to them?' he whispered. 'I'm no good at it.'

Aline nodded and stood boldly forth. 'Your Majesty and nobles of the court,' she said, 'we shall now prove the statements we made about the treachery of Merseia.

'We of Terra found out that the Merseians were planning to seize Alfzar and hold it and yourselves until their own fleet could arrive to complete the occupation. To that end they are assembling this very night in Gunazar Valley of the Borthudian range. A flying squad will attack and capture the palace — '

She waited until the uproar had subsided. 'We could not tell your Majesty or any of the highest in the court,' she resumed coolly, 'for the Merseian spies were everywhere and we had reason to believe that one of them could read your minds. If they had known anyone knew of their plans, they would have acted at once. Instead we contacted General Bronson, who was not high enough to merit their attention, but who did have enough power to act as the situation required.

'We planted a trap for the enemy. For one thing, we mounted telescopic telecameras in the valley. With your permission, I will now show what is going on there this instant.'

She turned a switch and the scene came to life — naked crags and cliffs reaching up towards the red moons, and a stir of activity in the shadows. Armoured forms were moving about, setting up atomic guns, warming the engines of spaceships — and they were Merseians.

The Sartaz snarled. Someone asked, 'How do we know this is not a falsified transmission?'

'You will be able to see their remains for yourself,' said Aline. 'Our plan was very simple. We planted atomic land mines in the ground. They are radio controlled.' She held up a small switch-box wired to the televisor, and her smile was grim. 'This is the control. Perhaps your Majesty would like to press the button?'

'Give it to me,' said the Sartaz thickly. He thumbed the switch.

A blue-white glare of hell-flame lit the screen. They had a vision of the ground fountaining upward, the cliffs toppling down, a cloud or radioactive dust boiling up towards the moons, and then the screen went dark.

'The cameras have been destroyed,' said Aline quitely. 'Now, your Majesty, I suggest that you send scouts there immediately. They will find enough remains to verify what the televisor has shown. I would further suggest that a power which maintains armed forces within your own territory is not a friendly one!'

Korvash and Aycharaych were to be deported with whatever other Merseians were left in the system — once Betelgeuse had broken diplomatic relations with their state and begun negotiating an alliance with Terra. The evening before they left, Flandry gave a small party for them in his apartment. Only he and Aline were there to meet them when they entered.

'Congratulations,' said Aycharaych wryly. 'The Sartaz was so furious he wouldn't even listen to our protestations. I can't blame him — you certainly put us in a bad light.'

'No worse than your own,' grunted Korvash angrily. 'Hell

take you for a lying hypocrite, Flandry. You know that Terra
has her own forces and agents in the Betelgeusean System,
hidden on wild moons and asteroids. It's part of the game.'

'Of course I know it,' smiled the Terran. 'But does the
Sartaz? However, it's as you say — the game. You don't hate
the one who beats you in chess. Why then hate us for winning
this round?'

'Oh, I don't,' said Aycharaych. 'There will be other rounds.'

'You've lost much less than we would have,' said Flandry.
'This alliance has strengthened Terra enough for her to halt
your designs, at least temporarily. But we aren't going to use
that strength to launch a war against you, though I admit that
we should. The Empire want only to keep the peace.'

'Because it doesn't dare fight a war,' snapped Korvash.

They didn't answer. Perhaps they were thinking of the cities
that would not be bombed and the young men that would
not go out to be killed. Perhaps they were simply enjoying
a victory.

Flandry poured wine. 'To our future amiable enmity,' he
toasted.

'I still don't see how you did it,' said Korvash.

'Aline did it,' said Flandry. 'Tell them, Aline.'

She shook her head. She had withdrawn into a quietness
which was foreign to her. 'Go ahead, Dominic,' she murmured.
'It was really your show.'

'Well,' said Flandry, not loath to expound, 'when we realised
that Aycharaych could read our minds, it looked pretty hopeless. How can you possibly lie to a telepath? Aline found the
answer — by getting information which just isn't true.

'There's a drug in this system called *sorgan* which has the
property of making its user believe anything he's told. Aline fed
me some without my knowledge and then told me that fantastic
lie about Terra coming in to occupy Alfzar. And, of course, I
accepted it as absolute truth. Which you, Aycharaych, read in
my mind.'

'I was puzzled,' admitted the Chereionite. 'It just didn't look
reasonable to me; but as you said, there didn't seem to be any
way to lie to a telepath.'

'Aline's main worry was then to keep out of mind-reading
range,' said Flandry. 'You helped us there by going off to prepare a warm reception for the Terrans. You gathered all your
forces in the valley, ready to blast our ships out of the sky.'

'Why didn't you go to the Sartaz with what you knew — or thought you knew?' asked Korvash accusingly.

Aycharaych shrugged. 'I realised Captain Flandry would be doing his best to prevent me from doing that and to discredit any information I could get that high,' he said. 'You yourself agreed that our best opportunity lay in repulsing the initial attack ourselves. That would gain us far more favour with the Sartaz; moreover, since there would have been overt acts on both sides, war between Betelgeuse and Terra would then have been inevitable — whereas if the Sartaz had learned in time of the impending assault, he might have tried to negotiate.'

'I suppose so,' said Korvash glumly.

'Aline, of course, prevailed on Bronson to mine the valley,' said Flandry. 'The rest you know. When you yourselves showed up —'

'To tell the Sartaz, now that it was too late,' said Aycharaych.

' — we were afraid that the ensuing argument would damage our own show. So we used violence to shut you up until it had been played out.' Flandry spread his hands in a gesture of finality. 'And that, gentlemen, is that.'

'There will be other tomorrows,' said Aycharaych gently. 'But I am glad we can meet in peace tonight.'

The party lasted well on towards dawn. When the aliens left, with many slightly tipsy expressions of good will and respect, Aycharaych took Aline's hand in his own bony fingers. His strange golden eyes searched hers, even as she knew his mind was looking into the depths of her own.

'Goodbye, my dear,' he said, too softly for the others to hear. 'As long as there are women like you, I think Terra will endure.'

She watched his tall form go down the corridor and her vision blurred a little. It was strange to think that her enemy knew what the man beside her did not.

HUNTERS

OF

THE

SKY

CAVE

I

It pleased Ruethen of the Long Hand to give a feast and ball at the Crystal Moon for his enemies. He knew they must come. Pride of race had slipped from Terra, while the need to appear well-bred and sophisticated had waxed correspondingly. The fact that spaceships prowled and fought, fifty light-years beyond Antares, made it all the more impossible a gaucherie to refuse an invitation from the Merseian representative. Besides, one could feel delightfully wicked and ever so delicately in danger.

Captain Sir Dominic Flandry, Imperial Naval Intelligence Corps, allowed himself a small complaint. 'It's not that I refuse any being's liquor,' he said, 'and Ruethen has a chef for his human-type meals who'd be worth a war to get. But I thought I was on furlough.'

'So you are,' said Diana Vinogradoff, Right Noble Lady Guardian of the Mare Crisium. 'Only I saw you first.'

Flandry grinned and slid an arm about her shoulders. He felt pretty sure he was going to win his bet with Ivar del Bruno. They relaxed in the lounger and he switched off the lights.

This borrowed yacht was ridiculously frail and ornate; but a saloon which was one bubble of clear plastic, ah! Now in the sudden darkness, space leaped forth, crystal black and a wintry blaze of stars. The banded shield of Jupiter swelled even as they watched, spilling soft amber radiance into the ship. Lady Diana became a figure out of myth, altogether beautiful; her jewels glittered like raindrops on long gown and heaped tresses. Flandry stroked his neat moustache. *I don't suppose I look too hideous myself*, he thought smugly, and advanced to the attack.

'No . . . please . . . not now.' Lady Diana fended him off, but in a promising way. Flandry reclined again. No hurry. The banquet and dance would take hours. Afterward, when the yacht made its leisured way home towards Terra, and champagne bubbles danced in both their heads. . . . 'Why did you say that about being on furlough?' she asked, smoothing her coiffure with slim fingers. Her luminous nail polish danced about in the twilight like flying candle flames.

Flandry got a cigarette from his own shimmerite jacket and inhaled it to life. The glow picked out his face, long, narrow, with high cheekbones and grey eyes, seal-brown hair and straight nose. He sometimes thought his last biosculp had made it too handsome, and he ought to change it again. But what the devil, he wasn't on Terra often enough for the girls to get bored with his looks. Besides, his wardrobe, which he did take pains to keep fashionable, was expensive enough to rule out many other vanities.

'The Nyanza business was a trifle wearing, y' know,' he said to remind her of yet another exploit of his on yet another exotic planet. 'I came Home for a rest. And the Merseians are such damnably strenuous creatures. It makes me tired just to look at one, let alone spar with him.'

'You don't have to tonight, Sir Dominic,' she smiled. 'Can't you lay all this feuding aside, just for a little while, and be friends with them? I mean, we're all beings, in spite of these silly rivalries.'

'I'd love to relax with them, my lady. But you see, they never do.'

'Oh, come now! I've talked to them, often, and — '

'They can radiate all the virile charm they need,' said Flandry. For an instant his light tone was edged with acid. 'But destroying the Terrestrial Empire is a full-time job.'

Then, quickly, he remembered what he was about, and picked up his usual line of banter. He wasn't required to be an Intelligence agent all the time. Was he? When a thousand-credit bet with his friend was involved? Ivar del Bruno had insisted that Lady Diana Vinogradoff would never bestow her favours on anyone under the rank of earl. The challenge was hard to refuse, when the target was so intrinsically tempting, and when Flandry had good reason to be complacent about his own abilities. It had been a hard campaign, though, and yielding to her whim to attend the Merseian party was only a small fraction of the lengths to which he had gone.

But now, Flandry decided, if he played his cards right for a few hours more, the end would be achieved. And afterwards, a thousand credits would buy a really good orgy for two at the Everest House.

Chives, valet cum pilot cum private gunman, slipped the yacht smoothly into berth at the Crystal Moon. There was no flutter of weight change, though deceleration had been swift and the internal force-field hard put to compensate. Flandry stood up, cocked his beret at a carefully rakish angle, swirled his scarlet cloak, and offered an arm to Lady Diana. They stepped through the airlock and along a transparent tube to the palace.

The woman caught a delighted gasp. 'I've never seen it so close up,' she whispered. 'Who ever made it?'

The artificial satellite had Jupiter for background, and the Milky Way and the huge cold constellations. Glass-clear walls faced infinity, curving and tumbling like water. Planar gravity fields held faceted synthetic jewels, ruby, emerald, diamond, topaz, massing several tons each, in orbit around the central minaret. One outward thrust of bubble was left at zero gee, a conservatory where mutant ferns and orchids rippled on rhythmic breezes.

'I understand it was built for Lord Tsung-Tse about a century back,' said Flandry. 'His son sold it for gambling debts, and the then Merseian ambassador acquired it and had it put in orbit around Jupiter. Symbolic, eh?'

She arched questioning brows, but he thought better of explaining. His own mind ran on: *Eh, for sure. I suppose it's inevitable and so forth. Terra has been too rich for too long: we've grown old and content, no more high hazards for us. Whereas the Merseian Empire is fresh, vigorous, disciplined, dedicated, et tedious cetera. Personally, I enjoy decadence; but somebody has to hold off the Long Night for my own lifetime, and it looks as if I'm elected.*

Then they neared the portal, where a silver spiderweb gate stood open. Ruethen himself greeted them at the head of an iridescent slideramp. Such was Merseian custom. But he bowed in Terran style and touched horny lips to Lady Diana's hand. 'A rare pleasure, I am certain.' The bass voice gave to fluent Anglic an indescribable nonhuman accent.

She considered him. The Merseian was a true mammal, but with more traces of reptile ancestry than humankind: pale green skin, hairless and finely scaled; a low spiny ridge from the head down along the backbone to the end of a long thick tail. He was broader than a man, and would have stood a sheer two metres did he not walk with a forward-stooping gait. Except for its baldness and lack of external ears, the face was quite humanoid, even good-looking in a heavy rough way. But the eyes beneath the overhanging brow ridges were two small pits of jet.

Ruethen wore the austere uniform of his class, form-fitting black with silver trim. A blaster was belted at his hip.

Lady Diana's perfectly sculped mouth curved in a smile. 'Do you actually know me, my lord?' she murmured.

'Frankly, no.' A barbaric bluntness. Any nobleman of Terra would have been agile to disguise his ignorance. 'But while this log does burn upon the altar stone, peace-holy be it among us. As my tribe would say in the Cold Valleys.'

'Of course you are an old friend of my escort,' she teased.

Ruethen cocked an eye at Flandry. And suddenly the man sensed tautness in that massive frame. Just for a moment, then Ruethen's whole body became a mask. 'We have met now and then,' said the Merseian dryly. 'Welcome, Sir Dominic. The cloakroom slave will furnish you with a mind-screen.'

'What?' Despite himself, Flandry started.

'If you want one.' Ruethen bared powerful teeth at Lady Diana. 'Will my unknown friend grant me a dance later?'

She lost her own coolness for a second, then nodded graciously. 'That would be a . . . unique experience, my lord,' she said.

It would, at that. Flandry led her on into the ballroom. His mind worried Ruethen's curious offer, like a dog with a bone. Why — ?

He saw the gaunt black shape among the rainbow Terrans, and he knew. It went cold along his spine.

II

He wasted no time on excuses but almost ran to the cloakroom. His feet whispered along the crystalline floor, where Orion glittered hundreds of light-years beneath. 'Mind-screen,' he snapped.

The slave was a pretty girl. Merseians took pleasure in buying humans for menial jobs. 'I've only a few, sir,' she said. 'His lordship told me to keep them for — '

'Me!' Flandry snatched the cap of wires, transistors, and power cells from her hesitant fingers. Only when it was on his head did he relax. Then he took out a fresh cigarette and steered through lilting music towards the bar. He needed a drink, badly.

Aycharaych of Chereion stood beneath high glass pillars. No

one spoke to him. Mostly the humans were dancing while non-humans of various races listened to the music. A performer from Lulluan spread heaven-blue feathers on a small stage, but few watched that rare sight. Flandry elbowed past a Merseian who had just drained a two-litre tankard. 'Scotch,' he said. 'Straight, tall, and quick.'

Lady Diana approached. She seemed uncertain whether to be indignant or intrigued. 'Now I know what they mean by cavalier treatment.' She pointed upward. 'What *is* that thing?'

Flandry tossed off his drink. The whisky smoked down his throat, and he felt his nerves ease. 'I'm told it's my face,' he said.

'No, no! Stop fooling! I mean that horrible wire thing.'

'Mind-screen.' He held out his glass for a refill. 'It heterodynes the energy radiation of the cerebral cortex in a random pattern. Makes it impossible to read what I'm thinking.'

'But I thought that was impossible anyway,' she said, bewildered. 'I mean, unless you belong to a naturally telepathic species.'

'Which man isn't,' he agreed, 'except for rare cases. The nontelepath develops his own private "language," which is gibberish to anyone who hasn't studied him for a long time as a single individual. Ergo, telepathy was never considered a particular threat in my line of work, and you've probably never heard of the mind-screen. It was developed just a few years ago. And the reason for its development is standing over there.'

She followed his eyes. 'Who? That tall being in the black mantle?'

'The same. I had a brush with him, and discovered to my . . . er . . . discomfiture, shall we say? . . . that he has a unique gift. Whether or not all his race does, I couldn't tell you. But within a range of a few hundred metres, Aycharaych of Chereion can read the mind of any individual of any species, whether he's ever met his victim before or not.'

'But — why, then — '

'Exactly. He's *persona non grata* throughout our territory, of course, to be shot on sight. But as you know, my lady,' said Flandry in a bleak tone, 'we are not now in the Terrestrial Empire. Jupiter belongs to the Dispersal of Ymir.'

'Oh,' said Lady Diana. She coloured. 'A telepath!'

Flandry gave her a lopsided grin. 'Aycharaych is the equivalent of a gentleman,' he said. 'He wouldn't tell on you. But I'd better go talk to him now.' He bowed. 'You are certain not to lack company. I see a dozen men converging here already.'

'So there are.' She smiled. 'But I think Aycharaych — how *do* you pronounce it, that guttural *ch* baffles me — I think he'll be much more intriguing.' She took his arm.

Flandry disengaged her. She resisted. He closed a hand on her wrist and shoved it down with no effort. Maybe his visage was a fake, he told himself once in a while, but at least his body was his own, and the dreary hours of calisthenics had some reward. 'I'm sorry, my lady,' he said, 'but I am about to talk shop, and you're not initiated in the second oldest profession. Have fun.'

Her eyes flared offended vanity. She whirled about and welcomed the Duke of Mars with far more enthusiasm than that foolish young man warranted. Flandry sighed. *I suppose I owe you a thousand credits, Ivar.* He cocked his cigarette at a defiant angle, and strolled across the ballroom.

Aycharaych smiled. His face was also closely humanoid, but in a bony, sword-nosed fashion; the angles of mouth and jaw were exaggerated into V's. It might almost have been the face of some Byzantine saint. But the skin was a pure golden hue, the brows were arches of fine blue feathers, the bald skull carried a feather crest and pointed ears. Broad chest, wasp waist, long skinny legs were hidden by the cloak. The feet, with four clawed toes and spurs on the ankles, showed bare.

Flandry felt pretty sure that intelligent life on Chereion had evolved from birds, and that the planet must be dry, with a thin cold atmosphere. He had hints that its native civilisation was incredibly old, and reason to believe it was not a mere subject of Merseia. But beyond that, his knowledge emptied into darkness. He didn't even know where in the Merseian sphere the sun of Chereion lay.

Aycharaych extended a six-fingered hand. Flandry shook it. The digits were delicate within his own. For a brutal moment he thought of squeezing hard, crushing the fine bones. Aycharaych stood a bit taller than he, but Flandry was a rather big human, much broader and more solid.

'A pleasure to meet you again, Sir Dominic,' said Aycharaych. His voice was low, sheer beauty to hear. Flandry looked at rust-red eyes, with a warm metallic lustre, and released the hand.

'Hardly unexpected,' he said. 'For you, that is.'

'You travel about so much,' Aycharaych said. 'I was sure a few men of your corps would be here tonight, but I could not be certain of your own whereabouts.'

'I wish I ever was of yours,' said Flandry ruefully.

'Congratulations upon your handling of *l'affaire Nyanza*. We are going to miss A'u on our side. He had a certain watery brilliance.'

Flandry prevented himself from showing surprise. 'I thought that aspect of the business had been hushed up,' he said. 'But little pitchers seem to have big ears. How long have you been in the Solar System?'

'A few weeks,' said Aycharaych. 'Chiefly a pleasure trip.' He cocked his head. 'Ah, the orchestra has begun a Strauss waltz. Very good. Though of course Johann is not to be compared to Richard, who will always be *the* Strauss.'

'Oh?' Flandry's interest in ancient music was only slightly greater than his interest in committing suicide. 'I wouldn't know.'

'You should, my friend. Not even excepting Xingu, Strauss is the most misunderstood composer of known galactic history. Were I to be imprisoned for life with only one tape, I would choose his *Death and Transfiguration* and be satisfied.'

'I'll arrange it,' offered Flandry at once.

Aycharaych chuckled and took the man's arm. 'Come, let us find a more peaceful spot. But I pray you, do not waste so amusing an occasion on me. I own to visiting Terra clandestinely, but that part of it was entirely for the easement of my personal curiosity. I had no intention of burgling the Imperial offices —'

'Which are equipped with Aycharaych alarms anyway.'

'Telepathising detectors? Yes, so I would assume. I am a little too old and stiff, and your gravity a little too over-powering, to indulge in my own thefts. Nor have I the type of dashing good looks needed, I am told by all the teleplays, for cloak and dagger work. No, I merely wished to see the planet which bred such a race as yours. I walked in a few forests, inspected certain paintings, visited some chosen graves, and returned here. Whence I am about to depart, by the way. You need not get your Imperium to put pressure on the Ymirites to expel me; my courier ship leaves in twenty hours.'

'For where?' asked Flandry.

'Hither and yon,' said Aycharaych lightly.

Flandry felt his stomach muscles grow hard. 'Syrax?' he got out.

They paused at the entrance to the null-gee conservatory. A single great sphere of water balanced like silver at its very heart, with fern jungle and a thousand purple-scarlet blooms forming a cavern around it, the stars and mighty Jupiter beyond. Later, no doubt, the younger and drunker humans would be peeling off their clothes and going for a free-fall swim in that serene globe. But now only the music dwelt here. Aycharaych kicked himself over the threshold. His cloak flowed like black wings as he arrowed across the bubble-dome. Flandry came after, in clothes that were fire and trumpeting. He needed a moment before he adjusted to weightlessness. Aycharaych, whose ancestors once whistled in Chereion's sky, appeared to have no such trouble.

The non-human stopped his flight by seizing a bracken frond. He looked at a violet burst of orchids and his long hawk-head inclined. 'Black against the quicksilver water globe,' he mused; 'the universe black and cold beyond both. A beautiful arrangement, and with that touch of horror necessary to the highest art.'

'Black?' Flandry glanced startled at the violet flowers. Then he clamped his lips.

But Aycharaych had already grasped the man's idea. He smiled. '*Touché.* I should not have let slip that I am colour-blind in the blue wavelengths.'

'But you see further into the red than I do,' predicted Flandry.

'Yes. I admit, since you would infer so anyhow, my native sun is cooler and redder than yours. If you think that will help you identify it, among all the millions of stars in the Merseian sphere, accept the information with my compliments.'

'The Syrax Cluster is middle Population One,' said Flandry. 'Not too suitable for your eyes.'

Aycharaych stared at the water. Tropical fish were visible within its globe, like tiny many-coloured rockets. 'It does not follow I am going to Syrax,' he said tonelessly. 'I certainly have no personal wish to do so. Too many warcraft, too many professional officers. I do not like their mentality.' He made a free-fall bow. 'Your own excepted, of course.'

'Of course,' said Flandry. 'Still, if you could do something to break the deadlock out there, in Merseia's favour — '

'You flatter me,' said Aycharaych. 'But I fear you have not yet outgrown the romantic view of military politics. The fact is that neither side wants to make a total effort to control the Syrax stars. Merseia could use them as a valuable base, outflanking Antares and thus a spearhead poised at that entire sector of your empire. Terra wants control simply to deny us the cluster. Since neither government wishes, at present, to break the nominal state of peace, they manoeuvre about out there, mass naval strength, spy and snipe and hold running battles ... but the game of all-out seizure is not worth the candle of all-out war.'

'But if you could tip the scales, personally, so our boys lost out at Syrax,' said Flandry, 'we wouldn't counter-attack your imperial sphere. You know that. It'd invite counter-counter-attack on us. Heavens, Terra itself might be bombed! We're much too comfortable to risk such an outcome.' He pulled himself up short. Why expose his own bitterness, and perhaps be arrested on Terra for sedition?

'If we possessed Syrax,' said Aycharaych, 'it would, with 71 per cent probability, hasten the collapse of the Terran hegemony by a hundred years, plus or minus ten. That is the verdict of our military computers — though I myself feel the faith our High Command has in them is naïve and rather touching. However, the predicted date of Terra's fall would still lie 150 years hence. So I wonder why your government cares.'

Flandry shrugged. 'A few of us are a bit sentimental about our planet,' he answered sadly. 'And then, of course, we ourselves aren't out there being shot at.'

'That is the human mentality again,' said Aycharaych. 'Your instincts are such that you never accept dying. You, personally, down underneath everything, do you not feel death is just a little bit vulgar, not quite a gentleman?'

'Maybe What would you call it?'

'A completion.'

Their talk drifted to impersonalities. Flandry had never found anyone else whom he could so converse with. Aycharaych could be wise and learned and infinitely kind when he chose: or flick a whetted wit across the pompous face of empire. To speak with him, touching now and then on the immortal questions, was almost like a confessional — for he was not human

93

and did not judge human deeds, yet he seemed to understand the wishes at their root.

At last Flandry made a reluctant excuse to get away. *Nu*, he told himself, *business is business*. Since Lady Diana was studiously ignoring him, he enticed a redhaired bit of fluff into an offside room, told her he would be back in ten minutes, and slipped through a rear corridor. Perhaps any Merseian who saw him thus disappear wouldn't expect him to return for an hour or two; might not recognise the girl when she got bored waiting and found her own way to the ballroom again. One human looked much like another to the untrained non-human eye, and there were at least a thousand guests by now.

It was a flimsy camouflage for his exit, but the best he could think of.

Flandry re-entered the yacht and roused Chives. 'Home,' he said. 'Full acceleration. Or secondary drive, if you think you can handle it within the System in this clumsy gold-plated hulk.'

'Yes, sir. I can.'

At faster-than-light, he'd be at Terra in minutes, rather than hours. Excellent! It might actually be possible to arrange for Aycharapch's completion.

More than half of Flandry hoped the attempt would fail.

III

It happened to be day over North America, where Vice Admiral Fenross had his offices. Not that that mattered; they were like as not to work around the clock in Intelligence, or else Flandry could have gotten his superior out of bed. He would, in fact, have preferred to do so.

As matters worked out, however, he created a satisfactory commotion. He saved an hour by having Chives dive the yacht illegally through all traffic lanes above Admiralty Centre. With a coverall over his party clothes, he dove from the airlock and rode a grav repulsor down to the 40th flange of the Intelligence tower. While the yacht was being stopped by a sky monitor, Flandry was arguing with a marine on guard duty. He looked down the muzzle of a blaster and said: 'You know me, sergeant. Let me by. Urgent.'

'I guess I do know your face, sir,' the marine answered. 'But faces can be changed and nobody gets by me without a pass. just stand there while I buzzes a patrol.'

Flandry considered making a jump for it. But the Imperial Marines were on to every trick of judo he knew. Hell take it, an hour wasted on identification — Wait. Memory clicked into place. 'You're Mohandas Parkinson,' said Flandry. 'You have four darling children, your wife is unreasonably monogamous, and you were playing Go at Madame Cepheid's last month.'

Sergeant Parkinson's gun wavered. 'Huh?' he said. Then, loudly. 'I do' know whatcher talking about!'

'Madame Cepheid's Go board is twenty metres square,' said Flandry, 'and the pieces are live girls. In the course of a game — Does that ring a bell, sergeant? I was there too, watching, and I'm sure your wife would be delighted to hear you are still capable of such truly epic — '

'Get on your way, you ... blackmailer!' choked Parkinson. He gulped and added, 'Sir.'

Captain Flandry grinned, patted him on his helmet, holstered his weapon for him, and went quickly inside.

Unlike most, Fenross had no beautiful receptionist in his outer office. A robovoice asked the newcomer's business. 'Hero,' he said blandly. The robot said Admiral Fenross was occupied with a most disturbing new development. Flandry said he was also, and got admission.

Hollow-cheeked and shaky, Fenross looked across his desk. His eyes were not too bloodshot to show a flick of hatred. 'Oh,' he said. 'You. Well, Captain, what interrupts your little tête-à-tête with your Merseian friends?'

Flandry sat down and took out a cigarette. He was not surprised that Fenross had set spies on him, but the fact was irritating nonetheless. *How the devil did this feud ever get started?* he wondered. *Is it only that I took that girl ... what was her name, anyway? Marjorie? Margaret? ... was it only that I once took her from him when we were cadets together? Why, I did it for a joke. She wasn't very good-looking in spite of everything biosculp could do.*

'I've news too hot for any com circuit,' he said. 'I just now — '

'You're on furlough,' snapped Fenross. 'You've got no business here.'

'What? Look, it was Aycharaych! Himself! At the Crystal Moon!'

95

A muscle twitched in Fenross' cheek. 'I can't hear an unofficial report,' he said. 'All ruin is exploding beyond Aldebaran. If you think you've done something brilliant, file an account in the regular channels.'

'But — for God's sake!' Flandry sprang to his feet. 'Admiral Fenross, sir, whatever the hell you want me to call you, he's leaving the Solar System in a matter of hours. Courier boat. We can't touch him in Ymirite space, but if we waylaid him on his way out — He'll be tricky, the ambush might not work, but name of a little green pig, if we can get Aycharaych it'll be better than destroying a Merseian fleet!'

Fenross reached out a hand which trembled ever so faintly, took a small pillbox and shook a tablet loose. 'Haven't slept in forty hours,' he muttered. 'And you off on that yacht. . . . I can't take cognizance, Captain. Not under the circumstances.' He glanced up again. Slyness glistened in his eyes. 'Of course,' he said, 'if you want to cancel your own leave —'

Flandry stood a moment, rigid, staring at the desk-bound man who hated him. Memory trickled back: *After I broke off with her, yes, the girl did go a bit wild. She was killed in an accident on Venus, wasn't she . . . drunken party flying over the Saw . . . yes, I seem to've heard about it. And Fenross has never even looked at another woman.*

He sighed. 'Sir, I am reporting myself back on active duty.'

Fenross nodded. 'File that with the robot as you leave. Now I've got work for you.'

'But Aycharaych —'

'We'll handle him. I've got a more suitable assignment in mind.' Fenross grinned, tossed down his pill and followed it with a cup of water from the desk fountain. 'After all, a dashing field agent ought to dash don't you think?'

Could it be just the fact that he's gotten more rank but I've had more fun? wondered Flandry. *Who knows? Does he himself?* He sat down again, refusing to show expression.

Fenross drummed the desk top and stared at a blank wall. His uniform was as severe as regulations permitted — Flandry's went in the opposite direction — but it still formed an unnecessarily gorgeous base for his tortured red head. 'This is under the strictest secrecy,' he began in a rapid, toneless voice. 'I have no idea how long we can suppress the news, though. One of our colonies is under siege. Deep within the Imperial sphere.'

Flandry was forced to whistle. 'Where? Who?'

'Ever heard of Vixen? Well, I never had either before this. It's a human-settled planet of an F6 star about a hundred light-years from Sol, somewhat north and clockwise of Aldebaran. Oddball world, but moderately successful as colonies go. You know that region is poor in systems of interest to humans, and very little explored. In effect, Vixen sits in the middle of a desert. Or does it? You'll wonder when I tell you that a space fleet appeared several weeks ago and demanded that it yield to occupation. The ships were of exotic type, and the race crewing them can't be identified. But some, at least, spoke pretty good Anglic.'

Flandry sat dead still. His mind threw up facts, so familiar as to be ridiculous, and yet they must now be considered again. The thing which had happened was without precedent.

An interstellar domain can have no definite borders; stars are scattered too thinly, their types too intermingled. And there are too many of them. In very crude approximation, the Terrestrial Empire was a sphere of some 400 light-years diameter, centered on Sol, and contained an estimated four million stars. But of these less than half had even been visited. A bare 100,000 were directly concerned with the Imperium, a few multiples of that number might have some shadowy contact and owe a theoretical allegiance. Consider a single planet; realise that it is a *world*, as big and varied and strange as this Terra ever was, with as many conflicting elements of race and language and culture among its natives; estimate how much government even one planet requires, and see how quickly a reign over many becomes impossibly huge. Then consider, too, how small a percentage of stars are of any use to a given species (too hot, too cold, too turbulent, too many companions) and, of those, how few will have even one planet where that species is reasonably safe. The Empire becomes tenuous indeed. And its inconceivable extent is still the merest speck in one outlying part of one spiral arm of one galaxy; among a hundred billion or more great suns, those known to any single world are the barest, tiniest handful.

However — attack that far within the sphere? No! Individual ships could sneak between the stars easily enough. But a war fleet could never come a hundred light-years inward from the farthest Imperial bases. The instantaneous 'wake' of disturbed space-time, surging from so many vessels, would be certain of detection somewhere along the line. Therefore —

'Those ships were built within our sphere,' said Flandry slowly. 'And not too many parsecs from Vixen.'

Fenross sneered. 'Your genius dazzles me. As a matter of fact, though, they might have come further than usual, unde-tected, because so much of the Navy is out at Syrax now. Our interior posts are stripped, some completely deserted. I'll agree the enemy must base within several parsecs of Vixen. But that doesn't mean they live there. Their base might be a space station, a rogue planet, or something else we'll never find; they could have sent their fleet to it a ship at a time, over a period of months.'

Flandry shook his head. 'Supply lines. Having occupied Vixen, they'll need to maintain their garrison till it's self-sufficient. No, they have a home somewhere in the Imperial sphere, surely in the same quadrant. Which includes only about a million stars! Say, roughly, 100,000 possibilities, some never even catalogued. How many years would it take how many ships to check out 100,000 systems?'

'Yeh. And what would be happening meanwhile?'

'What has?'

'The Vixenites put up a fight. There's a small naval base on their planet, unmanned at present, but enough of the civilian population knew how to make use of its arsenal. They got cour-iers away, of course, and Aldebaran Station sent what little help it could. When last heard from, Vixen was under siege. We're dispatching a task force, but it'll take time to get there. That wretched Syrax business ties our hands. Reports indicate the aliens haven't overwhelming strength; we could send enough ships to make mesons of them. But if we withdrew that many from Syrax, they'd come back to find Merseia entrenched in the Cluster.'

'Tie-in?' wondered Flandry.

'Who knows? I've got an idea, though, and your assignment will be to investigate it.' Fenross leaned over the desk. His sunken eyes probed at Flandry's. 'We're all too ready to think of Merseia when anything goes wrong,' he said bleakly. 'But after all, they live a long ways off. There's another alien power right next door . . . and as closely interwoven with Merseia as it is with us.'

'You mean Ymir?' Flandry snorted. 'Come now, dear chief, you're letting your xenophobia run away with you.'

'Consider,' said Fenross. 'Somebody, or something, helped

98

those aliens at Vixen build a modern war fleet. They couldn't have done it alone: we'd have known it if they'd begun exploring stellar space, and knowledge has to precede conquest. Somebody, very familiar with our situation, has briefed the aliens on our language, weapons, territorial layout — the works. Somebody, I'm sure, told them when to attack: right now, when nearly our whole strength is at Syrax. *Who?* There's one item. The aliens use a helium-pressure power system like the Ymirites. That's unmistakable on the detectors. Helium-pressure is all right, but it's not as convenient as the hydrogen-heavy atom cycle; not if you live under terrestroid conditions, and the aliens very definitely do. The ships, their shape I mean, also have a subtly Ymirite touch. I'll show you pictures that have arrived with the reports. Those ships look as if they'd been designed by some engineer more used to working with hydrolithium than steel.'

'You mean the Ymirites are behind the aliens? But — '

'But nothing. There's an Ymirite planet in the Vixen system too. Who knows how many stars those crawlers have colonised . . . stars we never even heard about? Who knows how many client races they might lord it over? And they travel blithely back and forth, across our sphere and Merseia's and — Suppose they are secretly in cahoots with Merseia. What better way to smuggle Merseian agents into our systems? We don't stop Ymirite ships. We aren't able to! But any of them could carry a force-bubble with terrestroid conditions inside. . . . I've felt for years we've been to childishly trustful of Ymir. It's past time we investigated them in detail. It may already be too late!'

Flandry stubbed out his cigarette. 'But what interest have they got in all this?' he asked mildy. 'What could any oxygen-breathing race have that they'd covet — or bribe them with?'

'That I don't know,' said Fenross. 'I could be dead wrong. But I want it looked into. You're going back to Jupiter, Captain. At once.'

'What?'

'We're chronically undermanned in this miserable stepchild of the service,' said Fenross. 'Now, worse than ever. You'll have to go alone. Snoop around as much as you can. Take all the time you need. But don't come back without a report that'll give some indication — one way or another!'

Or come back dead, thought Flandry. He looked into the

twitching face across the desk and knew that was what Fenross wanted.

IV

He got Chives out of arrest and debated with himself whether to sneak back to Ruethen's party. It was still going on. But no. Aycharaych would never have mentioned his own departure without assuming Flandry would notify headquarters. It might be his idea of a joke — it might be a straight-forward challenge, for Aycharaych was just the sort who'd enjoy seeing if he could elude an ambush — most likely, the whole thing was deliberate, for some darkling purpose. In any event, a junior Intelligence officer or two could better keep tabs on the Chereionite than Flandry, who was prominent. Having made arrangements for that, the man took Chives to his private flitter.

Though voluptuous enough inside, the *Hooligan* was a combat boat, with guns and speed. Even on primary, sub-light drive, it could reach Jupiter in so few hours that Flandry would have little enough time to think what he would do. He set the autopilot and bade Chives bring a drink. 'A stiff one,' he added.

'Yes, sir. Do you wish your whites laid out, or do you prefer a working suit?'

Flandry considered his rumpled elegance and sighed. Chives had spent an hour dressing him — for nothing. 'Plain grey zip-suit,' he said. 'Also sackcloth and ashes.'

'Very good, sir.' The valet poured whisky over ice. He was from Shalmu, quite humanoid except for bald emerald skin, prehensile tail, one-point-four metre height, and details of ear, hand, and foot. Flandry had bought him some years back, named him Chives, and taught him any number of useful arts. Lately the being had politely refused manumission. ('If I may made so bold as to say it, sir, I am afraid my tribal customs would now have a lack of interest for me matched only by their deplorable lack of propriety.')

Flandry brooded over his drink while. 'What do you know about Ymir?' he asked.

'Ymir is the arbitrary human name, sir, for the chief planet of a realm — if I may use that word advisedly — coterminous with the Terrestrial Empire, the Merseian, and doubtless a considerable part of the galaxy beyond.'

'Don't be so bloody literal-minded,' said Flandry. 'Especially when I'm being rhetorical. I mean, what do you know about their ways of living, thinking, believing, hoping? What do they find beautiful and what is too horrible to tolerate? Good galloping gods, what do they even use for a government? They call themselves the Dispersal when they talk Anglic — but is that a translation or a mere tag? How can we tell? What do you and I have in common with a being that lives at a hundred below zero, breathing hydrogen at a pressure which makes our ocean beds look like vacuum, drinking liquid methane and using allotropic ice to make his tools?

'We were ready enough to cede Jupiter to them: Jupiter-type planets throughout our realm. They had terrestroid planets to offer in exchange. Why, that swap doubled the volume of our sphere. And we traded a certain amount of scientific information with them, high-pressure physics for low-pressure, oxygen metabolisms versus hydrogen ... but disappointingly little, when you get down to it. They'd been in interstellar space longer than we had. (And how did they learn atomics under Ymirite air pressure? Me don't ask it!) They'd already observed our kind of life throughout ... how much of the galaxy? We couldn't offer them a thing of importance, except the right to colonise some more planets in peace. They've never shown as much interest in our wars — the wars of the oxygen breathers on the pygmy planets — as you and I would have in a fight between two ant armies. Why should they care? You could drop Terra or Merseia into Jupiter and it'd hardly make a decent splash. For a hundred years, now, the Ymirites have scarcely said a word to us. Or to Merseia, from all indications. Till now.

'And yet I glanced at the pictures taken out near Vixen, just before we left. And Fenross, may he fry, is right. Those blunt ships were made on a planet similar to Terra, but they have Ymirite lines ... the way the first Terran automobiles had the motor in front, because that was where the horse used to be. . . . It could be coincidence, I suppose. Or a red herring. Or — I don't know. How am I supposed to find out, one man on a planet with ten times the radius of Terra? Judas!' He drained his glass and held it out again.

Chives refilled, then went back to the clothes locker. 'A white scarf or a blue?' he mused. 'Hm, yes, I do believe the white, sir.'

The flitter plunged onward. Flandry needed a soberjolt by the time he had landed on Ganymede.

There was an established procedure for such a visit. It hadn't been used for decades, Flandry had had to look it up, but the robot station still waited patiently between rough mountains. He presented his credentials, radio contact was made with the primary planet, unknown messages travelled over its surface. A reply was quick: yes, Captain, the governor can receive you. A spaceship is on its way, and will be at your disposal.

Flandry looked out at the stony desolation of Ganymede. It was not long before a squat, shimmering shape had made grav-beam descent. A tube wormed from its lock to the flitter's. Flandry sighed. 'Let's go,' he said, and strolled across. Chives trotted after with a burden of weapons, tools, and instruments — none of which was likely to me much use. There was a queasy moment under Ganymede's natural gravity, then they had entered the Terra-conditioned bubble.

It looked like any third-class passenger cabin, except for the outmoded furnishings and a bank of large viewscreens. Hard to believe that this was only the material inner lining of a binding-force field: that that same energy, cousin to that which held the atomic nucleus together, was all which kept this room from being crushed beneath intolerable pressure. Or, at the moment, kept the rest of the spaceship from exploding outward. The bulk of the vessel was an alloy of water, lithium, and metallic hydrogen, stable only under Jovian surface conditions.

Flandry let Chives close the airlock while he turned on the screens. They gave him a full outside view. One remained blank, a communicator, the other showed the pilot's cabin.

An artificial voice, ludicrously sweet in the style of a century ago, said: 'Greeting, Terran. My name, as nearly as it may be rendered in sonic equivalents, is Horx. I am your guide and interpreter while you remain on Jupiter.'

Flandry looked into the screen. The Ymirite didn't quite register on his mind. His eyes weren't trained to those shapes and proportions, seen by that weirdly shifting red-blue-brassy light. (Which wasn't the real thing, even, but an electronic translation. A human looking straight into the thick Jovian air would only see darkness.) 'Hello, Horx,' he said to the great black multi-legged shape with the peculiarly tendrilled heads. He wet his lips, which seemed a bit dry. 'I, er, expect you haven't had such an assignment before in your life.'

'I did several times, a hundred or so Terra-years ago,' said Horx casually. He didn't seem to move, to touch any controls, but Ganymede receded in the viewscreens and raw space blazed forth. 'Since then I have been doing other work.' Hesitation. Or was it? At last: 'Recently, though, I have conducted several missions to our surface.'

'What?' choked Flandry.

'Merseian,' said Horx. 'You may enquire of the governor if you wish.' He said nothing else the whole trip.

Jupiter, already big in the screen, became half of heaven. Flandry saw blots march across its glowing many-coloured face, darknesses which were storms that could have swallowed all Terra. Then the sight was lost, he was dropping through the atmosphere. Still the step-up screens tried loyally to show him something: he saw clouds of ammonia crystals, a thousand kilometres long, streaked with strange blues and greens that were free radicals; he saw lightning leap across a purple sky, and the distant yellow flare of sodium explosions. As he descended, he could even feel, very dimly, the quiver of the ship under enormous winds, and hear the muffled shriek and thunder of the air.

They circled the night side, still descending, and Flandry saw a methane ocean, beating waves flattened by pressure and gravity against a cliff of black allotropic ice, which crumbled and was lifted again even as he watched. He saw an endless plain where things half trees and half animals — except that they were neither, in any Terrestrial sense — lashed snaky fronds after ribbon-shaped flyers a hundred metres in length. He saw bubbles stream past on a red wind, and they were lovely in their myriad colours and they sang in thin crystal voices which somehow penetrated the ship. But they couldn't be true bubbles at this pressure. Could they?

A city came into view, just beyond the dawn line. If it was a city. It was, at least, a unified structure of immense extent, intricate with grottos and arabesques, built low throughout but somehow graceful and gracious. On Flandry's screen its colour was polished blue. Here and there sparks and threads of white energy would briefly flash. They hurt his eyes. There were many Ymirites about, flying on their own wings or riding in shell-shaped power gliders. You wouldn't think of Jupiter as a planet where anything could fly, until you remembered the air density; then you realised it was more a case of swimming.

The spaceship came to a halt, hovering on its repulsor field. Horx said: 'Governor Thua.'

Another Ymirite squatted suddenly in the outside communication screen. He held something which smoked and flickered from shape to shape. The impersonally melodious robot voice said for him, under the eternal snarling of a wind which would have blown down any city men could build: 'Welcome. What is your desire?'

The old records had told Flandry to expect brusqueness. It was not discourtesy; what could a human and an Ymirite make small talk about? The man puffed a cigarette to nervous life and said: 'I am here on an investigative mission for my government.' Either these beings were or were not already aware of the Vixen situation; if not, then they weren't allies of Merseia and would presumably not tell. Or if they did, what the devil difference? Flandry explained.

Thua said at once, 'You seem to have very small grounds for suspecting us. A mere similarity of appearances and nuclear technology is logically insufficient.'

'I know,' said Flandry, 'It could be a fake.'

'It could even be that one or a few Ymirite individuals have offered advice to the entities which instigated this attack,' said Thua. You couldn't judge from the pseudo-voice, but he seemed neither offended nor sympathetic: just monumentally uninterested. 'The Dispersal has been nonstimulate as regards individuals for many cycles. However, I cannot imagine what motive an Ymirite would have for exerting himself on behalf of oxygen breathers. There is no insight to be gained from such acts, and certainly no material profit.'

'An aberrated individual?' suggested Flandry with little hope. 'Like a man poking an anthill — an abode of lesser animals — merely to pass the time?'

'Ymirites do not aberrate in such fashion,' said Thua stiffly.

'I understand there've been recent Merseian visits here.'

'I was about to mention that. I am doing all I can to assure both empires of Ymir's strict neutrality. It would be a nuisance if either attacked us and forced us to exterminate their species.'

Which is the biggest brag since that fisherman who caught the equator, thought Flandry, *or else is sober truth.* He said aloud, choosing his words one by one: 'What, then, were the Merseians doing here?'

'They wished to make some scientific observations of the Jovian surface,' said Thua. 'Horx guided them, like you. Let him describe their activities.'

The pilot stirred in his chamber, spreading black wings. 'We simply cruised about a few times. They had optical instruments, and took various spectroscopic readings. They said it was for research in solid-state physics.'

'Curiouser and curiouser,' said Flandry. He stroked his moustache. 'They have as many Jovoid planets in their sphere as we do. The detailed report on Jovian conditions which the first Ymirite settlers made to Terra, under the treaty, has never been secret. No, I just don't believe that research yarn.'

'It did seem dubious,' agreed Thua, 'but I do not pretend to understand every vagary of the alien mind. It was easier to oblige them than argue about it.'

Chives cleared his throat and said unexpectedly: 'If I may take the liberty of a question, sir, were all these recent visitors of the Merseian species?'

Thua's disgust could hardly be mistaken: 'Do you expect me to register insignificant differences between one such race and another?'

Flandry sighed. 'It looks like deadlock, doesn't it?' he said.

'I can think of no way to give you positive assurance that Ymir is not concerned, except my word,' said Thua. 'However, if you wish you may cruise about this planet at random and see if you observe anything out of the ordinary.' His screen went blank.

'Big fat chance!' muttered Flandry. 'Give me a drink, Chives.'

'Will you follow the governor's proposal?' asked Horx.

'Reckon so.' Flandry flopped into a chair. 'Give us the standard guided tour. I've never been on Jupiter, and might as well have something to show for my time.'

The city fell behind, astonishingly fast. Flandry sipped the whisky Chives had gotten from the supplies they had along, and watched the awesome landscape with half an eye. Too bad he was feeling so sour; this really was an experience such as is granted few men. But he had wasted hours on a mission which any second-year cadet could have handled . . . while guns were gathered at Syrax and Vixen stood alone against all hell . . . or even while Lady Diana danced with other men and Ivar del Bruno waited grinning to collect his bet. Flandry said an improper word. 'What a nice subtle bed of coals for Fenross to rake me over,' he added. 'The man has a genius for it.' He gulped his drink and called for another.

'We're rising, sir,' said Chives much later.

Flandry saw mountains which trembled and droned, blue mists that whirled about their metallic peaks, and then the Jovian ground was lost in darkness. The sky began to turn blood colour. 'What are we heading for now?' he asked. He checked a map. 'Oh, yes, I see.'

'I venture to suggest to the pilot, sir, that our speed may be a trifle excessive,' said Chives.

Flandry heard the wind outside rise to a scream, with subsonic undertones that shivered in his marrow. Red fog flew roiled and tattered past his eyes. Beyond, he saw crimson clouds the height of a Terrestrial sierra, with lightning leaping in their bellies. The light from the screens washed like a dull fire into the cabin.

'Yes,' he muttered. 'Slow down, Horx. There'll be another one along in a minute, as the story has it — '

And then he saw the pilot rise up in his chamber, fling open a door, and depart. An instant afterward Flandry saw Horx beat wings against the spaceship's furious slipstream; then the Ymirite was whirled from view. And then Chives saw the thing which hung in the sky before them, and yelled. He threw his tail around Flandry's waist while he clung with hands and legs to a bunk stanchion.

And then the world exploded into thunder and night.

V

Flandry awoke. He spent centuries wishing he hadn't. A blurred green shape said: 'Your aneurine, sir.'

'Go 'way,' mumbled Flandry. 'What was I drinking?'

'Pardon my taking the liberty, sir,' said Chives. He pinned the man's wrists down with his tail, held Flandry's nose with one hand and poured the drug down his mouth with the other. 'There, now, we are feeling much better, aren't we?'

'Remind me to shoot you, slowly.' Flandry gagged for a while. The medicine took hold and he sat up. His brain cleared and he looked at the screen bank.

Only one of the viewers still functioned. It showed thick, drifting redness, shot through with blues and blacks. A steady rough growling, like the breakup of a polar ice pack, blasted its way through the ultimate rigidity of the force bubble — God,

106

what must the noise be like outside? The cabin was tilted. Slumped in its lower corner, Flandry began to glide across the floor again; the ship was still being rolled about. The internal gravity field had saved their lives by cushioning the worst shock, but then it had gone dead. He felt the natural pull of Jupiter upon him, and every cell was weary from its own weight.

He focused on a twisted bunkframe. 'Did I do that with my own little head?'

'We struck with great force, sir,' Chives told him. 'I permitted myself to bandage your scalp. However, a shot of growth hormone will heal the cuts in a few hours, sir, if we escape the present dilemma.'

Flandry lurched to his feet. His bones seemed to be dragging him back downward. He felt the cabin walls tremble and heard them groan. The force bubble had held, which meant that its generator and the main power plant had survived the crash. Not unexpectedly; a ship like this was built on the 'fail safe' principle. But there was no access whatsoever from this cabin to the pilot room — unless you were an Ymirite. It made no difference whether the ship was still flyable or not. Human and Shalmuan were stuck here till they starved. Or, more likely, till the atomic-power plant quit working, under some or other of the buffers this ship was receiving.

Well, when the force-field collapsed and Jovian air pressure flattened the cabin, it would be a merciful death.

'The hell with that noise,' said Flandry. 'I don't want to die so fast I can't feel it. I want to see death coming, and make the stupid thing fight for every centimetre of me.'

Chives gazed into the sinister crimson which filled the last electronic window. His slight frame stooped, shaking in the knees; he was even less adapted to Jovian weight than Flandry. 'Where are we, sir?' he husked. 'I was thinking primarily about what to make for lunch, just before the collision, and —'

'The Red Spot area,' said Flandry. 'Or, rather, the fringe of it. We must be on an outlying berg, or whatever the deuce they're called.'

'Our guide appears to have abandoned us, sir.'

'Hell, he got us into this mess. On purpose! I know for a fact there's at least one. Ymirite working for the enemy — whoever the enemy is. But the information won't be much use if we become a pair of grease spots.'

The ship shuddered and canted. Flandry grabbed a stanchion for support, eased himself down on the bunk, and said, very quickly, for destruction roared around him:

'You've seen the Red Spot from space, Chives. It's been known for a long time, even before space travel, that it's a . . . a mass of aerial pack ice. Lord, what a fantastic place to die! What happens is that at a certain height in the Jovian atmosphere, the pressure allows a red crystalline form of ice — not the white stuff we splash whisky on to, or the black allotrope down at the surface, or the super-dense variety in the mantle around the Jovian core. Here the pressure is right for red ice, and the air density is identical, so it floats. An initial formation created favourable conditions for the formation of more . . . so it accumulated in this one region, much as polar caps build up on cozier type planets. Some years a lot of it melts away — changes phase — the Red Spot looks paler from outside. Other years you get a heavy pile-up, and Jupiter seems to have a moving wound. But always, Chives, the Red Spot is a pack of flying glaciers, stretching broader than all Terra. And we've been crashed on one of them!'

'Then our present situation can scarcely be accidental, sir,' nodded Chives imperturbably. 'I daresay, with all the safety precautions built into this ship, Horx thought this would be the only way to destroy us without leaving evidence. He can claim a stray berg was tossed in our path, or some such tale.' Chives sniffed. 'Not sportsmanlike at all, sir. Just what one would expect of a . . . a native.'

The cabin yawed. Flandry caught himself before he fell out of the bunk. At this gravity, to stumble across the room would be to break a leg. Thunders rolled. White vapors hissed up against crimson in the surviving screen.

'I'm not on to these scientific esoterica,' said Flandry. His chest pumped, struggling to supply oxygen for muscles toiling under nearly three times their normal weight. Each rib felt as if cast in lead. 'But I'd guess what is happening is this. We maintain a temperature in here which for Jupiter is crazily high. So we're radiating heat, which makes the ice go soft and — We're slowly sinking into the berg.' He shrugged and got out a cigarette.

'Is that wise, sir?' asked Chives.

'The oxygen recyclers are still working,' said Flandry. 'It's not at all stuffy in here. Air is the least of our worries.' His coolness cracked over, he smote a fist on the wall and said between his teeth: 'It's this being helpless! We can't go out of the cabin, we can't do a thing but sit here and take it!'

'I wonder, sir.' Slowly, his thin face sagging with gravity, Chives pulled himself to the pack of equipment. He pawed through it. 'No, sir. I regret to say I took no radio. It seemed we could communicate through the pilot.' He paused. 'Even if we did find a way to signal, I daresay any Ymirite who received our call would merely interpret it as random static.'

Flandry stood up, somehow. 'What do we have?' A tiny excitement shivered along his nerves. Outside, Jupiter boomed at him.

'Various detectors, sir, to check for installations. A pair of spacesuits. Sidearms. Your burglar kit, though I confess uncertainty what value it would have here. A microrecorder. A —'

'Wait a minute!'

Flandry sprang towards his valet. The floor rocked beneath him. He staggered towards the far wall. Chives shot out his tail and helped brake the man. Shaking, Flandry eased himself down and went on all fours to the corner where the Shalmuan squatted.

He didn't even stop to gibe at his own absent-mindedness. His heart thuttered. 'Wait a minute, Chives,' he said. 'We've got an airlock over there. Since the force-bubble necessarily reinforces its structure, it must still be intact; and its machinery can open the valves even against this outside pressure. Of course, we can't go through ourselves. Our space armour would be squashed flat. But we can get at the mechanism of the lock. It also, by logical necessity, has to be part of the Terra-conditioned system. We can use the tools we have here to make a simple automatic cycle. First the outer valve opens. Then it shuts, the Jovian air is exhausted from the chamber and Terrestrial air replaces same. Then the valve opens again ... and so on. Do you see?'

'No, sir,' said Chives. A deadly physical exhaustion filmed his yellow eyes. 'My brain feels so thick ... I regret —'

'A signal!' yelled Flandry. 'We flush oxygen out into a hydrogen-cum-methane atmosphere. We supply an electric spark in the lock chamber to ignite the mixture. Whoosh! A flare! Feeble and blue enough — but not by Jovian standards. Any Ymirite anywhere within tens of kilometres is bound to see it as brilliant as we see a magnesium torch. And it'll repeat. A steady cycle, every four or five minutes. If the Ymirites aren't made of concrete, they'll be curious enough to investigate . . . and when they find the wreck on this berg, they'll guess our need and — '

His voice trailed off. Chives said dully. 'Can we spare the oxygen, sir?'

'We'll have to,' said Flandry. 'We'll sacrifice as much as we can stand, and then halt the cycle. If nothing has happened after several hours, we'll expend half of what left in one last fireworks.' He took an ultimate pull on his cigarette, ground it out with great care, and fought back to his feet. 'Come on, let's get going. What have we to lose?'

The floor shook. It banged and crashed outside. A fog of free radicals drifted green past the window, and the red iceberg spun in Jupiter's endless gale.

Flandry glanced at Chives. 'You have one fault, laddy,' he said, forcing a smile to his lips. 'You aren't a beautiful woman.' And then, after a moment, sighing: 'However, it's just as well. Under the circumstances.'

VI

— And in that well-worn nick of time, which goes to prove that the gods, understandably, love me, help arrived. An Ymirite party spotted our flare. Having poked around, they went off, bringing back another force-bubble ship to which we transferred our nearly suffocated carcasses. No, Junior, I don't know what the Ymirites were doing in the Red Spot area. It must be a dank cold place for them too. But I had guessed they would be sure to maintain some kind of monitors, scientific stations, or what have you around there, just as we monitor the weather-breeding regions of Terra.

Governor Thua didn't bother to apologise. He didn't even notice my valet's indignant demand that the miscreant Horx be forthwith administered a red-ice shaft, except to say that future visitors would be given a different guide (how can they tell?) and that this business was none of his doing and he wouldn't waste any Ymitire's time with investigations or punishments or any further action at all. He pointed out the treaty provision, that he wasn't bound to admit us, and that any visits would always be at the visitor's own risk.

The fact that some Ymirites did rescue us proves that the

conspiracy, if any, does not involve their whole race. But how highly placed the hostile individuals are in their government (if they have anything corresponding to government as we know it) — I haven't the groggiest.

Above summary for convenience only. Transcript of all conversation, which was taped as per ungentlemanly orders, attached.

Yes, Junior, you may leave the room.

Flandry switched off the recorder. He could trust the confidential secretary, who would make a formal report out of his dictation, to clean it up. Though he wished she wouldn't.

He leaned back, cocked feet on desk, trickled smoke through his nostrils, and looked out the clear wall of his office. Admiralty Centre gleamed, slim faerie spires in soft colours, reaching for the bright springtime sky of Terra. You couldn't mount guard across 400 light-years without millions of ships; and that meant millions of policy makers, scientists, engineers, strategists, tacticians, co-ordinators, clerks . . . and they had families, which needed food, clothing, houses, schools, amusements . . . so the heart of the Imperial Navy became a city in its own right. *Damn company town*, thought Flandry. And yet, when the bombs finally roared out of space, when the barbarians howled among smashed buildings and the smoke of burning books hid dead men in tattered bright uniforms — when the Long Night came, as it would, a century or a millennium hence, what difference? — something of beauty and gallantry would have departed the universe.

To hell with it. Let civilisation hang together long enough for Dominic Flandry to taste a few more vintages, ride a few more horses, kiss a lot more girls and sing another ballad or two. That would suffice. At least, it was all he dared hope for.

The intercom chimed. 'Admiral Fenross wants to see you immediately, sir.'

'Now he tells me,' grunted Flandry. 'I wanted to see him yesterday, when I got back.'

'He was busy then, sir,' said the robot, as glibly as if it had a conscious mind. 'His lordship the Earl of Sidrath is visiting Terra, and wished to be conducted through the operations centre.'

Flandry rose, adjusted his peacock-blue tunic, admired the crease of his gold-frogged white trousers, and covered his sleek hair with a jewel-banded officer's cap. 'Of course,' he said,

'Admiral Fenross couldn't possibly delegate the tour to an aide.'

'The Earl of Sidrath is related to Grand Admiral the Duke of Asia,' the robot reminded him.

Flandry sang beneath his breath, *'Brown is the colour of my true love's nose,'* and went out the door. After a series of slide-ways and gravshafts, he reached Fenross' office.

The admiral nodded his close-cropped head beyond the desk. 'There you are.' His tone implied Flandry had stopped for a beer on the way. 'Sit down. Your preliminary verbal report on the Jovian mission has been communicated to me. Is that really all you could find out?'

Flandry smiled. 'You told me to get an indication, one way or another, of the Ymirite attitude, sir,' he purred. 'That's what I got: an indication, one way or another.'

Fenross gnawed his lip. 'All right, all right. I should have known, I guess. Your forte never was working with an organisation, and we're going to need a special project, a very large project, to learn the truth about Ymir.'

Flandry sat up straight. 'Don't,' he said sharply.

'What?'

'Don't waste men that way. Sheer arithmetic will defeat them. Jupiter alone has the area of a hundred Terras. The population must be more or less proportional. How are our men going to percolate around, confined to the two or three space-ships that Thua has available for them? Assuming Thua doesn't simply refuse to admit any further oxygen-breathing nuisances. How are they going to question, bribe, eavesdrop, get any single piece of information? It's a truism that the typical Ingelligence job consists of gathering a million unimportant little facts and fitting them together into one big fact. We've few enough agents as is, spread ghastly thin. Don't tie them up in an impossible job. Let them keep working on Merseia, where they've a chance of accomplishing something!'

'And if Ymir suddenly turns on us?' snapped Fenross.

'Then we roll with the punch. Or we die.' Flandry shrugged and winced; his muscles were still sore from the pounding they had taken. 'But haven't you thought, sir, this whole business may well be a Merseian stunt — to divert our attention from them, right at this crisis? It's exactly the sort of bear trap Aycharaych loves to set.'

'That may be,' admitted Fenross. 'But Merseia lies beyond

Syrax; Jupiter is next door. I've been given to understand that His Imperial Majesty is alarmed enough to desire — ' He shrugged too, making it the immemorial gesture of a baffled underling.

'Who dropped that hint?' drawled Flandry. 'Surely not the Earl of Sidrath, whom you were showing the sights yesterday while the news came in that Vixen had fallen?'

'Shut up!' Almost, it was a scream. A jag of pain went over Fenross' hollowed countenance. He reached for a pill. 'If I didn't oblige the peerage,' he said thickly, 'I'd be begging my bread in Underground and someone would be in this office who'd never tell them no.'

Flandry paused. He started a fresh cigarette with unnecessary concentration. *I suppose I am being unjust to him,* he thought. *Poor devil. It can't be much fun being Fenross.*

Still, he reflected, Aycharaych had left the Solar System so smoothly that the space ambush had never even detected his boat. Twenty-odd hours ago, a battered scoutship had limped in to tell the Imperium that Vixen had perforce surrendered to its nameless besiegers, who had landed *en masse after* reducing the defences. The last despatch from Syrax described clashes which had cost the Terrans more ships than the Merseians. Jupiter blazed a mystery in the evening sky. Rumour said that after his human guests had left, Ruethen and his staff had rolled out huge barrels of bitter ale and caroused like trolls for many hours; they must have known some reason to be merry.

You couldn't blame Fenross much. But would the whole long climb of man, from jungle to stars, fall back in destruction — and no single person even deserve to have his knuckles rapped for it?

'What about the reinforcements that were being sent to Vixen?' asked Flandry.

'They're still on their way.' Fenross gulped his pill and relaxed a trifle. 'What information we have, about enemy strength and so on, suggests that another stand-off will develop. The aliens won't be strong enough to kick our force out of the system — '

'Not with Tom Walton in command. I hear he is.' A very small warmth trickled into Flandry's soul.

'Yes. At the same time, now the enemy is established on Vixen, there's no obvious way to get them off without total blasting — which would sterilise the planet. Of course, Walton can try to cut their supply lines and starve them out; but once they get their occupation organised, Vixen itself will supply them. Or he can try to find out where they come from, and counter-attack their home. Or perhaps he can negotiate something. I don't know. The Emperor himself gave Admiral Walton what amounts to carte blanche.'

It must have been one of His Majesty's off days, decided Flandry. *Actually doing the sensible thing.*

'Our great handicap is that our opponents know all about us and we know almost nothing about them,' went on Fenross. 'I'm afraid the primary effort of our Intelligence must be diverted towards Jupiter for the time being. But someone has to gather information at Vixen too, about the aliens.' His voice jerked to a halt.

Flandry filled his lungs with smoke, held it a moment, and let it out in a slowflood. 'Eek,' he said tonelessly.

'Yes. That's your next assignment.'

'But . . . me, alone, to Vixen? Surely Walton's force carries a bunch of our people.'

'Of course. They'll do what they can. But parallel operations are standard espionage procedure, as even you must know. Furthermore, the Vixenites made the dramatic rather than the logical gesture. After their planet had capitulated, they got one boat out, with one person aboard. The boat didn't try to reach any Terrestrial ship within the system. That was wise, because the tiny force Aldebaran had sent was already broken in battle and reduced to sneak raids. But neither did the Vixenite boat go to Aldebaran itself. No, it came straight here, and the pilot expected a personal audience with the Emperor.'

'And didn't get it,' foretold Flandry. 'His Majesty is much too busy gardening to waste time on a mere commoner representing a mere planet.'

'Gardening?' Fenross blinked.

'I'm told His Majesty cultivates beautiful pansies,' murmured Flandry.

Fenross gulped and said in great haste: 'Well, no, of course not. I mean, I myself interviewed the pilot, and read the report carried along. Not too much information, though helpful. However, while Walton has a few Vixenite refugees along as guides and advisors, this pilot is the only one who's seen the aliens close up, on the ground, digging in and trading rifle shots with humans; has experienced several days of occupation before get-ing away. Copies of the report can be sent after Walton. But that first-hand knowledge of enemy behaviour, regulations, all the little unpredictable details ... that may also prove essential.'

'Yes,' said Flandry. 'If a spy is to be smuggled back on to Vixen's surface. Namely me.'

Fenross allowed himself a prim little smile. 'That's what I had in mind.'

Flandry nodded, unsurprised. Fenross would never give up trying to get him killed. Though in all truth, Dominic Flandry doubtless had more chance of pulling such a stunt and getting back unpunctured than anyone else.

He said idly: 'The decision to head straight for Sol wasn't illogical. If the pilot had gone to Aldebaran, then Aldebaran would have sent us a courier reporting the matter and asking for orders. A roundabout route. This way, we got the news days quicker. No, that Vixenite has a level head on his shoulders.'

'Hers,' corrected Fenross.

'Huh?' Flandry sat bolt upright.

'She'll explain any details,' said Fenross. 'I'll arrange an open requisition for you: draw what equipment you think you'll need. And if you survive, remember, I'll want every millo's worth accounted for. Now get out and get busy! I've got work to do.'

VII

The *Hooligan* snaked out of Terran sky, ran for a time on primary drive at an acceleration which it strained the internal grav-field to compensate for, and, having reached a safe distance from Sol, sprang over into secondary. Briefly the viewscreens went wild with Doppler effect and aberration. Then their circuits adapted to the rate at which the vessel pulsed in and out of normal space-time-energy levels; they annulled the optics of pseudo-speed, and Flandry looked again upon cold many-starred night as if he were at rest.

He left Chives in the turret to make final course adjustments and strolled down to the saloon. 'All clear,' he smiled. 'Estimated time to Vixen, thirteen standard days.'

'What?' The girl, Catherine Kittredge, half rose from the

luxuriously cushioned bench. 'But it took me a month the other way, an' I had the fastest racer on our planet.'

'I've tinkered with this one,' said Flandry, 'Or, rather, found experts to do so.' He sat down near her, crossing long legs and leaning an elbow on the mahogany table which the bench half-circled. 'Give me a screwdriver and I'll make any firearm in the cosmos sit up and speak. But space drives have an anatomy I can only call whimsical.'

He was trying to put her at ease. Poor kid, she had seen her home assailed, halfway in from the Imperial marches that were supposed to bear all the wars; she had seen friends and kinfolk slain in battle with unhuman unknowns, and heard the boots of an occupying enemy racket in once-familiar streets; she had fled to Terra like a child to its mother, and been coldly interviewed in an office and straightway bundled back on to a spaceship, with one tailed alien and one suave stranger. Doubtless an official had told her she was a brave little girl and now it was her duty to return as a spy and quite likely be killed. And meanwhile rhododendrons bloomed like cool fire in Terra's parks, and the laughing youth of Terra's aristocracy flew past on their way to some newly opened pleasure house.

No wonder Catherine Kittredge's eyes were wide and bewildered.

They were her best feature, Flandry decided: large, set far apart, a gold-flecked hazel under long lashes and thick dark brows. Her hair would have been nice too, a blonde helmet, if she had not cut it off just below the ears. Otherwise she was nothing much to look at — a broad, snub-nosed, faintly freckled countenance, generous mouth and good chin. As nearly as one could tell through a shapeless grey coverall, she was of medium height and on the stocky side. She spoke Anglic with a soft regional accent that sounded good in her low voice; but all her mannerisms were provincial, fifty years out of date. Flandry wondered a little desperately what they could talk about.

Well, there was business enough. He flicked buttons for autoservice. 'What are you drinking?' he asked. 'We've anything within reason, and a few things out of reason, on board.'

She blushed. 'Nothin', thank you,' she mumbled.

'Nothing at all? Come, now. Daiquiri? Wine? Beer? Buttermilk, for heaven's sake?'

'Hm?' She raised a fleeting glance. He discovered Vixen had no dairy industry, cattle couldn't survive there, and dialled ice cream for her. He himself slugged down a large gin-and-bitters. He was going to need alcohol — two weeks alone in space with Little Miss Orphan!

She was pleased enough by discovering ice cream to relax a trifle. Flandry offered a cigarette, was refused, and started one for himself. 'You'll have plenty of time to brief me en route,' he said, 'so don't feel obliged to answer questions now, if it distresses you.'

Catherine Kittredge looked beyond him, out the viewscreen and into the frosty sprawl of Andromeda. Her lips twitched downward, ever so faintly. But she replied with a steadiness he liked: 'Why not? 'Twon't bother me more'n sittin' an' broodin'.'

'Good girl. Tell me, how did you happen to carry the message?'

'My brother was our official courier. You know how 'tis on planets like ours, without much population or money: whoever's got the best spaceship gets a subsidy an' carries any special despatches. I helped him. We used to go off jauntin' for days at a time, an' — No,' she broke off. Her fists closed. 'I *won't* bawl. The aliens forced a landin'. Hank went off with our groun' forces. He didn't come back. Sev'ral days after the surrender, when things began to settle down a little, I got the news he'd been killed in action. A few of us decided the Imperium had better be given what information we could supply. Since I knew Hank's ship best, they tol' me to go.'

'I see.' Flandry determined to keep this as dry as possible, for her sake. 'I've a copy of the report your people made up, of course, but you had all the way to Sol to study it, so you must know more about it than anyone else off Vixen. Just to give me a rough preliminary idea, I understand some of the invaders knew Anglic and there was a certain amount of long-range parleying. What did they call themselves?'

'Does that matter?' she asked listlessly.

'Not in the faintest, at the present stage of things, except that it's such a weary cliché to speak of Planet X.'

She smiled, a tiny bit. 'They called themselves the Ardazirho, an' we gathered the *ho* was a collective endin'. So we figure their planet is named Ardazir. Though I can't come near pronouncin' it right.'

Flandry took a stereopic from the pocket of his iridescent shirt. It had been snapped from hiding, during the ground

117

battle. Against a background of ruined human homes crouched a single enemy soldier. Warrior? Acolyte? Unit? Armed, at least, and a killer of men.

Preconceptions always got in the way. Flandry's first startled thought had been *Wolf*! Now he realised that of course the Ardazirho was not lupine, didn't even look notably wolfish. Yet the impression lingered. He was not surprised when Catherine Kittredge said the aliens had gone howling into battle.

They were described as man-size bipeds, but digitigrade, which gave their feet almost the appearance of a dog's walking on its hind legs. The shoulders and arms were very humanoid, except that the thumbs were on the opposite side of the hands from mankind's. The head, arrogantly held on a powerful neck, was long and narrow for an intelligent animal, with a low forehead, most of the brain space behind the pointed ears. A black-nosed muzzle, not as sharp as a wolf's and yet somehow like it, jutted out of the face. Its lips were pulled back in a snarl, showing bluntly pointed fangs which suggested a flesh-eater turned omnivore. The eyes were oval, close set, and grey as sleet. Short thick fur covered the entire body, turning to a ruff at the throat; it was rusty red.

'Is this a uniform?' asked Flandry.

The girl leaned close to see. The pictured Ardazirho wore a sort of kilt, in checkerboard squares of various hues. Flandry winced at some of the combinations: rose next to scarlet, a glaring crimson offensively between two delicate yellows. 'Barbarians indeed,' he muttered. 'I hope Chives can stand the shock.' Otherwise the being was dressed in boots of flexible leather and a harness from which hung various pouches and equipment. He was armed with what was obviously a magnetronic rifle, and had a wicked-looking knife at his belt.

'I'm not sure,' said the girl. 'Either they don't use uniforms at all, or they have such a variety that we've not made any sense of it. Some might be dressed more or less like him, others in a kind o' tunic an' burnoose, others in breastplates an' fancy plumed helmets.'

'Him,' pounced Flandry. 'They're all male, then?'

'Yes, sir, seems that way. The groun' fightin' lasted long enough for our biologists to dissect an' analyse a few o' their dead. Accordin' to the report, they're placental mammals. It's clear they're from a more or less terrestroid planet, probably with a somewhat stronger gravity. The eye structure suggests

118

heir sun is bright, type A5 or thereabouts. That means they hould feel pretty much at home in our badlands.' Catherine Kittredge shrugged sadly. 'Figure that's why they picked us to tart on.'

'They might have been conquering for some time,' said Flandry. 'A hot star like an A5 is no use to humans; and I imagine he F-type like yours is about as cool as they care for. They may well have built up a little coterminous kingdom, a number of B, A, and F suns out in your quadrant, where we don't even have a complete astronomical mapping — let alone having explored much ... Hm. Didn't you get a chance to interrogate any live prisoners?'

'Yes. 'Twasn't much use. Durin' the fightin', one of our regiments did encircle a unit o' theirs an' knock it out with stun beams. When two o' them woke up an' saw they were captured, they died.'

'Preconditioning,' nodded Flandry. 'Go on.'

'The rest didn't speak any Anglic, 'cept one who'd picked up a little bit. They questioned him.' The girl winced. 'I don't figure 'twas very nice. The report says towards the end his heart kept stoppin' an' they'd revive it, but at last he died for good ... Anyway, it seems a fair bet he was tellin' the truth. An' he didn't know where his home star was. He could understan' our co-ordinate system, an' translate it into the one they used. But that was zeroed arbitrarily on S Doradus, an' he didn't have any idea about the co-ordinates of Ardazir.'

'Memory blank.' Flandry scowled. 'Probably given to all the enlisted ranks. Such officers as must retain full information are conditioned to die on capture. What a merry monarch they've got.' He twisted his moustache between nervous fingers. 'You know, though, this suggests their home is vulnerable. Maybe we should concentrate on discovering where it is.'

The girl dropped her eyes. She lost a little colour. 'Do you think we can, my lord?' she whispered. 'Or are we just goin' to die too?'

'If the mission involves procedures illegal or immoral, I should have no trouble.' Flandry grinned at her. 'You can do whatever honourable work is necessary. Between us, why, God help Ardazir. Incidentally, I don't rate a title.'

'But they called you Sir Dominic.'

'A knighthood is not a patent of nobility. I'm afraid my relationship to the peerage involves a bar sinister. You see, one

day my father wandered into this sinister bar, and — ' Flandry
rambled on, skirting the risqué, until he heard her laugh. Then
he laughed back and said: 'Good girl! What do they call you at
home? Kit, I'll swear. Very well, we're off to the wars, you the
Kit and I the caboodle. Now let's scream for Chives to lay out
caviar and cheeses. Afterwards I'll show you to your stateroom.'
Her face turned hot, and he added, 'Its door locks on the
inside.'

'Thank you,' she said, so low he could scarcely hear it.
Smoky lashes fluttered on her cheeks. 'When I was told to
come — with you — I mean, I didn't know —'

'My dear girl,' said Flandry, 'credit me with enough experience to identify a holstered needle gun among more attractive
curves beneath that coverall.'

VIII

There was always something unreal about a long trip through
space. Here, for a time, you were alone in the universe. No
radio could outpace you and be received, even if unimaginable
distance would not soon have drowned it in silence. No other
signal existed, except another spaceship, and how would it find
you unless your feeble drive-pulsations were by the merest
chance detected? A whole fleet might travel many parsecs
before some naval base sensed its wake with instruments; your
one mote of a craft could hurtle to the ends of creation and
never be heard. There was nothing to be seen, no landscape, no
weather, simply the enormous endless pageantry of changing
constellations, now and then a cold nebular gleam between
flashing suns, the curdled silver of the Milky Way and the
clotted stars near Sagittarius. Yet you in your shell were warm,
dry, breathing sweet recycled air; on a luxury vessel like the
Hooligan, you might listen to recorded Lysarcian bells, sip
Namorian maoth and taste Terran grapes.

Flandry worked himself even less mercifully than he did
Chives and Kit. It was the hard, dull grind which must underlie
all their hopes: study, rehearsal, analysis of data, planning and
discarding and planning again, until brains could do no more
and thinking creaked to a halt. But then recreation became pure
necessity — and they were two humans with one unobtrusive
servant, cruising among the stars.

Flandry discovered that Kit could give him a workout, when they played handball down in the hold. And her stubborn chess game defeated his swashbuckling tactics most of the time. She had a puckish humour when she wasn't remembering her planet. Flandry would not soon forget her thumbnail impression of Vice Admiral Fenross: 'A mind like a mousetrap, only he ought to some o' those poor little mice go.' She could play the lorr, her fingers dancing over its twelve primary strings with that touch which brings out the full ringing resonance of the secondaries; she seemed to know all the ballads from the old brave days when men were first hewing their home out of Vixen's wildness, and they were good to hear.

Flandry grew slowly aware that she was the opposite of bad-looking. She just hadn't been sculped into the monotonously aristocratic appearance of Terra's high-born ladies. The face, half boyish, was her own, the body full and supple where it counted. He swore dismally to himself and went on a more rigorous calisthenic programme.

Slowly the stars formed new patterns. There came a time when Aldebaran stood like red flame, the brightest object in all heaven. And then the needle-point of Vixen's sun, the star named Cerulia, glistened keen and blue ahead. And Flandry turned from the viewscreen and said quietly: 'Two more days to go. I think we'll have captain's dinner tonight.'

'Very good, sir,' said Chives. 'I took it upon myself to bring along some live Maine lobster. And I trust the Liebfraumilch '51 will be satisfactory?'

'That's the advantage of having a Shalmuan for your batman,' remarked Flandry to Kit. 'Their race has more sensitive palates than ours. They can't go wrong on vintages.'

She smiled, but her eyes were troubled.

Flandry retired to his own cabin and an argument. He wanted to wear a peach-coloured tunic with his white slacks; Chives insisted that the dark blue, with a gold sash, was more suitable. Chives won, naturally. The man wandered into the saloon, which was already laid out for a feast, and poured himself an apéritif. Music sighed from the recorder, nothing great but sweet to hear.

A footfall came lightly behind him. He turned and nearly dropped his glass. Kit was entering in a sheer black dinner gown; one veil the colour of fire flickered from her waistline. A

filigree tiara crowned shining hair, and a bracelet of Old Mar
tian silver coiled massive on her wrist.

'Great hopping electrons,' gasped Flandry. 'Don't *do* such
things without warning! Where did the paintbrush come from
to lay on the glamour that thick?'

Kit chuckled and pirouetted. 'Chives,' she said. 'Who else?
He's a darlin'. He brought the jew'llery along, an' he's been
makin' the dress at odd moments this whole trip.'

Flandry shook his head and clicked his tongue. 'If Chives
would accept manumission, he could set himself up in business
equipping lady spies to seduce poor officers like me. He'd own
the galaxy in ten years.'

Kit blushed and said hastily: 'Did he select the tape too? I
always have loved Mendelssohn's Violin Concerto.'

'Oh, is that what it is? Nice music for a sentimental occasion,
anyway. My department is more the administration of drinks. I
prescribe this before dinner: Ansan aurea. Essentially, it's a
light dry vermouth, but for once a non-Terran soil has im-
proved the flavour of a Terran plant.'

She hesitated. 'I don't — I never — '

'Well, high time you began.' He did not glance at the viewscreen, where Cerulia shone like steel, but they both knew there
might not be many hours left for them to savour existence. She
took the glass, sipped, and sighed.

'Thank you, Dominic. I've been missin' out on such a
lot.'

They seated themselves. 'We'll have to make that up, after
this affair is over,' said Flandry. A darkening passed through
him, just long enough to make him add: 'However, I suspect
that on the whole you've done better in life than I.'

'What do you mean?' Her eyes, above the glass, reflected the
wine's hue and became almost golden.

'Oh ... hard to say.' His mouth twisted ruefully upward.
'I've no romantic illusions about the frontier. I've seen too
much of it. I'd a good deal rather loll in bed sipping my morning chocolate than bounce into the fields before dawn to cul-
tivate the grotch or scag the thimbs or whatever dreary
technicalities it is that pioneers undergo. And yet, well, I've no
illusions about my own class either, or my own way of life. You
frontier people are the healthy ones. You'll be around — most
of you — long after the Empire is a fireside legend. I envy you
that.'

He broke off. 'Pardon me. I'm afraid spiritual jaundice is an occupational disease in my job.'

'Which I'm still not sure what it — Oh, dear.' Kit chuckled. 'Does alcohol act that fast? But really, Dominic, I wish you'd talk a little about your work. All you've said is, you're in Naval Intelligence. I'd like to know what you do.'

'Why?' he asked.

She flushed and blurted: 'To know you better.'

Flandry saw her confusion and moved to hide it from them both: 'There's not a lot to tell. I'm a field agent, which means I go out and peek through windows instead of sitting in an office reading the reports of window peekers. Thanks to the circumstance that my immediate superior doesn't like me, I spend most of my working time away from Terra, on what amounts to a roving commission. Good old Fenross. If he was ever replaced by some kindly father-type who dealt justly with all subordinates, I'd dry up and blow away.'

'I think that's revoltin'.' Anger flashed in her voice.

'What? The discrimination? But my dear lass, what is any civilisation but an elaborate structure of special privileges? I've learned to make my way around among them. Good frogs, d'you think I *want* a nice secure desk job with a guaranteed pension?'

'But still, Dominic — a man like you, riskin' his life again an' again, sent almost alone against all Ardazir . . . because someone doesn't like you!' Her face still burned, and there was a glimmer of tears in the hazel eyes.

'Hard to imagine how that could be,' said Flandry with calculated smugness. He added, lightly and almost automatically: 'But after all, think what an outrageous special privilege your personal heredity represents: so much beauty, charm, and intelligence lavished on one little girl.'

She grew mute, but faintly she trembled. With a convulsive gesture, she tossed off her glass.

Easy, boy, thought Flandry. A not unpleasurable alertness came to life. *Emotional scenes are the last thing we want out here.* 'Which brings up the general topic of you,' he said in his chattiest tone. 'A subject well worth discussing over the egg flower soup which I see Chives bringing in . . . or any other course, for that matter. Let's see, you were a weather engineer's assistant for a living, isn't that right? Sounds like fun, in an earnest high-booted way.' *And might prove useful*, added that part of him which never took a vacation.

She nodded, as anxious as he to escape what they had skirted. They took pleasure in the meal, and talked of many things. Flandry confirmed his impression that Kit was not an unsophisticated peasant. She didn't know the latest delicious gossip about you-know-who and that actor. But she had measured the seasons of her strange violent planet; she could assemble a machine so men could trust their lives to it; she had hunted and sported, seen birth and death; the intrigues of her small city were as subtle as any around the Imperial throne. Withal, she had the innocence of most frontier folk — or call it optimism, or honour, or courage — at any rate, she had not begun to despair of the human race.

But because he found himself in good company, and this was a special occasion, he kept both their glasses filled. After a while he lost track of how many times he had poured.

When Chives cleared the table and set out coffee and liqueur, Kit reached eagerly for her cup. 'I need this,' she said, not quite clearly. ' 'Fraid I had too much to drink.'

'That was the general idea,' said Flandry. He accepted a cigar from Chives. The Shalmuan went noiselessly out. Flandry looked across the table. Kit sat with her back to the broad viewscreen, so that the stars were jewels clustered around her tiara.

'I don't believe it,' she said after a moment.

'You're probably right,' said Flandry. 'What don't you believe?'

'What you were sayin' . . . 'bout the Empire bein' doomed.'

'It's better not to believe that,' he said gently.

'Not because o' Terra,' she said. She leaned forward. The light was soft on her bare young shoulders. 'The little bit I saw there was a hard blow. But Dominic, as long's the Empire has men like, like you — we'll take on the whole universe an' win.'

'Blessings,' said Flandry in haste.

'No.' Her eyes were the least bit hazed, but they locked steadily with his. She smiled, more in tenderness than mirth. 'You won't wriggle off the hook with a joke this time, Dominic. You gave me too much to drink, you see, an' — I mean it. A planet with you on its side has still got hope enough.'

Flandry sipped his liqueur. Suddenly the alcohol touched his own brain with its pale fires, and he thought, *Why not be honest with her? She can take it. Maybe she even deserves it.*

124

'No, Kit,' he said. 'I know my class from the inside out, because it is my class and I probably wouldn't choose another even if some miracle made me able to. But we're hollow, and corrupt, and death has marked us for its own. In the last analysis, however we disguise it, however strenuous and hazardous and even lofty our amusements are, the only reason we can find for living is to have fun. And I'm afraid that isn't reason enough.'

'But it is!' she cried.

'You think so,' he said, 'because you're lucky enough to belong to a society which still has important jobs uncompleted. But we aristocrats of Terra, we enjoy life instead of enjoying what we're doing ... and there's a cosmos of difference.

'The measure of our damnation is that every one of us with any intelligence — and there are some — every one sees the Long Night coming. We've grown too wise; we've studied a little psycho-dynamics, or perhaps only read a lot of history, and we can see that Manuel's Empire was not a glorious resurgence. It was the Indian summer of Terran civilisation. (But you've never seen Indian summer, I suppose. A pity: no planet has anything more beautiful and full of old magics.) Now even that short season is past. Autumn is far along; the nights are cold and the leaves are fallen and the last escaping birds call through a sky which has lost all colour. And yet, we who see winter coming can also see it won't be here till after our lifetimes ... so we shiver a bit, and swear a bit, and go back to playing with a few bright dead leaves.'

He stopped. Silence grew around them. And then, from the intercom, music began again, a low orchestral piece which spoke to deep places of their awareness.

'Excuse me,' said Flandry. 'I really shouldn' have wished my sour pessimism on you.'

Her smile this time held a ghost of pity. 'An' o' course 'twouldn't be debonair to show your real feelin's, or try to find words for them.'

'*Touché!*' He cocked his head. 'Think we could dance to that?'

'The music? Hardly. The *Liebestod* is background for somethin' else. I wonder if Chives knew.'

'Hm?' Flandry looked surprised at the girl.

'I don't mind at all,' she whispered. 'Chives is a darlin'.'

Suddenly he understood.

But the stars were chill behind her. Flandry thought of guns

125

and dark fortresses waiting for them both. He thought of knightly honour, which would not take advantage of the help-lessness which is youth — and then, with a little sadness, he decided that practical considerations were what really turned the balance for him.

He raised the cigar to his mouth and said softly, 'Better drink your coffee before it gets cold, lass.'

With that the moment was safely over. He thought he saw disappointed gratitude in Kit's hurried glance, but wasn't sure. She turned around, gazing at the stars merely to avoid facing him for the next few seconds.

Her breath sighed outward. She sat looking at Cerulia for a whole minute. Then she stared down at her hands and said tonelessly: 'Figure you're right 'bout the Empire. But then what's to become o' Vixen?'

'We'll liberate it, and squeeze a fat indemnity out of Ar-dazir,' said Flandry as if there were no doubt.

'Uh-uh.' She shook her head. Bitterness began to edge her voice. 'Not if 'tisn't convenient. Your Navy might decide to fight the war out where 'tis. An' then my whole planet, my people, the little girl next door an' her kitten, trees an' flowers an' birds, why, 'twill just be radioactive ash blowin' over dead gray hills. Or maybe the Imperium will decide to compromise, an' let Ardazir keep Vixen. Why not? What's one planet to the Empire? A swap might, as you say, buy them peace in their own lifetimes. A few million human bein's, that's nothin', write them off in red ink.' She shook her head again in a dazed way. 'Why are we goin' there, you an' I? What are we workin' for? Whatever we do can come to nothin,' from one stroke of a pen in some bored bureaucrat's hand. Can't it?'

'Yes,' said Flandry.

IX

Cerulia, being a main-sequence star, did not need vastly more mass than Sol to shine more fiercely. Vixen, the fourth planet out, circled its primary in one and a half standard years, along such an orbit that it received, on the average, about as much radition as Terra.

'The catch lies in that word "average",' murmured Flandry.

He floated in the turret with Chives, hands on the control

126

panel and body weightless in a cocoon of pilot harness. To port, the viewscreens were dimmed, lest the harsh blue sun burn out his eyes. Elsewhere, distorted constellations sprawled stark against night. Flandry picked out the Jupiter-type planet called Ogre by the humans of Vixen: a bright yellow glow, its larger moons visible like sparks. And what were its Ymirite colonists thinking?

'Ogre's made enough trouble for Vixen all by itself,' complained Flandry. 'Its settlers ought to be content with that and not go plotting with Ardazir. If they are, I mean.' He turned to Chives. 'How's Kit taking this free-fall plunge?'

'I regret to say Miss Kittredge did not look very comfortable sir,' answered the Shalmuan. 'But she said she was.'

Flandry clicked his tongue. Since the advent of gravity control, there had been little need for civilians ever to undergo weightlessness; hence Kit, susceptible to it, didn't have the training that would have helped. Well, she'd be a lot sicker if an Ardazirho missile homed on the *Hooligan*. Nobody ever died of space nausea: no such luck!

Ardazir would undoubtedly have mounted tight guard over conquered Vixen. Flandry's detectors were confirming this. The space around the planet quivered with primary-drive vibrations, patrolling warcraft, and there must be a network of orbital robot monitors to boot. A standard approach was certain to be spotted. There was another way to land, though, if you were enough of a pilot and had enough luck. Flandry had decided to go ahead with it, rather than contact Walton's task force. He couldn't do much there except report himself in . . . and then proceed to Vixen anyway, with still more likelihood of detection and destruction.

Engines cold, the *Hooligan* plunged at top meteoric velocity straight towards her goal. Any automaton was sure to register her as a siderite, and ignore her. Only visual observation would strip that disguise off; and space is so vast that even with the closest blockade, there was hardly a chance of passing that close to an unwarned enemy. Escape from the surface would be harder, but this present stunt was foolproof. Until you hit atmosphere!

Flandry watched Vixen swelling in the forward viewscreens. To one side Cerulia burned, ominously big. The planet's northern dayside was like a slice of incandescence; polarising telescopes showed bare mountains, stony deserts, rivers gone wild with melted snows. In the southern hemisphere, the continents were still green and brown, the oceans deeply blue, like polished cobalt. But cloud banded that half of the world, storms marched roaring over hundreds of kilometres, lightning flared through rain. The equator was hidden under a nearly solid belt of cloud and gale. The northern aurora was cold flame; the south pole, less brilliant, still shook great banners of light into heaven. A single small moon, 100,000 kilometres from the surface, looked pale against that luminance.

The spaceship seemed tomb silent when Flandry switched his attention back to it. He said, just to make a noise, 'And this passes for a terrestroid, humanly habitable planet. What real estate agents they must have had in the pioneer days!'

'I understand that southern Cerulia IV is not unsalubrious most of the year, sir,' said Chives. 'It is only now, in fact, that the northern part becomes lethal.'

Flandry nodded. Vixen was the goat of circumstance: huge Ogre had exactly four times the period, and thus over millions of years resonance had multiplied perturbation and brought the eccentricity of Vixen's orbit close to one-half. The planet's axial inclination was 24°, and northern midsummer fell nearly at periastron. Thus, every eighteen months, Cerulia scorched that hemisphere with fourfold the radiation Terra got from Sol. This section of the orbit was hastily completed, and most of Vixen's year was spent in cooler regions. 'But I daresay the Ardazirho timed their invasion for right now,' said Flandry. 'If they're from an A-type star, the northern weather shouldn't be too hard on them.'

He put out his final cigarette. The planet filled the bow screen. Robot mechanisms could do a lot, but now there must also be live piloting . . . or a streak in Vixen's sky and a crater blasted from its rock.

At the *Hooligan*'s speed, she crossed the tenuous upper air layers and hit stratosphere in a matter of seconds. It was like a giant's fist. Flandry's harness groaned as his body hurtled forward. There was no outside noise, yet, but the flitter herself shrieked in metallic pain. The screens became one lurid fire, air heated to incandescence.

Flandry's arm trembled with weight. He slammed it down on the drive switches. Chives' slight from could not stir under these pressures, but the green tail darted, button to dial to vernier. Engines bellowed as they fought to shed velocity. The vessel glowed red; but her metal was crystallised to endure more than furnace heat. Thunder banged around her, within her. Flandry felt his ribs shoved towards his lungs, as direction shifted. Still he could only see flame outside. But his blurring eyes read instruments. He knew the vessel had levelled off, struck denser atmosphere, skipped like a stone, and was now, rounding the planet in monstrous shuddering bounces.

First then did he have time to reactivate the internal compensators? A steady one gee poured its benediction through him. He drew uneven breath into an aching chest. 'For this we get *paid*?' he mumbled.

While Chives took over, and the thermostat brought the turret near an endurable temperature, Flandry unbuckled and went below to Kit's stateroom. She lay unstirring in harness, a trickle of blood from the snub nose. He injected her with stimulol. Her eyes fluttered open. Briefly, she looked so young and helpless that he must glance away. 'Sorry to jolt you back to consciousness in this fashion,' he said. 'It's bad practice. But right now, we need a guide.'

'O' course.' She preceded him to the turret. He sat down and she leaned over his shoulder, frowning at the viewscreens. The *Hooligan* burrowed into atmosphere on a steep downward slant. The roar of cloven air boomed through the hull. Mountains rose jagged on a night horizon. 'That's the Ridge,' said Kit. 'Head yonder, over Moonstone Pass.' On the other side, a shadowed valley gleamed with rivers, under stars and a trace of aurora. 'There's the Shaw, an' the King's Way cuttin' through. Land anywhere near, 'tisn't likely the boat will be found.'

The Shaw belied its name; it was a virgin forest, 40,000 square kilometres of tall trees. Flandry set his craft down so gently that not a twig was broken, cut the engines and leaned back. 'Thus far,' he breathed gustily, 'we is did it, chillun!'

'Sir,' said Chives, 'may I once again take the liberty of suggesting that if you and the young lady go off alone, without me, you need a psychiatrist.'

'And may I once again tell you where to stick your head,' answered Flandry. 'I'll have trouble enough passing myself off as a Vixenite, without you along. You stay with the boat and keep ready to fight. Or, more probably, to scramble out of here like an egg.'

He stood up. 'We'd better start now, Kit,' he added. 'That drug won't hold you up for very many hours.'

Both humans were already dressed in the soft green coveralls Chives had made according to Kit's description of professional hunters. That would also explain Flandry's little radio transceiver, knife and rifle; his accent might pass for that of a man lately moved here from the Avian Islands. It was a thin enough disguise . . . but the Ardazirho wouldn't have an eye for fine details. The main thing was to reach Kit's home city, Garth, undetected. Once based there, Flandry could assess the situation and start making trouble.

Chives wrung his hands, but bowed his master obediently out the airlock. It was midwinter, but also periastron; only long nights and frequent rains marked the season in this hemisphere. The forest floor was thick and soft underfoot. Scant light came through the leaves, but here and there on the high trunks glowed yellow phosphorescent fungi, enough to see by. The air was warm, full of strange green scents. Out in the darkness there went soft whistlings, callings, croakings, patterings, once a scream which cut off in a gurgle, the sounds of a foreign wilderness.

It was two hours' hike to the King's Way. Flandry and Kit fell into the rhythm of it and spoke little. But when they finally came out on the broad starlit ribbon of road, her hand stole into his. 'Shall we walk on?' she asked.

'Not if Garth is fifty kilometres to go,' said Flandry. He sat down by the road's edge. She lowered herself into the curve of his arm.

'Are you cold?' he asked, feeling her shiver.

' 'Fraid,' she admitted.

His lips brushed hers. She responded shyly, unpracticed. It beat hiking. Or did it? *I never liked hors d'oeuvres alone for a meal*, thought Flandry, and drew her close.

Light gleamed far down the highway. A faint growl waxed. Kit disengaged herself. 'Saved by the bell,' murmured Flandry, 'but don't stop to wonder which of us was.' She laughed, a small and trembling sound beneath unearthly constellations.

Flandry got up and extended his arm. The vehicle ground to a halt: a ten-car truck. The driver leaned out. 'Boun' for Garth?' he called.

'That's right.' Flandry helped Kit into the cab and followed. The truck started again, its train rumbling for 200 metres behind.

'Goin' to turn in your gun, are you?' asked the driver. He was

130

a burly bitter-faced man. One arm carried the traces of a recent blaster wound.

'Figure so,' Kit replied. 'My husban' an' I been trekkin' in the Ridge this last three months. We heard 'bout the invasion an' started back, but floods held us up — rains, you know — an' our radio's given some trouble too. So we aren't sure o' what's been happenin'.'

'Enough.' The driver spat out of the window. He glanced sharply at them. 'But what the gamma would anybody be doin' in the mountains this time o' year?'

Kit began to stammer. Flandry said smoothly, 'Keep it confidential please, but this is when the cone-tailed radcat comes off the harl. It's dangerous, yes, but we've filled six caches of grummage.'

'Hm ... uh ... yeh. Sure. Well, when you reach Garth, better not carry your gun yourself to the wolf headquarters. They'll most likely shoot you first an' ask your intentions later. Lay it down somewhere an' go ask one o' them would he please be so kind as to come take it away from you.'

'I hate to give up this rifle,' said Flandry.

The driver shrugged. 'Keep it, then, if you want to take the risk. But not aroun' me. I fought at Burnt Hill, an' played dead all night while those howlin' devils hunted the remnants of our troop. Then I got home somehow, an' that's enough. I got a wife an' children to keep.' He jerked his thumb backward. 'Load o' rare earth ore this trip. The wolves'll take it, an' Hobden's mill will turn it into fire-control elements for 'em, an' they'll shoot some more at the Empire's ships. Sure, call me a quislin' — an' then wait till you've seen your friends run screamin' down your street with a pack o' batsnakes flappin' an' snappin' at them an' the wolves boundin' behind laughin'. Ask yourself if you want to go through that, for an Empire that's given us up already.'

'Has it?' asked Flandry. 'I understood from one 'cast that there were reinforcements coming.'

'Sure. They're here. One o' my chums has a pretty good radio an' sort o' followed the space battle when Walton's force arrived, by receivin' stray messages. It petered out pretty quick, though. What can Walton do, unless he attacks this planet, where the wolves are now based, where they're already makin' their own supplies an' munitions? An' if he does that — ' The headlight reflections shimmered off sweat on the man's face.

'No more Vixen. Just a cinder. You pray God, chum, that the Terrans don't try to blast Ardazir off Vixen.'

'What's happening, then, in space?' asked Flandry.

He didn't expect a coherent reply. To the civilian, as to the average fighter, war is one huge murky chaos. It was a pure gift when the driver said: 'My chum caught radio 'casts beamed at us from the Terran fleet. The wolves tried to jam it, of course, but I heard, an' figure 'tis mostly truth. Because 'tis bad enough! There was a lot o' guff about keepin' up our courage, an' sabotagin' the enemy, an' — ' The driver rasped an obscenity. 'Sorry, ma'm. But wait till you see what 'tis really like aroun' Garth an' you'll know how I feel about *that* idea. Admiral Walton says his fleet's seized some asteroid bases an' theirs isn't tryin' to get him off 'em. Stalemate, you see, till the wolves have built up enough strength. Which they're doin', fast. The reason the admiral can't throw everything he's got against them in space is that he has to watch Ogre too. Seems there's reason to suspect Ymir might be in cahoots with Ardazir. The Ymirites aren't sayin'. You know what they're like.'

Flandry nodded. 'Yes. "If you will not accept our word that we are neutral, there is no obvious way to let you convince yourselves, since the whole Terran Empire could not investigate a fraction of Dispersal territory. Accordingly, we shall not waste our time discussing the question." '

'That's it, chum. You've got the very tone. They might be honest, sure. Or they might be waitin' for the minute Walton eases up his watch on 'em, to jump him.'

Flandry glanced out. The stars flashed impersonally, not caring that a few motes of flesh named them provinces for a few centuries. He saw that part of this planet's sky had no stars, a hole into forever. Kit had told him it was called the Hatch. But that was only a nearby dark nebula, not even a big one. The clear white spark of Rigel was more sinister, blazing from the heart of Merseia's realm. And what of Ogre, tawny above the tree?

'What do you think will happen?' Kit's voice could scarcely be heard through the engine grumble.

'I don't even dare guess,' said the driver. 'Maybe Walton'll negotiate something — might leave us here, to become wolf-cattle, or might arrange to evacuate us an' we can become beggars on Terra. Or he might fight in space . . . but even if he doesn't attack their forts here on Vixen, we'll all be hostages to

Ardazir, won't we? Or the Ymirites might . . . No, ma'm, I'm
just drivin' my truck an' drawin' my pay an' feedin' my family.
Shorter rations every week, it seems. Figure there's nothin' else
any one person can do. Is there?'

Kit began to cry, a soft hopeless sobbing on Flandry's shoulder. He laid an arm around her and they sat thus all the way to
Garth.

X

Night again, after a short hot winter day full of thunderstorms.
Flandry and Emil Bryce stood in the pit blackness of an alley,
watching a nearly invisible street. Rain sluiced over their
cloaks. A fold in Flandry's hood was letting water trickle in, his
tunic was soaked, but he dared not move. At any moment now,
the Ardazirho would come by.

The rain roared slow and heavy, down over the high-peaked
roofs of Garth, through blacked-out streets and gurgling into
the storm drains. All wind had stopped, but now and then lightning glared. There was a brief white view of pavement that
shimmered wet, half-timbered houses with blind shutters
crowded side by side, a skeletal transmitter tower for one of the
robotic weather-monitor stations strewn over the planet. Then
night clamped back down, and thunder went banging through
enormous hollow spaces.

Emil Bryce had not moved for half an hour. But he really
was a hunter by trade, thought Flandry. The Terran felt an
unreasonable resentment of Bryce's guild. Damn them, it
wasn't fair, in that trade they stood waiting for prey since they
were boys — and *he* had to start cold. No, hot. It steamed beneath his rain cape.

Feet resounded on the walk. They did not have a human
rhythm. And they did not smack the ground first with a boot-
heel, but clicked metal-shod toes along the pavement. A flashbeam bobbed, slashing darkness with a light too blue and
sharp for human comfort. Watery reflections touched Bryce's
broad red face. His mouth alone moved, and Flandry could
read fear upon it. *Wolves!*

But Bryce's dart gun slithered from under this cloak. Flandry eased steel knucks on to one hand. With the other, he gestured Bryce back. He, Flandry, must go first, pick out the

precise enemy he wanted — in darkness, in rain, and all their faces non-human. Nor would uniforms help; the Ardazirho bore such a wild variety of dress.

But ... Flandry was trained. It had been worth a rifle, to have an excuse for entering local invader headquarters. Their garrison in Garth was not large: a few hundred, for a city of a quarter million. But modern heavy weapons redressed that, robotanks, repeating cannon, the flat announcement that any town where a human uprising actually succeeded would be missiled. (The glassy crater which had been Marsburg proved it.) The Garth garrison was there chiefly to man observation posts and anti-spacecraft defences in the vicinity; but they also collected firearms, directed factories to produce for their army, prowled in search of any citizens with spirit left to fight. Therefore, Flandry told himself, their chief officer must have a fair amount of knowledge — and the chief officer spoke Anglic, and Flandry had gotten a good look at him while surrendering the rifle, and Flandry was trained to tell faces apart, even non-human faces —

And now Clanmaster Temulak, as he had called himself, was going off duty, from headquarters to barracks. Bryce and others had been watching the Ardazirho for weeks. They had told Flandry that the invaders went on foot, in small armed parties, whenever practicable. Nobody knew quite why. Maybe they preferred the intimacy with odours and sounds which a vehicle denied; it was known they had better noses than man. Or perhaps they relished the challenge: more than once, humans had attacked such a group, been beaten off and hunted down and torn to pieces. Civilians had no chance against body armour, blast-weapons, and reflexes trained for combat.

But I'm not a civilian, Flandry told himself, *and Bryce has some rather special skills.*

The quarry passed by. Scattered flashbeam light etched the ruffed, muzzled heads against flowing dimness. There were five. Flandry identified Temulak, helmeted and corseleted, near the middle. He glided out of the alley, behind them.

The Ardazirho whipped about. How keen were their ears? Flandry kept going. One red-furred alien hand dropped towards a holstered blaster. Flandry smashed his steel-knuckled fist at Temulak's face. The enemy bobbed his head, the knucks clanged off the helmet. And light metal sheathed his

134

belly, no blow would have effect there. The blaster came out. Flandry chopped down his left palm, edge on, with savage precision. He thought he felt wristbones crack beneath it. Temulak's gun glattered to the pavement. The Ardazirho threw back his head and howled ululating noise hurled into the rain. And HQ only half a kilometre away, barracks no further in the opposite direction —

Flandry threw a karate kick to the jaw. The officer staggered back. But he was quick, twisting about to seize the man's ankle before it withdrew. They went down together. Temulak's right hand still hung useless, but his left snatched for Flandry's throat. The Terran glimpsed fingernails reinforced with sharp steel plectra. He threw up an arm to keep his larynx from being torn. Temulak howled again. Flandry chopped at the hairy neck. The Ardazirho ducked and sank teeth into Flandry's wrist. Anguish went like flame along the nerves. But now Temulak was crouched before him. Flandry slammed down a rabbit punch. Temulak slumped. Flandry got on his back and throttled him.

Looking up, gasping, the man saw shadows leap and yell in the glow of the dropped flashlight. There had been no way to simply needle Temulak. He was wanted alive, and Flandry didn't know what anaesthetics might be fatal to an Ardazirho. But Bryce had only to kill the guards, as noiselessly as possible. His airgun spat cyanide darts, quick death for any oxygen breather. And his skilled aim sent those darts into exposed flesh, not uselessly breaking on armour. Two sprawled in the street. Another had somehow jumped for Bryce's throat. The hunter brought up one boot. It clanged on a breastplate, but sheer force sent the alien lurching backward. Bryce shot him. By then the last one had freed his blaster. It crashed and blazed through rain. Bryce had already dropped. The ion bolt sizzled where he had been. Bryce fired, missed, rolled away from another blast, fired again and missed. Now howling could be heard down the street, as a pack of invaders rallied to come and help.

Flandry reached across Temulak's gaunt body, picked up the Clanmaster's gun, and waited. He was nearly blind in this night. The other Ardazirho's blaster flamed once more. Flandry fired where it showed. The alien screamed, once, and thudded to the street. Scorched hair and meat smoked sickly in the wet air.

'Out o' here!' gasped Bryce. He sprang erect. 'They're comin'! An' they'll track us by scent —'

'I came prepared for *that*,' said Flandry. A brief hard grin peeled his teeth. He let Bryce pick up Temulak while he got a flat plastibottle from his tunic. He turned a pressure nozzle and sprayed a litre of gasoline around the area. 'If their noses are any good for several minutes after this, I give up. Let's go.'

Bryce led the way, through the alley to the next street, down a block of horribly open paving, then hand-over-hand across a garden wall. No private human vehicles could move after dark without being shot at from the air, but it wasn't far to the underground hideout. In fact, too close, thought Flandry. But then, who on Vixen had any experience with such operations? Kit had looked up those friends in Garth who smuggled her out, and they had led Flandry straight to their bitter little organisation. It expedited matters this time, yes, but suppose the Ardazirho had supplied a ringer? Or . . . it was only a matter of time before they started questioning humans in detail, under drugs and duress. Then you needed cells, changing passwords, widely scattered boltholes, or your underground was done for.

Flandry stumbled through drenched flowerbeds. He helped Bryce carry Temulak down into the hurricane cellar: standard for every house in Garth. A tunnel had been dug from this one; its door, at least, was well concealed. Flandry and Bryce groped for several hundred metres to the other end. They emerged beneath a house whose address they should not have been permitted to know.

Judith Hurst turned about with a small shriek when the cellar door opened. Then dim light picked out Bryce's heavy form, and Temulak still limp in the hunter's arms. Flandry came behind, shedding his cape with a relieved whistle. 'Oh,' gasped Judith. 'You got him!'

Bryce's eyes went around the circle of them. A dozen men stood with taut brown faces in the light of a single small fluoro. Their shadows fell monstrous in the corners and across the window shutters. Knives and forbidden guns gleamed at their belts. Kit was the only person seated, still slumped in the dull sadness of stimulol reaction.

'Damn near didn't,' grunted Bryce. 'Couldn't have, without the captain here. Sir Dominic, I apologise for some things I'd been thinkin' lately 'bout Terra.'

'An' I.' Judith Hurst trod forward, taking both the Navy

man's hands. She was among the few women in the underground, and Flandry thought it a crime to risk such looks being shot up. She was tall, with long auburn hair and skin like cream; her eyes were sleepy brown in a full, pouting face; her figure strained at shorts and bolero. 'I never thought I'd see you again,' she said. 'But you've come back with the first real success this war's had for us.'

'Two swallows do not make a drinking bout,' warned Flandry. He gave her his courtliest bow. 'Speaking of which, I could use something liquid, and cannot imagine a more ornamental cupbearer. But first, let's deal with friend Temulak. This way, isn't it?'

As he passed Kit, her exhausted eyes turned up to him. Slow tears coursed down her face. 'Oh, Dominic, you're alive,' she whispered. 'That makes everything else seem like nothin'.' She rose to wobbly legs. He threw her a preoccupied smile and continued on past, his brain choked with technicalities.

Given a proper biopsych lab, he could have learned how to get truth out of Temulak with drugs and electronics. But now he just didn't have enough data on the species. He would have to fall back on certain widely applicable, if not universal, rules of psychology.

At his orders, an offside room in the cellar had been provided with a comfortable bed. He stripped Temulak and tied him down, firmly, but using soft bonds which wouldn't chafe. The prisoner began to stir. By the time Flandry was through and Temulak immobile, the grey alien eyes were open and the muzzle wrinkled back over white teeth. A growl rumbled in Temulak's throat.

'Feeling better?' asked the man unctuously.

'Not as well as I shall when we pull you down in the street.' The Anglic was thickly accented, but fluent, and it bore a haughtiness like steel.

'I shudder.' Flandry kindled a cigarette. 'Well, comrade, if you want to answer some questions now, it will save trouble all around. I presume, since you're alive, you've been blanked of your home sun's co-ordinates. But you retain clues.' He blew a thoughtful smoke ring. 'And, to be sure, there are the things you obviously do know, since your rank requires it. Oh, all sorts of things, dear heart, which my side is just dying to find out.' He chuckled. 'I don't mean that literally. Any dying will be done by you.'

Temulak stiffened. 'If you think I would remain alive, at the price of betraying the *orbekh* — '

'Nothing so clear-cut.'

The red fur bristled, but Temulak snarled: 'Nor will pain in any degree compel me. And I do not believe you understand the psycho-physiology of my race well enough to undertake total reconditioning.'

'No,' admitted Flandry, 'not yet. However, I haven't time for reconditioning in any event, and torture is so strenuous ... besides offering no guarantee that when you talk, you won't fib. No, no, my friend, you'll want to spill to me pretty soon. Whenever you've had enough, just call and I'll come hear you out.'

He nodded to Dr. Reineke. The physician wheeled forth the equipment he had abstracted from Garth General Hospital at Flandry's request. A blindfolding hood went over Temulak's eyes, sound-deadening wax filled his ears and plugged his nose, a machine supplied him with intravenous nourishment and another removed body wastes. They left him immobile and, except for the soft constant pressure of bonds and bed, sealed into a darkness like death. No sense impressions could reach him from outside. It was painless, it did no permanent harm, but the mind is not intended for such isolation. When there is nothing by which it may orient itself, it rapidly loses all knowledge of time; an hour seems like a day, and later like a week or a year. Space and material reality vanish. Hallucinations come, and the will begins to crumble. Most particularly is this true when the victim is among enemies, tensed to feel the whip or knife which his own ferocious culture would surely use.

Flandry closed the door. 'Keep a guard,' he said. 'When he begins to holler, let me know.' He peeled off his tunic. 'From whom can I beg something dry to wear?'

Judith gave his torso a long look. 'I thought all Terrans were flabby, Sir Dominic,' she purred. 'I was wrong about that too.'

His eyes raked her. 'And you, my dear, make it abundantly plain that Vixenites are anything but,' he leered.

She took his arm. 'What do you plan to do next?'

'Scratch around. Observe. Whip this maquisard outfit into something efficient. There are so many stunts to teach you. To name just one, any time you've no other amusement, you can halt work at a war factory for half a day with an anonymous telecall warning that a time bomb's been planted and the staff had better get out. Then there's all the rest of your planet to

138

organise. I don't know how many days I'll have, but there's enough work to fill a year of 'em.' Flandry stretched luxuriously, 'Right now, though, I want that drink I spoke of.'

'Here you are, sir.' Bryce held out a flask.

Judith flicked a scowl at him. 'Is that white mule all you can offer the captain?' she cried. Her hair glowed along her back as she turned to smile again at Flandry. 'I know you'll think I'm terribly forward, but I have two bottles o' real Bourgogne at my house. 'Tis only a few blocks from here, an' I know a safe way to go.'

Oh-oh! Flandry licked his mental chops. 'Delighted,' he said.

'I'd invite the rest o' you,' said Judith sweetly, 'but 'tisn't enough to go aroun', an' Sir Dominic deserves it the most. Nothin's too good for him, that's what I think. Just nothin' at all.'

'Agreed,' said Flandry. He bowed good night and went out with her.

Kit stared after them a moment. As he closed the door, he heard her burst into weeping.

XI

Three of Vixen's 22-hour rotation periods went by, and part of a fourth, before the message came that Temulak had broken. Flandry whistled. 'It's about time! If they're all as tough as that —'

Judith clung to him. 'Do you have to go right now, darlin'?' she murmured. 'You've been away so much ... out prowlin', spyin', an' the streets still full o' packs huntin' for whoever attacked that squad — I'm terrified for you.'

Her look was more inviting than anxious. Flandry kissed her absent-mindedly. 'We're patriots and all that sort of rot,' he said. 'I could not love you so much, dear, et cetera. Now do let go.' He was out the door before she could speak further.

The way between her house and the underground's went mostly from garden to garden, but there was a stretch of public thoroughfare. Flandry put hands in pockets and sauntered along under rustling feather palms as if he had neither cares nor haste. The other humans about, afoot or in groundcars, were subdued, the pinch of hunger and shabbiness already upon them. Once a party of Ardazirho whirred past on motor unicycles;

139

their sharp red muzzles clove the air like prows, and they left a wake of frightened silence behind them. The winter sun burned low to northwest, big and dazzling white in a pale sky, among hurried stormclouds.

When Flandry let himself into the cellar, only Emil Bryce and Kit Kittredge were there. The hunter lounged on guard. From the closed door behind him came howling and sobbing. 'He babbled he'd talk,' said Bryce. 'But can you trust what he says?'

'Interrogation is a science too,' answered Flandry. 'If Temulak is enough like a human to break under isolation, he won't be able to invent consistent lies fast enough when I start throwing questions at him. Did you get that recorder I wanted?'

'Here.' Kit picked it up. She looked very small and alone in all the shadows. Sleeplessness had reddened her eyes. She brought the machine to Flandry, who met her several metres from Bryce. She leaned towards him on tiptoe and whispered shakily: 'What will you do now?'

Flandry studied her. He had gotten to know her well on the journey here, he thought. But that was under just one set of conditions — and how well does one human ever know another, in spite of all pretentious psychology? Since capturing the Ardazirho, he had only seen her on a single brief visit to this cellar. They had had a few moments alone, but nothing very personal was said. There had been no time for it. He saw how she trembled.

'I'm going to quiz brother Temulak,' he told her. 'And afterwards I could use some dinner and a stiff drink.'

'With Judith Hurst?' It startled him, how ferociously she spat it out.

'Depends,' he said in a careful tone.

'Dominic — ' She hugged herself, forlornly, to stop shivering. Her gaze blurred, seeing his. 'Don't. Please don't make me do . . . what I don't want — '

'We'll see.' He started towards the inner door. Kit began to cry, hopelessly this time.

Bryce got up. 'Why, what all's the matter?' he asked.

'She's overtired.' Flandry opened the door.

'Worse'n that.' The hunter looked from him to the girl and back again. Resentment smouldered in his growl: 'Maybe it's none o' my business — '

140

'It isn't.' Flandry stepped through, closing the door behind him.

Temulak lay shuddering and gasping. Flandry set up the recorder and unplugged the Ardazirho's ears. 'Did you want to speak to me?' he asked mildly.

'Let me go!' shrieked Temulak. 'Let me go, I say! *Zamara shammish ni ulan!*' He opened his mouth and howled. It was so much like a beast that a crawling went along Flandry's spine.

'We'll see, after you've co-operated.' The man sat down.

'I never thought ... you grey people ... grey hearts —' Temulak whimpered. He dribbled between his fangs.

'Good night, then,' said Flandry. 'Sweet dreams.'

'No! No, let me see! Let me smell! I will ... *zamara, zamara —*'

Flandry began to interrogate.

It took time. The basic principle was to keep hitting, snap out a question, yank forth the answer, toss the next question, pounce on the smallest discrepancies, always strike and strike and strike with never a second's pause for the victim to think. Without a partner, Flandry was soon tired. He kept going, on cigarettes and nerves; after the first hour, he lost count of time.

In the end, with a full tape, he relaxed a moment. The air was nearly solid with smoke. Sweat felt sticky under his clothes. He puffed yet another cigarette and noticed impersonally the shakiness of his hand. But Temulak whined and twitched, beaten close to mindlessness by sheer psychic exhaustion.

The picture so far was only a bare outline, thought Flandry in a dull far-off way. How much could be told in one night of an entire world, its greatness and rich variety, its many peoples and all their histories? How much, to this day, do we really know about Terra? But the tape held information worth entire ships.

Somewhere there was a sun, brighter even than Cerulia, and a planet called Ardazir by its principal nation. ('Nation' was the Anglic word; Flandry had an impression that 'clan alliance' or 'pack aggregate' might more closely translate *orbekh*.) Interplanetary travel had been independently achieved by that country. Then, some fifteen standard years ago, gravitics, superlight pseudo-speeds, the whole apparatus of the modern galaxy, had burst upon Ardazir. The war lords (chiefs, speakers, pack leaders?) of Urdahu, the dominant *orbekh*, had promptly used these to complete the subjugation of their own world. Then they turned outward. Their hunters ravened into a dozen backward systems, looting and enslaving; engineers followed, organising the conquered planets for further war.

And now the attack on the human empire had begun. The lords of Urdahu assured their followers that Ardazir had allies, mighty denizens of worlds so alien that there could never be any fear of attack — though these aliens had long been annoyed by humankind, and found in Ardazir an instrument to destroy and replace the Terran Empire . . . Temulak had not enquired more deeply, had not thought much about it at all. The Ardazirho seemed, by nature, somewhat more reckless and fatalistic than men, and somewhat less curious. If circumstances had provided a chance for adventure, glory, and wealth, that was enough. Precautions could be left in care of the *orbekh's* wise old females.

Flandry smoked in a thick silence. If Ymir were, indeed, behind Ardazir— it would be natural for Ymir to co-operate temporarily with Merseia, whipsawing Terra between the Syrax and Vixen crises. Maybe Merseia was next to Ymir's list. Thereafter Ardazir would hardly prove troublesome to wreck.

But what grudge could Ymir have against oxygen breathers, or even against Terra alone? There had been some small friction, yes, inevitably — but nothing serious, surely the monsters rubbed each other more raw than . . . *And yet Horx did his level best to kill me. Why? What could he have been hired with? What material thing from a terrestroid planet would not collapse in his hands on Jupiter? What reason would he have, except orders from his own governor, who was carrying out a policy hatched on Ymir itself . . .?*

Flandry clenched a fist. There was an answer to that question, but not one he dared rely on without further proof. He bent his mind back towards practicalities. Mostly the tape held such details: the number of Ardazirho ships and troops in this system, recognition signals, military dispositions across Vixen, the layout of forts and especially of the great headquarters den; the total population of Ardazir, resources, industry, army and navy . . . Temulak was not in on many state secrets, but he had enough indications to give Flandry gooseflesh. Two million or so warriors occupied Vixen; a hundred million were still at home or on the already conquered planets, where war matériel was being rapidly stockpiled; officers had all been informed hat there were plenty of other vulnerable Imperial outposts, human colonies or the home worlds of Terran-allied species . . . Yes, Ardazir was surely planning to strike elsewhere within the Empire, and soon. Another one or two such blows, and the Imperial Navy *must* surrender Syrax to Merseia, turn inward and defend the mother planet. At which point —

Not true that an army marches on its stomach, thought Flandry. *It needs information even more than food. Marches on its head. Which, no doubt, is why the Imperial High Command has so many flat-heads.*

He chuckled. Bad as it was, the joke strengthened him. And he was going to need strength.

'Will you let me see?' asked Temulak in a small, broken voice.

'I will deprive you no longer of my beauty,' said Flandry. He unhooded the rufous head and drew his wax plugs from the nose. Temulak blinked dazedly into smoke and one dull light. Flandry uncoupled the machines which had kept him alive. 'You'll remain our guest, of course,' he said. 'If it turns out you prevaricated, back you go in the dark closet.'

Temulak bristled. His teeth snapped together, missing the man's arm by a centimetre.

'Naughty!' Flandry stepped back. 'For that, you can stay tied up for a while.'

Temulak snarled from the cot: 'You grey-skinned hairless worm, if you think your *valkuza's* tricks will save you from the Black People — I myself will rip out your gullet and strangle you with your own bowels!'

'And foreclose my mortgage,' said Flandry. He went out, closing the door behind him.

Bryce and Kit started. They had fallen asleep in their chairs. The hunter rubbed his eyes. 'God o' the galaxy, you been at it a long time!' he exclaimed.

'Here.' Flandry tossed him the tape spool. 'This has to reach Admiral Walton's fleet. It's necessary, if not quite sufficient, for your liberation. Can do?'

'The enemy would pick up radio,' said Bryce doubtfully. 'We still got a few spaceships hid, but Kit's was the fastest. An' since then, too, the wolf space guard's been tightened till it creaks.'

Flandry sighed. 'I was afraid of that.' He scribbled on a sheet of paper. 'Here's a rough map to show you where my personal flitter is. D'you know this tune?' He whistled. 'No? That proves you've a clean mind. Well, learn it.' He rehearsed the Vixenite till he was satisfied. 'Good. Approach the flitter whistling that, and Chives won't shoot you without investigation. Give him this note. It says for him to take the tape to Walton. If anything can run that blockade without collecting a missile, it's Chives in the *Hooligan*.'

Kitt suppressed a gasp. 'But then you, Dominic — no escape — '

Flandry shrugged. 'I'm much too tired to care about aught except a nice soft bed.'

Bryce, sticking the spool under his tunic, grinned: 'Whose?'

Kit stood as if struck.

Flandry nodded slightly at her. 'That's the way of it.' He glanced at his chrono. 'Close to local midnight. Shove off, Bryce, lad. But stop by and tell Dr. Reineke to shift his apparatus and the prisoner elsewhere. It's always best to keep moving around, when you're being searched for. And nobody, except the pill peddler and whoever helps him, is to know where they stash Temulak next. All clear?'

'Dominic — ' Kit closed her fists till the knuckles stood white. She stared down at the floor; he could only see her short bright hair.

He said gently: 'I have to sleep or collapse, lass. I'll meet you at noon by the Rocket Fountain. I think we've a few private things to discuss.'

She turned and fled upstairs.

Flandry departed too. The night sky was aflicker with aurora; he thought he could hear its ionic hiss in the city's blacked-out silence. Once he scrambled to a rooftop and waited for an Ardazirho patrol to go by. Wan blue light glimmered off their metal and their teeth.

Judith made him welcome. 'I've been so worried, darlin' — '

He considered her a while. Weariness dragged at him. But she had put out a late supper, with wine and a cold game bird, as she knew he liked it; and her hair glowed red by candlelight. Sleep be damned, Flandry decided. He might be permanently asleep tomorrow.

He did nap for a few morning hours, and went out before noon. Explorers' Plaza had been a gay scene once, where folk sat leisurely in the surrounding gardens, sipping coffee and listening to harp trees in the wind and watching life stream past. Now it was empty. The metal fountain itself, in the form of an ancient space rocket, still jetted many-coloured heatless fires from its tail; but they seemed pale under the gloomy winter sky.

Flandry took out a cigarette, sat down on the fountain rim and waited. A few preliminary raindrops kissed his half lifted face.

A military truck careened out of a deserted street and ground to a halt. Three Ardazirho leaped from the cab. Kit was with them. She pointed at Flandry. Lightning blinked immediately overhead, and sudden thunder swamped her words. But the tone was vindictive.

'Halt, human!'

It must have been the only Anglic phrase any of the three invaders knew. They bayed it again and yet again as Flandry sprang to the plaza. He ducked and began to run, zigzagging.

No shots were fired. An Ardazirho yelped glee and opened the truck body. Wings snapped leathery. Flandry threw a glance behind. A score of metre-long snake bodies were streaming upward from the truck. They saw him, whistled and stooped.

Flandry ran. His heart began to pump, the wildness of irrational uncontrollable terror. The batsnakes reached him. He heard teeth click together behind his nape. A lean body coiled on his right arm. He jerked the limb up, frantic. Wings resisted him. Fangs needled into his flesh. The rest of the pack whirled and dived and whipped him with their tails.

He started to run again. The three Ardazirho followed, long bounds which took them over the ground faster than a man could speed. They howled, and there was laughter in their howling. The street was empty, resounding under boots. Shuttered windows looked down without seeing. Doors were closed and locked.

Flandry stopped. He spun around. His right arm was still cumbered. The left dived beneath his tunic. His needler came out. He aimed at the nearest of the laughing ruddy devils. A batsnake threw itself on his gun hand. It bit with trained precision, into the fingers. Flandry let the weapon fall. He snatched after the snake — to wring just one of their damned necks — !

It writhed free. Its reptile-like jaws grinned at him. Then the Ardazirho closed in.

XII

Most of the year, Vixen's northern half was simply desert, swamp, or prairie, where a quick vegetative life sprang up and animals that had been estivating crept from their burrows. The arctic even knew snow, when winter-long night had fallen. But in summer the snows melted to wild rivers, the rivers overflowed and became lakes, the lakes baked dry. Storms raged about the equator and into the southern hemisphere, as water precipitated again in cooler parts. Except for small seas dreary amidst salt flats, the north blistered arid. Fires broke loose, the pampas became barren again in a few red days. Under such erosive conditions, this land had no mountains. Most of it was plain, where dust and ash scoured on a furnace wind. In some places rose gnarled ranges, lifeless hills, twisted crags, arroyos carved by flash floods into huge earth scars.

The Ardazirho had established their headquarters in such a region, a little below the arctic circle. Thousands of lethal kilometers made it safe from human ground attack, the broken country was camouflage and protection from spaceships. Not that they tried to conceal their fortress absolutely. That would have been impossible. But it burrowed deep into the range and offered few specific targets.

Here and there Flandry saw a warship sitting insolently in the open, a missile emplacement, a detector station, a lookout tower black and lean against the blinding sky. Outer walls twisted through gullies and over naked ridges; Ardazirho sentries paced them, untroubled by dry cruel heat, blue-white hell-glare, pouring ultraviolet radiation. But mostly, the fortress went inside the hills, long vaulted tunnels where boots clashed and voices echoed from room to den-like room. Construction had followed standard dig-in methods: prodigal use of atomic energy to fuse the living rock into desired patterns, then swift robotic installation of the necessary mechanisms. But the layout was rougher, more tortuous, less private, than man or Merseian would have liked. The ancestral Ardazirho had laired in caves and hunted in packs.

Flandry was hustled into a small room equipped as a laboratory. A pair of warriors clamped him in place. A grizzled technician began to prepare instruments.

Often, in the next day or two, Flandry screamed. He couldn't help it. Electronic learning should not go that fast. But finally, sick and shaking, he could growl the Urdahu language. Indeed, he thought, the Ardazirho had been thoroughly briefed. They understood the human nervous system so well that they could stamp a new linguistic pattern on it in mere hours, and not drive the owner insane.

Not quite.

Flandry was led down endless booming halls. Their brilliant bluish fluorescence hurt his eyes; he must needs squint. Even so, he watched what passed. It might be a truckload of ammunition, driven at crazy speed by a warrior who yelped curses at foot traffic. Or it might be a roomful of naked red-furred shapes: sprawled in snarling, quarrelsome fellowship; gambling with tetrahedral dice for stakes up to a year's slavery; watching a wrestling match which employed teeth and nails; testing nerve by standing up in turn against a wall while the rest threw axes. Or it might be a sort of chapel, where a single scarred fighter wallowed in pungent leaves before a great burning wheel. Or it might be a mess hall and a troop lying on fur rugs, bolting raw meat and howling in chorus with one who danced on a monstrous drumhead.

The man came at last to an office. This was also an artificial cave, thick straw on the floor, gloom in the corners, a thin stream of water running down a groove in one wall. A big Ardazirho lay prone on a hairy dais, lifted on both elbows to a slanting desktop. He wore only a skirt of leather strips, a crooked knife and a very modern blaster. But the telescreen and intercom before him were also new, and Flandry's guards touched their black noses in his presence.

'Go,' he said in the Urdahu. 'Wait outside.' The guards obeyed. He nodded at Flandry. 'Be seated, if you wish.'

The human lowered himself. He was still weak from what he had undergone, filthy, ill-fed, and ragged. Automatically he smoothed back his hair, and thanked human laziness for its invention of long-lasting antibeard enzyme. He needed such morale factors.

His aching muscles grew tight. Things were in motion again.

'I am Svantozik of the Janneer Ya,' said the rough voice. 'I am told that you are Captain Dominic Flandry of Terran Naval Intelligence. You may consider my status approximately the same.'

'As one colleague to another,' husked Flandry, 'will you give me a drink?'

'By all means.' Svantozik gestured to the artesian stream.

Flandry threw him a reproachful look, but needed other things too badly to elaborate. 'It would be a kindly deed, and one meriting my gratitude, if you provided me at once with dark lenses and cigarettes.' The last word was perforce Anglic. He managed a grin. 'Later I will tell you what further courtesies ought to be customary.'

Svantozik barked laughter. 'I expected your eyes would suffer,' he said. 'Here.' He reached in the desk and tossed over a pair of green polarite goggles, doubtless taken off a Vixenite casualty. Flandry put them on and whistled relief. 'Tobacco is forbidden,' added Svantozik. 'Only a species with half-dead scent organs could endure it.'

'Oh, well. There was no harm in asking.' Flandry hugged his knees and leaned back against the cave wall.

'None. Now, I wish to congratulate you on your daring exploits.' Svantozik's smile looked alarming enough, but it seemed friendly. 'We searched for your vessel, but it must have escaped the planet.'

'Thanks,' said Flandry, quite sincerely. 'I was afraid you would have gotten there in time to blast it.' He cocked his head. 'In return ... see here, my friend [literally: croucher-in-my-blind], when dealing with my species, it is usually better to discourage them. You should have claimed you had caught my boat before it could escape, manufacturing false evidence if necessary to convince me. That would make me much more liable to yield my will to yours.'

'Oh, indeed?' Svantozik pricked up his ears. 'Now among the Black People, the effect would be just opposite. Good news tends to relax us, make us grateful and amenable to its bearer. Bad tidings raise the quotient of defiance.'

'Well, of course it is not that simple,' said Flandry. 'In breaking down the resistance of a man, the commonest technique is to chivvy him for a protracted time, and then halt the process, speak kindly to him — preferably, get someone else to do that.'

'Ah.' Svantozik drooped lids over his cold eyes. 'Are you not being unwise in telling me this — if it is true?'

'It is textbook truth,' said Flandry, 'as I am sure whatever race has instructed you in the facts about Terra's Empire will confirm. I am revealing no secret. But as you must be aware, textbooks have little value in practical matters. There is always the subtlety of the individual, which eludes anything except direct intuition based on wide, intimate experience. And you, being nonhuman, cannot ever have such an experience of men.'

'True.' The long head nodded. 'In fact, I remember now reading somewhat of the human trait you mention . . . but there was so much else to learn, prior to the Great Hunt we are now on, that it had slipped my memory. So you tantalise me with a fact I could use — if I were on your side!' A sudden deep chuckle cracked in the ruffed throat. 'I like you, Captain, the Sky Cave eat me if I do not.'

Flandry smiled back. 'We could have fun. But what are your intentions towards me now?'

'To learn what I can. For example, whether or not you were concerned in the murder of four warriors in Garth and the abduction of a fifth, not long ago. The informant who led us to you has used hysterics — real or simulated — to escape detailed questioning so far. Since the captured Ardazirho was a Clanmaster, and therefore possessed of valuable information, I suspect you had a hand in this.'

'I swear upon the Golden Ass of Apuleius I did not.'

'What is that?'

'One of our most revered books.'

' "The Powers only hunt at night," ' quoted Svantozik. 'In other words, oaths are cheap. I personally do not wish to hurt you unduly, being sceptical of the value of torture anyhow. And I know that officers like you are immunised to the so-called truth sera. Therefore, reconditioning would be necessary: a long, tedious process, the answers stale when finally you wanted to give them, and you of little further value to us or yourself.' He shrugged. 'But I am going back to Ardazir before long, to report and wait reassignment. I know who will succeed me here: an officer quite anxious to practice some of the techniques which we have been told are effective on Terrans. I recommend you co-operate with me instead.'

This must be one of their crack field operatives, thought Flandry, growing cold. *He did the basic Intelligence work on Vixen. Now, with Vixen in hand, he'll be sent to do the same job when the next Terran planet is attacked. Which will be soon!*

Flandry slumped. 'Very well,' he said in a dull tone. 'I captured Temulak.'

'Ha!' Svantozik crouched all-fours on the dais. The fur stood up along his spine, the iron-coloured eyes burned. 'Where is he now?'

'I do not know. As a precaution, I had him moved elsewhere, and did not enquire the place.'

'Wise.' Svantozik relaxed. 'What did you get from him?'

'Nothing. He did not crack.'

Svantozik stared at Flandry. 'I doubt that,' he said. 'Not that I scorn Temulak — a brave one — but you are an extraordinary specimen of a civilisation older and more learned than mine. It would be strange if you had not — '

Flandry sat up straight. His laughter barked harsh. 'Extraordinary?' he cried bitterly. 'I suppose so . . . the way I allowed myself to be caught like a cub!'

'No ground is free of possible pits,"' murmured Svantozik. He brooded a while. Presently: 'Why did the female betray you? She went to our headquarters, declared you were a Terran agent, and led our warriors to your meeting place. What had she to gain?'

'I don't know,' groaned Flandry. 'What difference does it make? She is wholly yours now, you know. The very fact she aided you once gives you the power to make her do it again — lest you denounce her to her own people.' Svantozik nodded, grinning. 'What do her original motives matter?' The man sagged back and picked at the straw.

'I am interested,' said Svantozik. 'Perhaps the same process may work again, on other humans.'

'No.' Flandry shook his head in a stunned way. 'This was personal. I suppose she thought I had betrayed her first — Why am I telling you this?'

'I have been informed that you Terrans often have strong feelings about individuals of the opposite sex,' said Svantozik. 'I was told it will occasionally drive you to desperate, meaningless acts.'

Flandry passed a tired hand across his brow. 'Forget it,' he mumbled. 'Just be kind to her. You can do that much, can you not?'

'As a matter of fact — ' Svantozik broke off. He sat for a moment, staring at emptiness.

'*Great unborn planets!*' he whispered.

'What?' Flandry didn't look up.

'No matter,' said Svantozik hastily. 'Ah, am I right in assuming there was a reciprocal affection on your part?'

'It is no concern of yours!' Flandry sat up and shouted it. 'I will hear no more! Say what else you will, but keep your filthy snout out of my own life!'

'So,' breathed Svantozik. 'Yes-s-s-s. ... Well, then, let us discuss other things.'

He hammered at Flandry a while, not with quite the ruthlessness the human had shown Temulak. Indeed, he revealed a kind of chivalry: there was respect, fellow feeling, even an acrid liking in him for this man whose soul he hunted. Once or twice Flandry managed to divert the conversation — they spoke briefly of alcoholic drinks and riding animals; they traded some improper jokes, similar in both cultures.

Nevertheless, Svantozik hunted. It was a rough few hours.

At last Flandry was taken away. He was too worn to notice very much, but the route did seem devious. He was finally pushed into a room, not unlike Svantozik's office, save that it had human-type furniture and illumination. The door clashed behind him.

Kit stood waiting.

XIII

For a moment he thought she would scream. Then, very quickly, her eyes closed. She opened them again. They remained dry, as if all her tears had been spent. She took a step toward him.

'Oh, God, Kit,' he croaked.

Her arms closed about his neck. He held her to him. His own gaze flickered around the room, until it found a small human-made box with a few controls which he recognised. He nodded to himself, ever so faintly, and drew an uneven breath. But he was still uncertain.

'Dominic, darlin' — ' Kit's mouth sought his.

He stumbled to the bunk, sat down and covered his face. 'Don't,' he whispered. 'I can't take much more.'

The girl sat down beside him. She laid her head on his shoulder. He felt how she trembled. But the words came in glorious anticlimax: 'That debuggin' unit is perfectly good, Dominic.'

He wanted to lean back and shout with sudden uproarious mirth. He wanted to kick his heels and thumb his nose and turn handsprings across the cell. But he held himself in, letting only a rip of laughter come from lips which he hid against her cheek.

He had more than half expected Svantozik to provide a bugscrambler. Only with the sure knowledge that any listening devices were being negated by electronic and sound-wave interference, would even a cadet of Intelligence relax and speak freely. He suspected, though, that a hidden lens was conveying a silent image. They could talk, but both of them must continue to pantomime.

'How's it been, Kit?' he asked. 'Rough?'

She nodded, not play-acting her misery at all. 'But I haven't had to give any names,' she gulped. 'Not yet.'

'Let's hope you don't,' said Flandry.

He had told her in the hurricane cellar — how many centuries ago? . . . 'This is picayune stuff. I'm not doing what any competent undercover agent couldn't: what a score of Walton's men will be trying as soon as they can be smuggled here. I've something crazier in mind. Quite likely it'll kill us, but then again it might strike a blow worth whole fleets. Are you game, kid? It means the risk of death, or torture, or life-long slavery on a foreign planet. What you'll find worst, though, is the risk of having to sell out your own comrades, name them to the enemy, so he will keep confidence in you. Are you brave enough to sacrifice twenty lives for a world? I believe you are — but it's as cruel a thing as I could ask of any living creature.'

'They brought me straight here,' said Kit, holding him. 'I don't think they know quite what to make o' me. A few minutes ago, one o' them came hotfootin' here with the scrambler an' orders for me to treat you . . .' a slow flush went over her face, '. . . kindly. To get information from you, if I could, by any means that seemed usable.'

Flandry waved a fist in melodramatic despair, while out of a contorted face his tone came levelly: 'I expected something like this. I led Svantozik, the local snooper-in-chief, to think that gentle treatment from one of my own species, after a hard grilling from him, might break me down. Especially if you were the one in question. Svantozik isn't stupid at all, but he's dealing with an alien race, us, whose psychology he knows mainly from sketchy second-hand accounts. I've an advantage: the Ardazirho are new to me, but I've spent a lifetime dealing with all shapes and sizes of other species. Already I see what the Ardazihro have in common with several peoples whom I hornswoggled in the past.'

The girl bit her lip to hold it steady. She looked around the stone-walled room, and he knew she thought of kilometres of tunnel, ramparts and guns, wolfish hunters, and the desert beyond where men could not live. Her words fell thin and frightened: 'What are we goin' to do now, Dominic? You never told me what you planned.'

'Because I didn't know,' he replied. 'Once here, I'd have to play by ear. Fortunately, my confidence in my own ability to land on my feet approaches pure conceit, or would if I had any faults. We're not doing badly, Kit. I've learned their principal language, and you've been smuggled into their ranks.'

'They don't trust me yet.'

'No. I didn't expect they would — very much. . . . But let's carry on our visual performance. I wouldn't flipflop over to the enemy side just because you're here, Kit; but when I am badly shaken, I lose discretion and ordinary carefulness. Svantozik will accept that.'

He gathered her back to him. She responded hungrily. He felt so much of himself return to his abused being, that his brain began to spark, throwing up schemes and inspecting them, discarding them and generating new ones, like a pyrotechnic display, like merry hell.

He said at last, while she quivered on his lap: 'I think I have a notion. We'll have to play things as they lie, and prearrange a few signals, but here's what we'll try for.' He felt her stiffen in his embrace. 'Why, what's the matter?'

She asked, low and bitter: 'Were you thinkin' o' your work all the time — just now?'

'Not that alone.' He permitted himself the briefest grin. 'Or, rather, I enjoyed my work immensely.'

'But still — Oh, never mind. Go on.' She slumped.

Flandry scowled. But he dared not stop for side issues. He said: 'Tell Svantozik, or whoever deals with you, that you played remorseful in my presence, but actually you hate my inwards, and my outwards too, because — uh — '

'Judith!' she snarled.

He had the grace to blush. 'I suppose that's as plausible a reason as any, at least in Ardazirho eyes.'

'Or human. If you knew how close I was to — No. Go on.'

'Well, tell the enemy that you told me you'd betrayed me in a fit of pique, and now you regretted it. And I, being wildly in love with you — which again is highly believable — ' She gave his predictable gallantry no response whatsoever. 'I told you there was a possible escape for you. I said this: The Ardazirho are under the impression that Ymir is behind them. Actually, Ymir leans toward Terra, since we are more peace-minded and therefore less troublesome. The Ymirites are willing to help us in small ways; we keep this fact secret because now and then it saves us in emergencies. If I could only set a spaceship's signal to a certain recognition pattern, you could try to steal that ship. The Ardazirho would assume you headed for Walton's fleet, and line out after you in that direction. So you could give them the slip, reach Ogre, transmit the signal pattern, and request transportation to safety in a force-bubble ship.'

Her eyes stretched wide with terror. 'But if Svantozik hears that — an' 'tisn't true — '

'He won't know it's false till he's tried, will he?' answered Flandry cheerfully. 'If I lied, it isn't your fault. In fact, since you hastened to tattle, even about what looked like an escape for you, it'll convince him you're a firm collaborationist.'

'But — no, Dominic. 'Tis . . . I don't dare — '

'Don't hand me that, Kit. You're one girl in ten to the tenth, and there's nothing you won't dare.'

Then she did begin to sob.

After she had gone, Flandry spent a much less happy time waiting. He could still only guess how his enemy would react: an experienced human would probably not be deceived, and Svantozik's ignorance of human psychology might not be as deep as hoped. Flandry swore and tried to rest. The weariness of the past days was grey upon him.

When his cell door opened, he sprang up with a jerkiness that told him how thin his nerves were worn.

Svantozik stood there, four guards poised behind. The Ardazirho officer flashed teeth in a grin. 'Good hunting, Captain,' he greeted. 'Is your den comfortable?'

'It will do,' said Flandry, 'until I can get one provided with a box of cigars, a bottle of whisky, and a female.'

'The female, at least, I tried to furnish,' riposted Svantozik.

Flandry added in his suavest tone: 'Oh, yes, I should also like a rug of Ardazirho skin.'

One of the guards snarled. Svantozik chuckled. 'I too have a favour to ask, Captain,' he said. 'My brothers in the engineering division are interested in modifying a few spaceships to make them more readily usable by humans. You understand how such differences as the location of the thumb, or that lumbar conformation which makes it more comfortable for us to lie prone on the elbows than sit, have influenced the design of our control panels. A man would have trouble steering an Ardazirho craft. Yet necessarily, in the course of time, if the Great Hunt succeeds and we acquire human subjects — we will find occasion for some of them to pilot some of our vehicles. The Kittredge female, for example, could profitably have a ship of her own, since we anticipate usefulness in her as a go-between among us and the human colonists here. If you would help her — simply in checking over one of our craft, and drawing up suggestions —'

Flandry grew rigid. 'Why should I help you at all?' he said through clenched jaws.

Svantozik shrugged. 'It is very minor assistance. We could do it ourselves. But it may pass the time for you.' Wickedly: 'I am not at all sure that good treatment, rather than abuse, may not be the way to break down a man. Also, Captain, if you must have a rationalisation, think: here is a chance to examine one of our vessels close up. If later, somehow, you escape, your own service would be interested in what you saw.'

Flandry stood a moment, altogether quiet. Thought lanced through him. *Kit told. Svantozik naturally prefers me not to know what she did tell. So he makes up this story — offers me what he hopes I'll think is a God-sent opportunity to arrange for Kit's escape —*

He said aloud, urbanely: 'You are most kind, my friend of the Janneer Ya. But Miss Kittredge and I could not feel at ease with ugly guards like yours drooling over our shoulders.'

He got growls from two warriors that time. Svantozik hushed them. 'That is easily arranged,' he said. 'The guards can stay out of the control turret.'

'Excellent. Then, if you have some human-made tools —'

They went down hollow corridors, past emplacements where artillery slept like nested dinosaurs, across the furious arctic day, and so to a spaceship near the outworks. Through goggles, the man studied her fiercely gleaming shape. About equivalent to a Terran Comet class. Fast, lightly armed, a normal complement of fifteen or so, but one could handle her if need be.

The naked hills beyond wavered in heat. When he had stepped through the airlock, he felt dizzy from that brief exposure.

Svantozik stopped at the turret companionway. 'Proceed,' he invited cordially. 'My warriors will wait here until you wish to return — at which time you and the female will come dine with me and I shall provide Terran delicacies.' Mirth crossed his eyes. 'Of course, the engines have been temporarily disconnected.'

'Of course,' bowed Flandry.

Kit met him as he shut the turret door. Her fingers closed cold on his arm. 'Now what'll we do?' she gasped.

'Easy, lass.' He disengaged her. 'I don't see a bugscrambler here.' *Remember, Svantozik thinks I think you are still loyal to me. Play it, Kit, don't forget, or we're both done!* 'There are four surly-looking guards slouched below,' he said. 'I don't imagine Svantozik will waste his own valuable time in their company. A direct bug to the office of someone who knows Anglic is more efficient. Consider me making obscene gestures at you, O great unseen audience. But is anyone else aboard, d'you know?'

'N-no —' Her eyes asked him, through fear: *Have you forgotten? Are you alerting them to your plan?*

Flandry wandered past the navigation table to the main radio transceiver. 'I don't want to risk someone getting officious,' he murmured. 'You see, I'd first like to peek at their communication system. It's the easiest thing to modify, if any alterations are needed. And it could look bad, unseen audience, if we were surprised at what is really a harmless inspection.' *I trust,* he thought with a devil's inward laughter, *that they don't know I know they know I'm actually supposed to install a password circuit for Kit.*

It was the sort of web he loved. But he remembered, as a cold tautening, that a bullet was still the ultimate simplicity which clove all webs.

He took the cover off and began probing. He could not simply have given Kit the frequencies and wave shapes in a recognition signal: because Ardazirho equipment would not be built just like Terran, nor calibrated in metric units. He must examine an actual set, dismantle parts, test them with oscilloscope and static metres — and, surreptitiously, modify it so that the required pattern would be emitted when a single hidden circuit was closed.

156

She watched him, as she should if she expected him to believe this was her means of escape. And doubtless the Ardazirho spy watched too, over a bugscreen. When Flandry's job was done, it would be Svantozik who took this ship to Ogre, generated the signal, and saw what happened.

Because the question of whose side the Ymirite Dispersal truly was on, overrode everything else. If Flandry had spoken truth to Kit, the lords of Urdahu must be told without an instant's pause.

The man proceeded, making up a pattern as he went and thinking wistfully how nice it would be if Ymir really did favour Terra. Half an hour later he resealed the unit. Then he spent another hour ostentatiously strolling around the turret examing all controls.

'Well,' he said at last, 'we might as well go home, Kit.'

He saw the colour leave her face. She knew what that sentence meant. But she nodded. 'Let's,' she whipered.

Flandry bowed her through the door. As she came down the companionway, the guards at its base got up. Their weapons aimed past her, covering Flandry, who strolled with a tigerish leisure.

Kit pushed through the line of guards. Flandry, still on the companionway, snatched at his pocket. The four guns leaped to focus on him. He laughed and raised empty hands. 'I only wanted to scratch an itch,' he called.

Kit slipped a knife from the harness of one guard and stabbed him in the ribs.

Flandry dived into the air. A bolt crashed past him, scorching his tunic. He struck the deck with flexed knees and bounced. Kit had already snatched the rifle from the yelling warrior she had wounded. It thundered in her hands, pointblank. Another Ardazirho dropped. Flandry knocked aside the gun of a third. The fourth enemy had whipped around towards Kit. His back was to Flandry. The man raised the blade of his hand and brought it down again, chop to the skull-base. He heard neckbones splinter. The third guard sprang back, seeking room to shoot. Kit blasted him open. The first one, stabbed, on his knees, reached for a dropped rifle. Flandry kicked him in the larynx.

'Starboard lifeboat!' he rasped.

He clattered back into the turret. If the Ardazirho watcher had left the bugscreen by now, he had a few minutes' grace.

Otherwise, a nuclear shell would probably write his private doomsday. He snatched up the navigator's manual and sprang out again.

Kit was already in the lifeboat. Its small engine purred, warming up. Flandry plunged through the lock, dogged it behind him. 'I'll fly,' he panted. 'I'm more used to non-Terran panels. You see if you can find some bailing out equipment. We'll need it.'

Where the devil was the release switch? The bugwatcher had evidently quit in time, but any moment now he would start to wonder why Flandry and Party weren't yet out of the spaceship —

There! He slapped down a lever. A hull panel opened. Harsh sunlight poured through the boat's viewscreen. Flandry glanced over its controls. Basically like those he had just studied. He touched the *Escape* button. The engine yelled. The boat sprang from its mother ship, into the sky.

Flandry aimed southward. He saw the fortress whirl dizzily away, fall below the horizon. And still no pursuit, not even a homing missile. They must be too dumbfounded. It wouldn't last, of course. . . . He threw back his head and howled out all his bottled-up laughter, great gusts of it to fill the cabin and echo over the scream of split atmosphere.

'What are you doin'?' Kit's voice came faint and frantic. 'We can't excape this way. Head spaceward before they overhaul us!'

Flandry wiped his eyes. 'Excuse me,' he said. 'I was laughing while I could.' Soberly: 'With the blockade, and a slow vessel never designed for human steering, we'd not climb 10,000 kilometres before they nailed us. What we're going to do is bail out and let the boat continue on automatic. With luck, they'll pursue it so far before catching up that they'll have no prayer of backtracking us. With still more luck, they'll blow the boat up and assume we were destroyed too.'

'Bail out?' Kit looked down at a land of stones and blowing ash. The sky above was like molten steel. 'Into that?' she whispered.

'If they do realise we jumped,' said Flandry, 'I trust they'll figure we perished in the desert. A natural conclusion, I'm sure, since our legs aren't so articulated that we can wear Ardazirho spacesuits.' He grew grimmer than she had known him before. 'I've had to improvise all along the way. Quite probably I've made mistakes, Kit, which will cost us a painful death. But if so, I'm hoping we won't die for naught.'

XIV

Even riding a grav repulsor down, Flandry felt how the air smote him with heat. When he struck the ground and rolled over, it burned his skin.

He climbed up, already ill. Through his goggles, he saw Kit rise. Dust veiled her, blown on a furnace wind. The desert reached in withered soil and bony crags for a few kilometres beyond her, then the heat-haze swallowed vision. The northern horizon seemed incandescent, impossible to look at.

Thunder banged in the wake of the abandoned lifeboat. Flandry stumbled towards the girl. She leaned on him. 'I'm sorry,' she said. 'I think I twisted an ankle.'

'And scorched it, too, I see. Come on lass, not far now.'

They groped over tumbled grey boulders. The weather monitor tower rippled before their eyes, like a skeleton seen through water. The wind blasted and whined. Flandry felt his skin prickle with ultraviolet and bake dry as he walked. The heat began to penetrate his bootsoles.

They were almost at the station when a whistle cut through the air. Flandry lifted aching eyes. Four torpedo shapes went overhead, slashing from horizon to horizon in seconds. The Ardazirho, in pursuit of an empty lifeboat. If they had seen the humans below — No. They were gone. Flandry tried to grin, but it split his lips too hurtfully.

The station's equipment huddled in a concrete shack beneath the radio transmitter tower. The shade, when they had staggered through the door, was like all hopes of heaven. Flandry uncorked a water bottle. That was all he had dared take out of the spaceboat supplies; alien food was liable to have incompatible proteins. His throat was too much like a mummy's to talk, but he offered Kit the flask and she gulped thirstily. When he had also swigged, he felt a little better.

'Get to work, wench,' he said. 'Isn't it lucky you're in Vixen's weather engineering department, so you knew where to find a station and what to do when we got there?'

'Go on,' she tried to laugh. It was a rattling in her mouth. 'You built your idea aroun' the fact. Let's see, now, they keep tools in a locker at every unit — ' She stopped. The shadow in this hut was so deep, against the fury seen through one little window, that she was almost invisible to him. 'I can tinker with the sender, easily enough,' she said. Slow terror rose in her voice. 'Sure, I can make it 'cast your message, 'stead o' tele-meterin' weather data. But ... I just now get to thinkin' ... s'pose an Ardazirho reads it? Or s'pose nobody does? I don't know if my service is even bein' manned now. We could wait here, an' wait, an' — '

'Easy.' Flandry came behind her, laid his hands on her shoulders and squeezed. 'Anything's possible. But I think the chances favour us. The Ardazirho can hardly spare personnel for something so routine and, to them, unimportant, as weather adjustment. At the same time, the human engineers are very probably still on the job. Humanity always continues as much in the old patterns as possible, people report to their usual work, hell may open but the city will keep every lawn mowed. ... Our real gamble is that whoever spots our call will have the brains, and the courage and loyalty, to act on it.'

She leaned against him a moment. 'An' d'you think there's a way for us to be gotten out o' here, under the enemy's nose?'

An obscure pain twinged in his soul. 'I know it's unfair, Kit,' he said. 'I myself am a hardened sinner and this is my job and so on, but it isn't right to hazard all the fun and love and accomplishment waiting for you. It must be done, though. My biggest hope was always to steal a navigation manual. Don't you understand, it will tell us where Ardazir lies!'

'I know.' Her sigh was a small sound almost lost in the boom of dry hot wind beyond the door. 'We'd better start work.'

While she opened the transmitter and cut out the metre circuits, Flandry recorded a message: a simple plea to contact Emil Bryce and arrange the rescue from Station 938 of two humans with vital material for Admiral Walton. How that was to be done, he had no clear idea himself. A Vixenite aircraft would have little chance of getting this far north undetected and undestroyed. A radio message — no, too easily intercepted, unless you had very special apparatus — a courier to the fleet — and if that was lost, another and another —

When she had finished, Kit reached for the second water bottle. 'Better not,' said Flandry. 'We've a long wait.'

'I'm dehydrated,' she husked.

'Me too. But we've no salt; heat stroke is a real threat. Drinking as little as possible will stretch our survival time. Why the devil aren't these places air conditioned and stocked with rations?'

'No need for it. They just get routine inspection . . . at midwinter in these parts.' Kit sat down on the one little bench. Flandry joined her. She leaned into the curve of his arm. A savage gust trembled in the hut walls, the window was briefly blackened with flying grit.

'Is Ardazir like this?' she wondered. 'Then 'tis a real hell for those devils to come from.'

'Oh, no,' answered Flandry. 'Temulak said their planet has a sane orbit. Doubtless it's warmer than Terra, on the average, but we could stand the temperature in most of its climatic zones, I'm sure. A hot star, emitting strongly in the UV, would split water molecules and kick the free hydrogen into space before it could recombine. The ozone layer would give some protection to the hydrosphere, but not quite enough. So Ardazir must be a good deal drier than Terra, with seas rather than oceans. At the same time, judging from the muscular strength of the natives, as well as the fact they don't mind Vixen's air pressure, Ardazir must be somewhat bigger. Surface gravity of one-point-five, maybe. That would retain an atmosphere similar to ours, in spite of the sun.'

He paused. Then: 'They aren't fiends, Kit. They're fighters and hunters. Possibly they've a little less built-in kindliness than our species. But I'm not even sure about that. We were a rambunctious lot too, a few centuries ago. We may well be again, when the Long Night has come and it's root, hog, or die. As a matter of fact, the Ardazirho aren't even one people. They're a whole planetful of races and cultures. The Urdahu conquered the rest only a few years ago. That's why you see all those different clothes on them — concession to parochialism, like an ancient Highland regiment. And I'll give odds that in spite of all their successes, the Urdahu are not too well liked at home. Theirs is a very new empire, imposed by overwhelming force; it could be split again, if we used the right tools. I feel almost sorry for them, Kit. They're the dupes of someone else — and Lord, what a someone that is! What a genius!'

He stopped, because the relentless waterless heat had shrivelled his gullet. The girl said, low and bitter: 'Go on. Sympathise with Ardazir an' admire the artistry o' this X who's behind it all. You're a professional too. But my kind o' people has to do the dyin'.'

'I'm sorry.' He ruffled her hair.

'You still haven't tol' me whether you think we'll be rescued alive.'

'I don't know.' He tensed himself until he could add: 'I doubt it. I expect it'll take days, and we can only hold out for hours. But if the ship comes — no, damn it, *when* the ship comes! — that pilot book will be here.'

'Thanks for bein' honest, Dominic,' she said. 'Thanks for everything.'

He kissed her, with enormous gentleness.

After that they waited.

The sun sank. A short night fell. It brought little relief, the wind still scourging, the northern sky still aflame. Kit tossed in a feverish daze beside Flandry. He himself could no longer think very clearly. He had hazed recollections of another white night in high-latitude summer — but that had been on Terra, on a cool upland meadow of Norway, and there had been another blonde girl beside him — her lips were like roses. . . .

The whistling down the sky, earthshaking thump of a recklessly fast landing, feet that hurried over blistering rock and hands that hammered on the door, scarcely reached through the charred darkness of Flandry's mind. But when the door crashed open and the wind blasted in, he swam up through waves of pain. And the thin face of Chives waited to meet him.

'Here, sir. Sit up. If I may take the liberty —'

'You green bastard,' croaked Flandry out of nightmare, 'I ordered you to —'

'Yes, sir. I delivered your tape. But after that, it seemed advisable to slip back and stay in touch with Mr. Bryce. Easy there, sir, if you please. We can run the blockade with little trouble. Really, sir, did you think *natives* could bar your own personal spacecraft? I shall prepare medication for the young lady, and tea is waiting in your stateroom.'

XV

Fleet Admiral Sir Thomas Walton was a big man, with grey hair and bleak faded eyes. He seldom wore any of his decorations, and visited Terra only on business. No sculp, but genes and war and unshed tears, when he watched his men die and then watched the Imperium dribble away what they had gained, had carved his face. Kit thought him the handsomest man she had ever met. But in her presence, his tongue locked with the shyness of an old bachelor. He called her Miss Kittredge, assigned her a private cabin in his flagship, and found excuses to avoid the officers' mess where she ate.

She was given no work, save keeping out of the way. Lonely young lieutenants buzzed about her, doing their best to charm and amuse. But Flandry was seldom aboard the dreadnought.

The fleet orbited in darkness, among keen sardonic stars. Little could actively be done. Ogre must be watched, where the giant planet crouched an enigma. The Ardazirho force did not seek battle, but stayed close to Vixen where ground support was available and where captured robofactories daily swelled its strength. Now and then the Terrans made forays. But Walton hung back from a decisive test. He could still win — *if* he used his whole strength and if Ogre stayed neutral. But Vixen, the prize, would be a tomb.

Restless and unhappy, Walton's men muttered in their ships.

After three weeks, Captain Flandry was summoned to the admiral. He whistled relief. 'Our scout must have reported back,' he said to his assistant. 'Now maybe they'll take me off this damned garbage detail.'

The trouble was, he alone had been able to speak Urdahu. There were a few hundred Ardazirho prisoners, taken off disabled craft by boarding parties. But the officers had destroyed all navigational clues and died, with the ghastly gallantry of preconditioning. None of the enlisted survivors knew Anglic, or co-operated with the Terran linguists. Flandry had passed on his command of their prime tongue, electronically; but not wishing to risk his sanity again, he had done it at the standard easy pace. The rest of each day had been spent interrogating — a certain percentage of prisoners were vulnerable to it in their own language. Now, two other humans possessed Urdahu: enough of a seedbed. But until the first spies sent to Ardazir itself got back, Flandry had been left on the grilling job. Sensible, but exhausting and deadly dull.

He hopped eagerly into a grav scooter and rode from the Intelligence ship to the dreadnought. It was Nova class; its hull curved over him, monstrous as a mountain, guns raking the

Milky Way. Otherwise he saw only stars, the distant sun Cerulia, the black nebula. Hard to believe that hundreds of ships, with the unchained atom in their magazines, prowled for a million kilometres around.

He entered the No. 7 lock and strode quickly towards the flag office. A scarlet cloak billowed behind him; his tunic was peacock blue, his trousers like snow, tucked into half-boots of authentic Cordovan leather. The angle of his cap was an outrage to all official dignity. He felt like a boy released from school.

'Dominic!'

Flandry stopped. 'Kit!' he whooped.

She ran down the corridor to meet him, a small lonely figure in brief Terran dress. Her hair was still a gold helmet, but he noted she was thinner. He put hands on her shoulders and held her at arm's length. 'The better to see you with,' he laughed. And then, soberly: 'Tough?'

'Lonesome,' she said. 'Empty. Nothin' to do but worry.' She pulled away from him. 'No, darn it, I hate people who feel sorry for themselves. I'm all right, Dominic.' She looked down at the deck and knuckled one eye.

'Come on!' he said.

'Hm? Dominic, where are you goin'? I can't — I mean — '

Flandry slapped her in the most suitable place and hustled her along the hall. 'You're going to sit in on this! It'll give you something to hope for. March!'

The guard outside Walton's door was shocked. 'Sir, my orders were to admit only you.'

'One side, junior.' Flandry picked up the marine by the gun belt and set him down a metre away. 'The young lady is my portable expert on hypersquidgeronics. Also, she's pretty.' He closed the door in the man's face.

Admiral Walton started behind his desk. 'What's this, Captain?'

'I thought she could pour beer for us,' burbled Flandry.

'I don't — ' began Kit helplessly. 'I didn't mean to — '

'Sit down.' Flandry pushed her into a corner chair. 'After all, sir, we might need first-hand information about Vixen.' His eyes clashed with Walton's. 'I think she's earned a ringside seat,' he added.

The admiral sat unmoving a moment. Then his mouth crinkled. 'You're incorrigible,' he said. 'And spare me that stock answer, "No, I'm Flandry." Very well, Miss Kittredge. You understand this is under top security. Captain Flandry, you know Commander Sugimoto.'

Flandry shook hands with the other Terran, who had been in charge of the first sneak expedition to Ardazir. They sat down. Flandry started a cigarette. 'D'you find the place all right?' he asked.

'No trouble,' said Sugimoto. 'Once you'd given me the correlation between their astronomical tables and ours, and explained the number system, it was elementary. Their star's not in our own catalogues, because it's on the other side of that dark nebula and there's never been any exploration that way. So you've saved us maybe a year of search. Incidentally, when the war's over the scientists will be interested in the nebula. Seen from the other side, it's faintly luminous: a proto-sun. No one ever suspected that Population One got *that* young right in Sol's own galactic neighbourhood! Must be a freak, though.'

Flandry stiffened. 'What's the matter?' snapped Walton.

'Nothing, sir. Or maybe something. I don't know. Go on, Commander.'

'No need to repeat in detail,' said Walton. 'You'll see the full report. Your overall picture of Ardazirho conditions, gained from your interrogations, is accurate. The sun is an A4 dwarf — actually no more than a dozen parsecs from here. The planet is terrestroid, biggish, rather dry, quite mountainous, three satellites. From all indications — you know the techniques, sneak landings, long-range telescopic spying, hidden cameras, random samples — the Urdahu hegemony is recent and none too stable.'

'One of our xenologists spotted what he swore was a typical rebellion,' said Sugimoto. 'To me, his films are merely a lot of red hairy creatures in one kind of clothes, firing with gunpowder weapons at a modern-looking fortress where they wear different clothes. The sound track won't mean a thing till your boys translate for us. But the xenologist says there are enough other signs to prove it's the uprising of a backward tribe against more civilised conquerors.'

'A chance, then, to play them off against each other,' nodded Flandry. 'Of course, before we can hope to do that, Intelligence must first gather a lot more information. Advertisement.'

'Have you anything to add, Captain?' asked Walton. 'Anything you learned since your last progress report?'

'No, sir,' said Flandry. 'It all hangs together pretty well. Except, naturally, the main question. The Urdahu couldn't have invented all the modern paraphernalia that gave them control of Ardazir. Not that fast. They were still in the early nuclear age, two decades ago. Somebody supplied them, taught them, and sent them out a-conquering. Who?'

'Ymir,' said Walton flatly. 'Our problem is, are the Ymirites working independently, or as allies of Merseia?'

'Or at all?' murmured Flandry.

'Hell and thunder! The Ardazirho ships and heavy equipment have Ymirite lines. The governor of Ogre ties up half our strength simply by refusing to speak. A Jovian colonist tried to murder you when you were on an official mission, didn't he?'

'The ships could be made that way on purpose, to mislead us,' said Flandry. 'You know the Ymirites are not a courteous race: even if they were, what difference would it make, since we can't investigate them in detail? As for my little brush with Horx —'

He stopped. 'Commander,' he said slowly, 'I've learned there are Jovoid planets in the system of Ardazir. Is any of them colonised?'

'Not as far as I could tell,' said Sugimoto. 'Of course, with that hot sun ... I mean, we wouldn't colonise Ardazir, so Ymir —'

'The sun doesn't make a lot of difference when atmosphere gets that thick,' said Flandry. 'My own quizzing led me to believe there are no Ymirite colonies anywhere in the region overrun by Ardazir. Don't you think, if they had interests there at all, they'd *live* there?'

'Not necessarily.' Walton's fist struck the desk. 'Everything's "not necessarily," ' he growled, like a baited lion. 'We're fighting in a fog. If we made an all-out attack anywhere, we'd expose ourselves to possible Ymirite action. This fleet is stronger than the Ardazirho force around Vixen — but weaker than the entire fleet of the whole Ardazirho realm — yet if we pulled in reinforcements from Syrax, Merseia would gobble up the Cluster! But we can't hang around here forever, either, waiting for somebody's next move!'

He stared at his big knobbly hands. 'We'll send more spies to Ardazir,' he rumbled. 'Of course some'll get caught, and then Ardazir will know we know, and they'll really exert themselves against us. ... By God, maybe the one thing to do is smash them here at Vixen, immediately, and then go straight to Ardazir and hope enough of our ships survive long enough to sterilise the whole hell-planet!'

Kit leaped to her feet. 'No!' she screamed.

Flandry forced her down again. Walton looked at her with eyes full of anguish. 'I'm sorry,' he mumbled. 'I know it would be the end of Vixen. I don't want to be a butcher at Ardazir either . . . all their little cubs, who never heard about war — But what can I do?'

'Wait,' said Flandry. 'I have a hunch.'

Silence fell, layer by layer, until the cabin grew thick with it. Finally Walton asked, most softly: 'What is it, Captain?'

Flandry stared past them all. 'Maybe nothing,' he said. 'Maybe much. An expression some of the Ardazirho use: the Sky Cave. It's some kind of black hole. Certain of their religions make it the entrance to hell. Could it be — I remember my friend Svantozik too. I surprised him, and he let out an oath which was not stock. *Great unborn planets*. Svantozik ranks high. He knows more than any other Ardazirho we've met. It's little enough to go on, but . . . can you spare me a flotilla, Admiral?'

'Probably not,' said Walton. 'And it couldn't sneak off. One ship at a time, yes, we can get that out secretly. But several. . . . The enemy would detect their wake, notice which way they were headed, and wonder. Or wouldn't that matter in this case?'

'I'm afraid it would.' Flandry paused. 'Well, sir, can you lend me a few men? I'll take my own flitter. If I'm not back soon, do whatever seems best.'

He didn't want to go. It seemed all too likely that the myth was right and the Sky Cave led to hell. But Walton sat watching him, Walton who was one of the last brave and wholly honourable men in all Terra's Empire. And Kit watched him too.

XVI

He would have departed at once, but a stroke of luck — *about time*, he thought ungratefully — made him decide to wait another couple of days. He spent them on the *Hooligan*, not telling Kit he was still with the fleet. If she knew he had leisure, he would never catch up on some badly needed sleep.

The fact was that the Ardazirho remained unaware that any human knew their language, except a few prisoners, and the late Dominic Flandry. So they were sending all messages in clear. By now Walton had agents on Vixen, working with the underground, equipped to communicate undetected with his fleet. Enemy transmissions were being monitored with growing thoroughness. Flandry remembered that Svantozik had been about to leave, and requested a special lookout for any information on this subject. A scanner was adjusted to spot that name on a recording tape. It did so; the contents of the tape were immediately relayed into space; and Flandry listened with sharp interest to a playback.

It was a normal enough order, relating to certain preparations. Mindhunter Svantozik of the Janneer Ya was departing for home as per command. He would not risk being spotted and traced back to Ardazir by some Terran, so would employ only a small ultra-fast flitter. (Flandry admired his nerve. Most humans would have taken at least a Meteor class boat.) The hour and date of his departure were given, in Urdahu terms.

'Rally 'round,' said Flandry. The *Hooligan* glided into action.

He did not come near Vixen. That was the risky business of the liaison craft. He could predict the exact manner of Svantozik's takeoff: there was only one logical way. The flitter would be in the middle of a squadron, which would roar spaceward on a foray. At the right time, Svantozik would give his own little boat a powerful jolt of primary drive; then, orbiting with cold engines away from the others, let distance accumulate. When he felt sure no Terran had spied him, he would go cautiously on gravs until well clear — then switch over into secondary and exceed the velocity of light. So small a craft, so far away from Walton's bases, would not be detected: especially with enemy attention diverted by the raiding squadron.

Unless, to be sure, the enemy had planted himself out in that region, with foreknowledge of Svantozik's goal and sensitive pulse-detectors running wide open.

When the alarm buzzed and the needles began to waver, Flandry allowed himself a yell. 'That's our boy!' His finger stabbed a button. The *Hooligan* went into secondary with a wail of abused converters. When the viewscreens had steadied, Cerulia was visibly dimming to stern. Ahead, outlined in diamond constellations, the nebula roiled ragged black. Flandry stared at his instruments. 'He's not as big as we are,' he said, but travelling like goosed lightning. Think we can overhaul short of Ardazir?'

'Yes, sir,' said Chives. 'In this immediate volume of space, which is dustier than average, and at these pseudo-speeds, friction becomes significant. We are more aerodynamic than he. I estimate twenty hours. Now, if I may be excused, I shall prepare supper.'

'Uh-uh,' said Flandry emphatically. 'Even if he isn't aware of us yet, he may try evasive tactics on general principles. An autopilot has a randomising predictor for such cases, but no poetry.'

'Sir?' Chives raised the eyebrows he didn't have.

'No feel ... intuition ... whatever you want to call it. Svantozik is an artist of Intelligence. He may also be an artist at the pilot panel. So are you, little chum. You and I will stand watch and watch here. I've assigned a hairy great CPO to cook.'

'Sir!' bleated Chives.

Flandry winced. 'I know. Navy cuisine. The sacrifices we unsung heroes made for Terra's cause — '

He wandered aft to get acquainted with his crew. Walton had personally chosen a dozen for this mission: eight humans; a Scothanian, nearly human-looking but for the horns in his yellow hair; a pair of big four-armed grey-furred shaggy-muzzled Gorzuni; a purple-and-blue giant from Donarr, vaguely like a gorilla torso centauroid on a rhinoceros body. All had Terran citizenship, all were career personnel, all had fought with every weapon from axe to operations analyser. They were as good a crew as could be found anywhere in the known galaxy. And far down underneath, it saddened Flandry that not one of the humans, except himself, came from Terra.

The hours passed. He ate, napped, stood piloting tricks. Eventually he was close upon the Ardazirho boat, and ordered combat armour all around. He himself went into the turret with Chives.

His quarry was a squat, ugly shape, dark against the distant star-clouds. The viewscreen showed a slim blast cannon and a torpedo launcher heavier than most boats that size would carry. The missiles it sent must have power enough to penetrate the *Hooligan's* potential screens, make contact, and vaporise the target in a single nuclear burst.

Flandry touched a firing stud. A tracer shell flashed out,

drawing a line of fire through Svantozik's boat. Or, rather through the space where shell and boat coexisted with differing frequencies. The conventional signal to halt was not obeyed.

'Close in,' said Flandry. 'Can you phase us?'

'Yes, sir.' Chives danced lean triple-jointed fingers over the board. The *Hooligan* plunged like a stooping osprey. She interpenetrated the enemy craft, so that Flandry looked for a moment straight through its turret. He recognised Svantozik at the controls, in person, and laughed his delight. The Ardazirho slammed on pseudo-deceleration. A less skillful pilot would have shot past him and been a million kilometers away before realising what had happened. Flandry and Chives, acting as one, matched the manoeuvre. For a few minutes they followed every twist and dodge. Then, grimly, Svantozik continued in a straight line. The *Hooligan* edged sideways until she steered a parallel course, twenty metres off.

Chives started the phase adjuster. There was an instant's sickness while the secondary drive skipped through a thousand separate frequency patterns. Then its in-and-out-of-space-time matched the enemy's. A mass detector informed the robot, within microseconds, and the adjuster stopped. A tractor beam clamped fast to the other hull's sudden solidity. Svantozik tried a different phasing, but the *Hooligan* equalled him without skipping a beat.

'Shall we lay alongside, sir?' asked Chives.

'Better not,' said Flandry. 'They might choose to blow themselves up, and us with them. Boarding tube.'

It coiled from the combat airlock to the other hull, fastened leech-like with magnetronic suckers, and clung. The Ardazirho energy cannon could not be brought to bear at this angle. A missile flashed from their launcher. It was disintegrated by a blast from the *Hooligan's* gun. The Donarrian, vast in his armour, guided a 'worm' through the boarding tube to the opposite hull. The machine's energy snout began to gnaw through metal.

Flandry sensed, rather than saw, the faint ripple which marked a changeover into primary drive. He slammed down his own switch. Both craft reverted simultaneously to intrinsic sublight velocity. The difference of fifty kilometres per second nearly ripped them across. But the tractor beam held, and so did the compensator fields. They tumbled onward, side by side.

'He's hooked!' shouted Flandry.

170

Still the prey might try a stunt. He must remain with Chives, carrying everything, while his crew had the pleasure of boarding. Flandry's muscles ached with the wish for personal combat. Over the intercom now, radio voices snapped: 'The worm's pierced through, sir. Our party entering the breach. Four hostiles in battle armour opposing with mobile weapons —'

Hell broke loose. Energy beams flamed against indurated steel. Explosive bullets burst, sent men staggering, went in screaming fragments through bulkheads. The Terran crew plowed unmercifully into the barrage, before it could break down their armour. They closed hand to hand with the Ardazirho. It was not too uneven a match in numbers: six to four, for half Flandry's crew must man guns against possible missiles. The Ardazirho were physically a bit stronger than humans. That counted little, when fists beat on plate. But the huge Gorzuni, the barbarically shrill Scothanian with his wrecking bar of collapsed alloy, the Donarrian happily ramping and roaring and dealing buffets which stunned through all insulation — they ended the fight. The enemy navigator, preconditioned, died. The rest were extracted from their armour and tossed in the *Holligan's* hold.

Flandry had not been sure Svantozik too was not channelled so capture would be lethal. But he had doubted it. The Urdahu were unlikely to be that prodigal of their very best officers, who if taken prisoner might still be exchanged or contrive to escape. Probably Svantozik had simply been given a bloc against remembering his home sun's co-ordinates, when a pilot book wasn't open before his face.

The Terran sighed. 'Clear the saloon, Chives,' he said wearily. 'Have Svantozik brought to me, post a guard outside, and bring us some refreshments.' As he passed one of the boarding gang, the man threw him a grin and an exuberant salute. 'Damn heroes,' he muttered.

He felt a little happier when Svantozik entered. The Ardazirho walked proudly, red head erect, kilt somehow made neat again. But there was an inward chill in the wolf eyes. When he saw who sat at the table, he grew rigid. The fur stood up over his whole lean body and a growl trembled in his throat.

'Just me,' said the human. 'Not back from the Sky Cave, either. Flop down.' He waved at the bench opposite his own chair.

Slowly, muscle by muscle, Svantozik lowered himself. He said at last, 'A proverb goes: "The hornbuck may run swifter than you think." I touch the nose to you, Captain Flandry.'

'I'm pleased to see my men didn't hurt you. They had particular orders to get you alive. That was the whole idea.'

'Did I do you so much harm in the Den?' asked Svantozik bitterly.

'On the contrary. You were a more considerate host than I would have been. Maybe I can repay that.' Flandry took out a cigarette. 'Forgive me. I have turned the ventilation up. But my brain runs on nicotine.'

'I suppose — ' Svantozik's gaze went to the viewscreen and galactic night, 'you know which of those stars is ours.'

'Yes.'

'It will be defended to the last ship. It will take more strength than you can spare from your borders to break us.'

'So you are aware of the Syrax situation.' Flandry trickled smoke through his nose. 'Tell me, is my impression correct that you rank high in Ardazir's space service and in the Urdahu *orbekh* itself?'

'Higher in the former than the latter,' said Svantozik dully. 'The Packmasters and the old females will listen to me, but I have no authority with them.'

'Still — look out there again. To the Sky Cave. What do you see?'

They had come so far now that they glimpsed the thinner part of the nebula, which the interior luminosity could penetrate, from the side. The black cumulus shape towered ominously among the constellations; a dim red glow along one edge touched masses and filaments, as if a dying fire smouldered in some grotto full of spiderwebs. Not many degrees away from it, Ardazir's sun flashed sword blue.

'The Sky Cave itself, of course,' said Svantozik wonderingly. 'The Great Dark. The Gate of the Dead, as those who believe in religion call it. . . .' His tone, meant to be sardonic, wavered.

'No light, then? It is black to you?' Flandry nodded slowly. 'I expected that. Your race is red-blind. You see further into the violet than I do: but in your eyes, I am grey and you yourself are black. Those atrociously combined red squares in your kilt all look equally dark to you.' The Urdahu word he used for 'red' actually designated the yellow-orange band; but Svantozik understood.

172

'Our astronomers have long known there is invisible radiation from the Sky Cave, radio and shorter wavelengths,' he said. 'What of it?'

'Only this,' said Flandry, 'that you are getting your orders from that nebula.'

Svantozik did not more a muscle. But Flandry saw how the fur bristled again, involuntarily, and the ears lay flat.

The man rolled his cigarette between his fingers, staring at it. 'You think the Dispersal of Ymir lies behind your own sudden expansion,' he said. 'They supposedly provided you with weapons, robot machinery, knowledge, whatever you needed, and launched you on your career of conquest. Their aim was to rid the galaxy of Terra's Empire making you dominant instead among the oxygen breathers. You were given to understand that humans and Ymirites simply did not get along. The technical experts on Ardazir itself, who helped you get started, were they Ymirite?'

'A few,' said Svantozik. 'Chiefly, of course, they were oxygen breathers. That was far more convenient.'

'You thought those were mere Ymirite clients, did you not?' pursued Flandry. 'Think, though. How do you know any Ymirites actually were on Ardazir? They would have to stay inside a force-bubble ship all the time. Was *anything* inside that ship, ever, except a remote-control panel? With maybe a dummy Ymirite? It would not be hard to fool you that way. There is nothing mysterious about vessels of that type, they are not hard to build, it is only that races like ours normally have no use for such elaborate additional apparatus — negagrav fields offer as much protection against material particles, and nothing protects against a nuclear shell which has made contact.

'Or, even if a few Ymirites did visit Ardazir . . . how do you know they were in charge? How can you be sure that their oxygen-breathing "vassals" were not the real masters?'

Svantozik laid back his lip and rasped through fangs: 'You flop bravely in the net, Captain. But a mere hypothesis — '

'Of course I am hypothesizing.' Flandry stubbed out his cigarette. His eyes clashed so hard with Svantozik's, flint grey striking steel grey, that it was as if sparks flew. 'You have a scientific culture, so you know the simpler hypothesis is to be preferred. Well, I can explain the facts much more simply than by some cumbersome business of Ymir deciding to meddle in the affairs of dwarf planets useless to itself. Because Ymir and

Terra have never had any serious trouble. We have no interest in each other! They know no terrestroid race could ever become a serious menace to them. They can hardly detect a difference between Terran and Merseian, either in outward appearance or in mentality. Why should they care who wins?'

'I do not try to imagine why,' said Svantozik stubbornly. 'My brain is not based on ammonium compounds. The fact is, however — '

'That a few individual Ymirites, here and there have performed hostile acts,' said Flandry. 'I was the butt of one myself. Since it is not obvious why they would, except as agents of their government, we have assumed that that was the reason. Yet all the time another motive was staring us in the face. I knew it. It is the sort of thing I have caused myself, in this dirty profession of ours, time and again. I have simply lacked proof. I hope to get that proof soon.

'When you cannot bribe an individual — blackmail him!'

Svantozik jerked. He raised himself from elbows to hands, his nostrils quivered, and he said roughly: 'How? Can you learn any sordid secrets in the private life of a hydrogen breather? I shall not believe you even know what that race would consider a crime.'

'I do not,' said Flandry. 'Nor does it matter. There is one being who could find out. He can read any mind at close range, without preliminary study, whether the subject is naturally telepathic or not. I think he must be sensitive to some underlying basic life energy our science does not yet suspect. We invented a mind-screen on Terra, purely for his benefit. He was in the Solar System, on both Terra and Jupiter, for weeks. He could have probed the inmost thoughts of the Ymirite guide. If Horx himself was not vulnerable, someone close to Horx may have been. Aycharaych, the telepath, is an oxygen breather. It gives me the cold shudders to imagine what it must feel like, receiving Ymirite thoughts in a protoplasmic brain. But he did it. How many other places has he been, for how many years? How strong a grip does he have on the masters of Urdahu?'

Svantozik lay wholly still. The stars flamed at his back, in all their icy millions.

'I say,' finished Flandry, 'that your people have been mere tools of Merseia. This was engineered over a fifteen-year period. Or even longer, perhaps. I do not know how old Aycharaych is. You were unleashed against Terra at a precisely chosen moment — when you confronted us with the choice of losing the vitae Syrax Cluster or being robbed and ruined in our own sphere. You, personally, as a sensible hunter, would co-operate with Ymir, which you understood would never directly threaten Ardazir, and which would presumably remain allied with your people after the war, thus protecting you forever. But dare you co-operate with Merseia? It must be plain to you that the Merseians are as much your rivals as Terra could ever be. Once Terra is broken, Merseia will make short work of your jerry-built empire. I say to you, Svantozik, that you have been the dupe of your overlords, and that they have been the help-less, traitorous tools of Aycharaych. I think they steal off into space to get their orders from a Merseian gang — which I think I shall go and hunt!'

XVII

As the two flitters approached the nebula, Flandry heard the imprisoned Ardazirho howl. Even Svantozik, who had been here before and claimed hard agnosticism, raised his ruff and licked dry lips. To red-blind eyes, it must indeed be horrible, watching that enormous darkness grow until it had gulped all the stars and only instruments revealed anything of the absolute night outside. And ancient myths will not die: within every Urdahu subconscious, this was still the Gate of the Dead. Surely that was one reason the Merseians had chosen it for the lair from which they controlled the destiny of Ardazir. De-moralising awe would make the Packmasters still more their abject puppets.

And then, on a practical level, those who were sum-moned — to report progress and receive their next instruc-tions — were blind. What they did not see, they could not let slip, to someone who might start wondering about dis-crepancies.

Flandry himself saw sinister grandeur: great banks and clouds of blackness, looming in utter silence on every side of him, gulfs and canyons and steeps, picked out by the central red glow. He knew, objectively, that the nebula was near-vacuum even in its densest portions: only size and distance created that picture of caverns beyond caverns. But his eyes told him that he sailed into Shadow Land, under walls and roofs larger than planetary systems, and his own tininess shook him.

The haze thickened as the boats plunged inward. So too did the light, until at last Flandry stared into the clotted face of the infra-sun. It was a broad blurred disc, deep crimson, streaked with spots and bands of sable, hazing at the edges into impossibly delicate coronal arabesques. Here, in the heart of the nebula, dust and gas were condensing, a new star was taking shape.

As yet it shone simply by gravitational energy, heating as it contracted. Most of its titanic mass was still ghostly tenuous. But already its core density must be approaching quantum collapse, a central temperature of megadegrees. In a short time (a few million years more, when man was bones and not even the wind remembered him) atomic fires would kindle and a new radiance light this sky.

Svantozik looked at the instruments of his own flitter. 'We orient ourselves by these three cosmic radio sources,' he said, pointing. His voice fell flat in a stretched quietness. 'When we are near the . . . headquarters . . . we emit our call signal and a regular ground-control beam brings us in.'

'Good.' Flandry met the alien eyes, half frightened and half wrathful, with a steady compassionate look. 'You know what you must do when you have landed.'

'Yes.' The lean grim head lifted. 'I shall not betray anyone again. You have my oath, Captain. I would not have broken troth with the Packmasters either, save that I think you are right and they have sold Urdahu.'

Flandry nodded and clapped the Ardazirho's shoulder. It trembled faintly beneath his hand. He felt Svantozik was sincere, though he left two armed humans aboard the prize, just to make certain the sincerity was permanent. Of course, Svantozik might sacrifice his own life to bay a warning — or he might have lied about there being only one installation in the whole nebula — but you had to take some risks.

Flandry crossed back to his own vessel. The boarding tube was retracted. The two boats ran parallel for a time.

Great unborn planets. It had been a slim clue, and Flandry would not have been surprised had it proved a false lead. But . . . it has been known for many centuries that when a rotating mass has condensed sufficiently, planets will begin to take shape around it.

By the dull radiance of the swollen sun, Flandry saw his goal. It was, as yet, little more than a dusty gassy belt of stones, strung out along an eccentric orbit in knots of local concentration, like beads. Gradually, the forces of gravitation, magnetism, and spin were bringing it together; ice and primeval hydrocarbons, condensed in the bitter cold on solid particles, made them unite on colliding, rather than shatter or bounce. Very little of the embryo world was visible: only the largest nucleus, a rough asteroidal mass, dark, scarred, streaked here and there by ice, crazily spinning, the firefly dance of lesser meteors, from mountains to dust motes, which slowly rained upon it.

Flandry placed himself in the turret by Chives. 'As near as I can tell,' he said, 'this is going to be a terrestroid planet.'

'Shall we leave a note for its future inhabitants, sir?' asked the Shalmuan, dead-pan.

Flandry's bark of laughter came from sheer tension. He added slowly, 'It does make you wonder, though, what might have happened before Terra was born — '

Chives held up a hand. The red light pouring in turned his green skin a hideous colour. 'I think that is the Merseian beam, sir.'

Flandry glanced at the instruments. 'Check. Let's scoot.'

He didn't want the enemy radar to show two craft. He let Svantozik's dwindle from sight while he sent the *Hooligan* leaping around the cluster. 'We'd better come in about ten kilometres from the base, to be safely below their horizon,' he said. 'Do you have them located, Chives?'

'I think so, sir. The irregularity of the central asteroid confuses identification, but. . . . Let me read the course, sir, while you bring us in.'

Flandry took the controls. This would come as close to seat-of-the-pants piloting as was ever possible in space. Instruments and robots, faster and more precise than live flesh could ever hope to be, would still do most of the work; but in an unknown, shifting region like this, there must also be a brain, continuously making the basic decisions. *Shall we evade this rock swarm at the price of running that ice cloud?*

He activated the negagrav screens and swooped straight for his target. No local object would have enough speed to overcome that potential and strike the hull. But sheer impact on the yielding force field could knock a small vessel galley west, dangerously straining its metal.

177

Against looming nebular curtains, Flandry saw two pitted meteors come at him. They rolled and tumbled, like iron dice. He threw in a double vector, killing some forward velocity while he applied a 'downward' acceleration. The *Hooligan* slid past. A jagged, turning cone, five kilometres long, lay ahead. Flandry whipped within metres of its surface. Something went by, so quickly his eyes registered nothing but an enigmatic fire-streak. Something else struck amidships. The impact rattled his teeth together. A brief storm of frozen gases, a comet, painted the viewscreens with red-tinged blizzard.

The the main asteroid swelled before him. Chives called out figures. The *Hooligan* slipped over the whirling rough surface. 'Here!' cried Chives. Flandry slammed to a halt. 'Sir,' added the Shalmuan. Flandry eased down with great care. Silence fell. Blackness lowered beyond the hull. They had landed.

'Stand by,' said Flandry. Chives' green face grew mutinous. 'That's an order,' he added, knowing how he hurt the other being, but without choice in the matter. 'We may possibly need a fast get-away. Or a fast pursuit. Or, if everything goes wrong, someone to report back to Walton.'

'Yes, sir.' Chives could scarcely be heard. Flandry left him bowed over the control panel.

His crew, minus the two humans with Svantozik, were already in combat armour. A nuclear howitzer was mounted on the Donarrian's centauroid back, a man astride to fire it. The pieces of a rocket launcher slanted across the two Gorzuni's double shoulders. The Scothanian cried a war chant and swung his pet wrecking bar so the air whistled. The remaining five men formed a squad in one quick metallic clash.

Flandry put on his own suit and led the way out.

He stood in starless night. Only the wan glow from detector dials, and the puddle of light thrown in vacuum by a flashbeam, showed him that his eyes still saw. But as they adjusted, he could make out the very dimmest of cloudy red above him, and blood-drop sparks where satellite meteors caught sunlight. The gravity underfoot was so low that even in armour he was near weightlessness. Yet his inertia was the same. It felt like walking beneath some infinite ocean.

He checked the portable neutrino tracer. In this roil of nebular matter, all instruments were troubled, the dust spoke in every spectrum, a million-year birth cry. But there was clearly a small nuclear-energy plant ahead. And that could only belong to one place.

'Join hands,' said Flandry. 'We don't want to wander from each other. Radio silence, of course. Let's go.'

They bounded over the invisible surface. It was irregular, often made slick by frozen gas. Once there was a shudder in the ground, and a roar travelling through their bootsoles. Some giant boulder had crashed.

Then the sun rose, vast and vague on the topplingly near horizon, and poured ember light across ice and iron. It climbed with visible speed. Flandry's gang released hands and fell into approach tactics: dodge from pit to crag, wait, watch, make another long flat leap. In their black armour, they were merely a set of moving shadows among many.

The Merseian dome came into view. It was a blue hemisphere, purple in this light, nestled into a broad shallow crater. On the heights around there squatted negafield generators, to maintain a veil of force against the stony rain. It had been briefly turned off to permit Svantozik's landing: the squat black flitter sat under a scrap, two kilometres from the dome. A small fast warcraft — pure Merseian, the final proof — berthed next to the shelter, for the use of the twenty or so beings whom it would accommodate. The ship's bow gun was aimed at the Ardazirho boat. Routine precaution, and there were no other defences. What had the Merseians to fear?

Flandry crouched on the rim and tuned his radio. Svantozik's beam dispersed enough for him to listen to the conversation: ' — no, my lords, this visit is on my own initiative. I encountered a situation on Vixen so urgent that I felt it should be made known to you at once, rather than delaying to stop at Ardazir — ' Just gabble, bluffing into blindness, to gain time for Flandry's attack.

The man checked his crew. One by one, they made the swab-O sign. He led them forward. The force field did not touch ground; they slithered beneath it, down the crater wall, and wormed towards the dome. The rough, shadow-blotted rock gave ample cover.

Flandry's plan was simple. He would sneak up close to the place and put a low-powered shell through. Air would gush out, the Merseians would die, and he could investigate their papers at leisure. With an outnumbered band, and so much urgency, he could not afford to be chivalrous.

' — thus you see, my lords, it appeared to me the Terrans — '

'All hands to space armour! We are being attacked!'

The shout ripped at Flandry's earphones. It had been in the Merseian Prime language, but not a Merseian voice. Somehow, incredibly, his approach had been detected.

'The Ardazirho is on their side! Destroy him!'

Flandry hit the ground. An instant later, it rocked. Through all the armour, he felt a sickening belly blow. It seemed as if he saw the brief thermonuclear blaze through closed lids and a sheltering arm.

Without air for concussion, the shot only wiped out Svantozik's boat. Volatilised iron whirled up, condensed, and sleeted down again. The asteroid shuddered to quiescence. Flandry leaped up. There was a strange dry weeping in his throat. He knew, with a small guiltiness, that he mourned more for Svantozik of the Janneer Ya than he did for the two humans who had died.

' — attacking party is about sixteen degrees north of the sunrise point, 300 metres from the dome —'

The gun turret of the Merseian warship swivelled about.

The Donarrian was already a-gallop. The armoured man on his back clung tight, readying his weapon. As the enemy gun found its aim, the nuclear howitzer spoke.

That was a lesser blast. But the sun was drowned in its noiseless blue-white hell-dazzle. Half the spaceship went up in a fiery cloud, a ball which changed from white to violet to rosy red, swelled away and was lost in the nebular sky. The stern tottered, a shaken stump down which molten steel crawled. Then, slowly, it fell. It struck the crater floor and rolled earthquaking to the cliffs, where it vibrated and was still.

Flandry opened his eyes again to cold wan light. 'Get at them!' he bawled.

The Donarrian loped back. The Gorzuni were crouched, their rocket launcher assembled in seconds, its chemical missile aimed at the dome. 'Shoot!' cried Flandry. It echoed in his helmet. The cosmic radio noise buzzed and mumbled beneath his command.

Flame and smoke exploded at the point of impact. A hole gaped in the dome, and air rushed out. Its moisture froze; a thin fog overlay the crater. Then it began to settle, but with slowness in this gravitational field, so that mists whirled around Flandry's crew as they plunged to battle.

The Merseians came swarming forth. There were almost a score, Flandry saw, who had had time to throw on armour after being warned. They crouched big and black in metal, articulated tail-plates lashing their boots with rage. Behind faceless helmets, the heavy mouths must be drawn into snarls. Their hoarse calls boomed over the man's earphones.

He raced forward. The blast from their sidearms sheeted over him. He felt heat glow through insulation, his nerves shrank from it. Then he was past the concerted barrage.

A dinosaurian shape met him. The Merseian held a blaster, focused to needle beam. Its flame gnawed at Flandry's cuirass. The man's own energy gun spat — straight at the other weapon. The Merseian roared and tried to shelter his gun with an armoured hand. Flandry held his beam steady. The battle gauntlet began to glow. The Merseian dropped his blaster with a shriek of anguish. He made a low-gravity leap towards his opponent, whipped around, and slapped with his tail.

The blow smashed at Flandry. He went tumbling across the ground, fetched against the dome with a force that stunned him, and sagged there. The Merseian closed in. His mighty hands snatched after the Terran's weapon. Flandry made a judo break: yanking his wrist out between the Merseian's fingers and thumb. He kept his gun arm in motion, till he poked the barrel into the enemy's eye slit. He pulled the trigger. The Merseian staggered back. Flandry followed, close in, evading all frantic attempts to break free of him. A second, two seconds, three, four, then his beam had pierced the thick super-glass. The Merseian fell, gruesomely slow.

Flandry's breath was harsh in his throat. He glared through the drifting red streamers of fog, seeking to understand what went on. His men were outnumbered still, but that was being whittled down. The Donarrian hurled Merseians to earth, tossed them against rocks, kicked and stamped with enough force to kill them through their armour by sheer concussion. The Gorzuni stood side by side, a blaster aflame in each of their hands; no metal could long withstand that concentration of fire. The Scothanian bounced, inhumanly swift, his wrecking bar leaping in and out like a battle axe — strike, pry, hammer at vulnerable joints and connections, till something gave way and air bled out. And the humans were live machines, bleakly wielding blaster and slug gun, throwing grenades and knocking Merseian weapons aside with karate blows. Two of them were down, dead; one slumped against the dome, and Flandry heard his pain over the radio. But there were more enemy casualties strewn over the crater. The Terrans were winning. In spite of all, they were winning.

But —

Flandry's eyes swept the scene. Someone, somehow, had suddenly realised that a band of skilled space fighters was stealing under excellent cover towards the dome. There was no way Flandry knew of to be certain of that, without instruments he had not seen planted around. Except —

Yes. He saw the tall gaunt figure mounting a cliff. Briefly it was etched against the bloody sun, then it slipped from view.

Aycharaych had been here after all.

No men could be spared from combat, even if they could break away. Flandry bounded off himself.

He topped the ringwall in three leaps. A black jumble of rocks fell away before him. He could not see any flitting shape, but in this weird shadowy land eyes were almost useless at a distance. He knew, though, which way Aycharaych was headed. There was only one escape from the nebula now, and the Chereionite had gotten what information he required from human minds.

Flandry began to travel. Leap — not high, or you will take forever to come down again — long, low bounds, with the dark metallic world streaming away beneath you and the firecoal sun slipping towards night again: silence, death, and aloneness. If you die here, your body will be crushed beneath falling continents, your atoms will be locked for eternity in the core of a planet.

A ray flared against his helmet. He dropped to the ground, before he had even thought. He lay in a small crater, blanketed with shadow, and stared into the featureless black wall of a giant meteor facing away from the sun. Somewhere on its slope —

Aycharaych's Anglic words came gentle, 'You can move faster than I. You could reach your vessel before me and warn your subordinate. I can only get in by a ruse, of course. He will hear me speak on the radio in a disguised voice of things known only to him and yourself, and will not see me until I have been admitted. And that will be too late for him. But first I must complete your life, Captain Flandry.'

The man crouched deeper into murk He felt the near-absolute cold of the rock creep through armour and touch his skin. 'You've tried often enough before,' he said.

Aycharaych's chuckle was purest music. 'Yes, I really thought I had said farewell to you, that night at the Crystal Moon. It seemed probable you would be sent to Jupiter — I have studied Admiral Fenross with care — and Horx had been instructed to kill the next Terran agent. My appearance at the feast was largely sentimental. You have been an ornament of my reality, and I could not deny myself a final conversation.'

'My friend,' grated Flandry, 'you're about as sentimental as a block of solid helium. You wanted us to know about your presence. You forsaw it would alarm us enough to focus our attention on Syrax, where you hinted you would go next — what part of our attention that superb red-herring operation had not fastened on Ymir. You had our Intelligence men swarming around Jupiter and out in the Cluster, going frantic in search of your handiwork: leaving you free to manipulate Ardazir.'

'My egotism will miss you,' said Aycharaych coolly. 'You alone, in this degraded age, can fully appreciate my efforts, or censure them intelligently when I fail. This time, the unanticipated thing was that you would survive on Jupiter. Your subsequent assignment to Vixen has, naturally, proven catastrophic for us. I hope now to remedy that disaster, but — ' The philosopher awoke. Flandry could all but see Aycharaych's ruddy eyes filmed over with a vision of some infinitude humans had never grasped. 'It is not certain. The totality of existence will always elude us: and in that mystery lies the very meaning. How I pity immortal God!'

Flandry jumped out of the crater.

Aycharaych's weapon spat. Flame splashed off the man's armour. Reflex — a mistake, for now Flandry knew where Aycharaych was, the Chereionite could not get away — comforting to realise, in this querning of worlds, that an enemy who saw twenty years ahead, and had controlled whole races like a hidden fate, could also make mistakes.

Flandry sprang up on to the meteor. He crashed against Aycharaych.

The blaster fired point-blank. Flandry's hand chopped down. Aycharaych's writ did not snap across, the armour protected it. But the gun went spinning down into darkness. Flandry snatched for his own weapon. Aycharaych read the intention and closed in, wrestling. They staggered about on the meteor in each other's arms. The sinking sun poured its baleful light across them: and Aycharaych could see better by it than Flandry. In minutes, when night fell, the man would be altogether blind and the Chereionite could take victory.

Aycharaych thrust a leg behind the man's and pushed. Flandry toppled. His opponent retreated. But Flandry fell slowly enough that he managed to seize the other's waist. They rolled down the slope together. Aycharaych's breath whistled in the radio, a hawk sound. Even in the clumsy spacesuit, he seemed like water, nearly impossible to keep a grip on.

They struck bottom. Flandry got his legs around the Chereionite's. He wriggled himself on to the back and groped after flailing limbs. A forearm around the alien helmet — he couldn't strangle, but he could immobilize and — his hands clamped on a wrist. He jerked hard.

A trill went through his radio. The struggle ceased. He lay atop his prisoner, gasping for air. The sun sank, and blackness closed about them.

'I fear you broke my elbow joint there,' said Aycharaych. 'I must concede.'

'I'm sorry,' said Flandry, and he was nothing but honest. 'I didn't mean to.'

'In the end,' sighed Aycharaych, and Flandry had never heard so deep a soul-weariness, 'I am beaten not by a superior brain or a higher justice, but by the brute fact that you are from a larger planet than I and thus have stronger muscles. It will not be easy to fit this into a harmonious reality.'

Flandry unholstered his blaster and began to weld their sleeves together. Broken arm or not, he was taking no chances. Bad enough to have that great watching mind next to his for the time needed to reach the flitter.

Aycharaych's tone grew light again, almost amused: 'I would like to refresh myself with your pleasure. So, since you will read the fact anyway in our papers, I shall tell you now that the overlords of Urdahu will arrive here for conference in five Terran days.'

Flandry grew rigid. Glory blazed within him. A single shell-burst, and Ardazir was headless!

Gradually the stiffness and the splendour departed. He finished securing his captive. They helped each other up. 'Come along,' said the human. 'I've work to do.'

XVIII

Cerulia did not lie anywhere near the route between Syrax and Sol. But Flandry went home that way. He didn't quite know why. Certainly it was not with any large willingness.

He landed at Vixen's main spaceport. 'I imagine I'll be back in a few hours, Chives,' he said. 'Keep the pizza flying.' He went lithely down the gangway, passed quarantine in a whirl of gold and scarlet, and caught an airtaxi to Garth.

The town lay peaceful in its midsummer. Now, at apastron, with Vixen's atmosphere to filter its radiation, the sun might almost have been Sol: smaller, brighter, but gentle in a blue sky where tall white clouds walked. Fields reached green to the Shaw; a river gleamed; the snowpeaks of the Ridge hovered dreamlike at world's edge.

Flandry looked up the address he wanted in a public telebooth. He didn't call ahead, but walked through bustling streets to the little house. Its peaked roof was gold above vine-covered walls.

Kit met him at the door. She stood unmoving a long time. Finally she breathed: 'I'd begun to fear you were dead.'

'Came close, a time or two,' said Flandry awkwardly.

She took his arm. Her hand shook. 'No,' she said, 'y-y-you can't be killed. You're too much alive. Oh, come in, darlin'!' She closed the door behind him.

He followed her to the living room and sat down. Sunlight streamed past roses in a trellis window, casting blue shadows over the warm small neatness of furnishings. The girl moved about, dialling the public pneumo for drinks, chattering with frantic gaiety. His eyes found it pleasant to follow her.

'You could have written,' she said, smiling too much to show it wasn't a reproach. 'When the Ardazirho pulled out o' Vixen, we went back to normal fast. The mailtubes were operatin' again in a few hours.'

'I was busy,' he said.

'An' you're through now?' She gave him a whisky and sat down opposite him, resting her own glass on a bare sunbrowned knee.

'I suppose so.' Flandry took out a cigarette. 'Until the next trouble comes.'

'I don't really understan' what happened,' she said. ' 'Tis all been one big confusion.'

'Such developments usually are,' he said, glad of a chance to speak impersonally. 'Since the Imperium played down all danger in the public mind, it could hardly announce a glorious victory in full detail. But things were simple enough. Once we'd clobbered the Ardazirho chiefs at the nebula, everything fell apart for their planet. The Vixen force withdrew to help defend the mother world, because revolt was breaking out all over their little empire. Walton followed. He didn't seek a decisive battle, his fleet being less than the total of theirs, but he held them at bay while our psychological warfare teams took Ardazir apart. Another reason for avoiding open combat as much as possible was that we wanted that excellent navy of theirs. When they reconstituted themselves as a loose federation of coequal *orbekhs*, clans, tribes, and what have you, they were ready enough to accept Terran supremacy — the Pax would protect them against one another!'

'As easy as that.' A scowl passed beneath Kit's fair hair. 'After all they did to us, they haven't paid a millo. Not that reparations would bring back our dead, but — should they go scot free?'

'Oh, they ransomed themselves, all right.' Flandry's tone grew sombre. He looked through a shielding haze of smoke at roses which nodded in a mild summer wind. 'They paid ten times over for all they did at Vixen: in blood and steel and agony, fighting as bravely as any people I've ever seen for a cause that was not theirs. We spent them like wastrels. Not one Ardazirho ship in a dozen came home. And yet the poor proud devils think it was a victory!'

'What? You mean —'

'Yes. We joined their navy to ours at Syrax. They were the spearhead of the offensive. It fell within the rules of the game, you see. Technically, Terra hadn't launched an all-out attack on the Merseian bases. Ardazir, a confederacy subordinate to us, had done so! But our fleet came right behind. The Merseians backed up. They negotiated. Syrax is ours now.' Flandry shrugged. 'Merseia can afford it. Terra won't use the Cluster as an invasion base. It'll only be a bastion. We aren't brave enough to do the sensible thing; we'll keep the peace, and to hell with our grandchildren.' He smoked in short ferocious drags. 'Prisoner exchange was a condition. All prisoners, and the Merseians meant *all*. In plain language, if they couldn't have Aycharaych back, they wouldn't withdraw. They got him.'

She looked a wide-eyed question.

'Never mind,' said Flandry scornfully. 'That's a mere detail. I don't suppose my work went quite for nothing. I helped end the Ardazir war and the Syrax deadlock. I personally, all by myself, furnished Aycharaych as a bargaining counter. I shouldn't demand more, should I?' He dropped his face into one hand. 'Oh, God, Kit, how tired I am!'

She rose, went over to sit on the arm of his chair, and laid a hand upon his head. 'Can you stay here an' rest?' she asked softly.

He looked up. A bare instant he paused, uncertain himself. Then rue twisted his lips upwards. 'Sorry. I only stopped in to say goodbye.'

'What?' she whispered, as if he had stabbed her. 'But, Dominic —'

He shook his head. 'No,' he cut her off. 'It won't do, lass. Anything less than everything would be too unfair to you. And I'm just not the forever-and-ever sort. That's the way of it.'

He tossed off his drink and stood up. He would go now, even sooner than he had planned, cursing himself that he had been so heedless of them both as to return here. He tilted up her chin and smiled down into the hazel eyes. 'What you've done, Kit,' he said, 'your children and their children will be proud to remember. But mostly . . . we had fun, didn't we?'

His lips brushed hers and tasted tears. He went out the door and walked down the street again, never looking back.

A vague, mocking part of him remembered that he had not yet settled his bet with Ivar del Bruno. And why should he? When he reached Terra, he would have another try. It would be something to do.

POUL ANDERSON

ENSIGN FLANDRY

Deadly green aliens threatened the Earth.

Dominic Flandry had a great future ahead of him as saviour of the civilized universe. In later years his talent for swift, decisive action would give him an intergalactic reputation. But at the age of nineteen and straight out of naval academy, he was just another raw ensign.

The mighty Merseian Empire had sworn to wipe the Earth from the face of the universe. The attack had already been launched . . . but no one knew how or where the ravening power of the savage green-skinned aliens would strike. Only Ensign Flandry had the answer, in the form of a code which he might — or might not — be able to decipher.

And so the Merseians were coming after Flandry with every weapon in their terrible arsenal. And just to make things worse, Earth's own armadas were after him too — for desertion, high treason and other assorted crimes. Even for a future saviour, times were looking pretty tough.

CORONET BOOKS

POUL ANDERSON

FLANDRY OF TERRA

Captain Sir Dominic Flandry was a top man in the Intelligence Corps of the Imperial Terrestrial Navy. He knew that on the outer edges of the empire, civilization was spread hideously thin. The stars faded towards barbarism, with the great evil Empire of Merseia beyond.

But there were times when Flandry abandoned his senior position of command to go out in the field. Then he operated like the cool and brilliant agent he was, a ruthless, highly-trained professional. And in these three fast-moving adventures Captain Dominic Flandry shows that a space-age secret agent has to stay on top of the job — or succumb to nameless horrors.

CORONET BOOKS

EDMUND COOPER

PRISONER OF FIRE

She possessed extraordinary telepathic powers — and in the 1990s telepathy was the ultimate weapon in psychological warfare. Vanessa, along with other gifted children, was virtually a prisoner at Random Hill Residential School, developing her abilities for Government exploitation.

So when she escaped, Vanessa became a political embarrassment. Questions were asked by the Opposition. It was vital for the Prime Minister, the ruthlessly dictatorial Sir Joseph Humbolt, that everything that marked Vanessa's existence should be erased. And orders were given that she should be hunted down — using telepaths like herself — and destroyed.

CORONET BOOKS

EDMUND COOPER

THE OVERMAN CULTURE

Michael was quite young when he discovered that some
of his playmates bled if they cut themselves, and some
didn't. For a long time he didn't think about it. Nor did
it seem strange to see Zeppelins being attacked by jet
fighters above London's force field, or glimpse Queen
Victoria walking with Winston Churchill in the Mall.
Not at first.

But later he thought about these things — he couldn't
help it. The world was real, and yet unreal. It was all
desperately worrying. So Michael and his friends formed
a society to investigate the world around them.

Despite the terrible things they discovered, things
that made some of them insane, they never actually
guessed the truth about the Overman culture: Until
Mr Shakespeare told them.

CORONET BOOKS

SCIENCE FICTION FROM CORONET BOOKS

POUL ANDERSON

☐ 16337 2   Beyond the Beyond   35p
☐ 16336 4   Tau Zero   35p
☐ 19864 8   Ensign Flandry   65p
☐ 20753 1   Flandry of Terra   70p

EDMUND COOPER

☐ 15132 3   The Uncertain Midnight   40p
☐ 15091 2   The Last Continent   40p
☐ 21242 X   Prisoner of Fire   60p
☐ 17860 4   The Overman Culture   60p
☐ 04364 4   A Far Sunset   60p

ROBERT SILVERBERG

☐ 21297 7   Born With The Dead   80p

*All these books are available at your local bookshop or newsagent, or can
be ordered direct from the publisher. Just tick the titles you want and fill
in the form below.*

Prices and availability subject to change without notice.

CORONET BOOKS, P.O. Box 11, Falmouth, Cornwall.
Please send cheque or postal order, and allow the following for postage
and packing:
U.K. — One book 19p plus 9p per copy for each additional book ordered,
up to a maximum of 73p.
B.F.P.O. and EIRE — 19p for the first book plus 9p per copy for the next
6 books, thereafter 3p per book.
OTHER OVERSEAS CUSTOMERS — 20p for the first book and 10p
per copy for each additional book.

Name ....

Address ....

....